MARVELLOUS MISS MARKHAM

by

Helen BeDe

A catalogue record for this work is available from the National Library of Australia

Fiction – Historical Romance

ISBN: (sc) 978-0-6454869-9-5

ISBN: (e) 978-1-7640324-0-7

Published by Footprints Publishing

Printed by iPrintPlus

CONTENTS

THE MARVELLOUS MISS MARKHAM

Welcome to a bright, sunny morning in Monthrope Village. Labourers are hurrying forth to haul the harvest under cover, and the cottage women, having wrung out the wash, are draping it across their lavender bushes. A few hours in the sun are all they can hope for, yeoman and dame alert to the tell-tale clouds boiling up on the horizon and auguring a wet finish to the day. Up at the Hall, the grooms are hard at work, knowing his lordship will be short and sharp if he is kept waiting, and the mistress has already sent the day's orders to the kitchen. She's never one to lay abed when there's work to be done.

Another normal day in peaceful Monthrope? No, it is a day of change and interest. How seldom does this village, drained by a burgeoning city, find itself expecting newcomers? Monthrope Hall is to have a new governess, and long overdue too. And if that's not a boon, there's news that tenants have been found for Claude Sutton's old home, now his mother's passed, poor lady. And to top it all, there is rumour of a Monthrope son returning, and not alone neither, which might ease the spite laid on that spinster sister of his.

THE NEW GOVERNESS

'*I* won't go there wearing black.' That was Laura, clad this fine morning in demure grey, and responding defiantly to Martha's raised eyebrows.

'You ought not to go at all,' that worthy announced. 'Much better that you stay here with me and Ben.' She took a few uneasy steps about the room and suddenly capitulated. 'Well, I suppose not. Your brother's …

'Existing on his stipend, with two dependent children and another on the way. And Emily. Do spare me poor dear Emily.'

Since the loss of her parents, Laura had moved to Surbury to live with Martha, her old nurse, now happily married to Ben Wilcox. They had opened their hearts and home to her, and Laura was thankful, but she had determined on independence. The hectic months since her parents' demise had altered Laura remarkably. The death of her parents had proved an outright shock, the dreaded influenza carrying them off so quickly, despite everything that she and good Dr Fairfax tried. 'It's almost as if they don't want to live,' he'd muttered and, confronted with the aftermath, she sometimes wondered if he was right. Papa had retired some years ago, saying he had determined to stay home and grow vegetables. Did it mean that his funds had collapsed? Where was his money? Similarly, with her mother's possessions. In rather a frantic search for assets, Laura had located her mother's jewellery case only to find it contained little more than her wedding ring and a receipt from Rundell and Bridge. Mama had apparently quietly disposed of her trinkets. She knew her father had a cashbox, but it took ingenuity to find it hidden behind the false back of a desk drawer. There were two sovereigns and a half crown in it.

Laura had grieved when her mother died but was almost overwhelmed when her father passed. He had been her rock, her measure of what was right and sensible in a changing world. But now her world was teetering wildly, and she struggled to maintain some sort of balance. Laura spent a night in anguished weeping with nobody to solace her, before emerging ready to face her biggest problem. 'What am I going to do?'

Laura had sent a message to inform the family lawyer and he had come immediately and sat down in the drawing room to read her the will. He explained that he'd been appointed her trustee and would oversee the management of her assets until she married and he could pass the role on to her husband. She had inherited everything, except the house. It was to be sold and the proceeds shared with her brother.

Laura had then asked him about her father's money, and they located an account ledger. Mr Davidson examined the pages, observing that it only showed her father withdrew the household money on the first of each month and, this being the last week of the current month, explained the lack of cash. He would find out where her father banked. Concluding with the remark that he would contact her in due course, Mr Davidson ambled off and Laura wrote to inform her brother of the loss of their parents.

The unexpectedness of their death was as nothing to the havoc that followed. Word spread of the tragedy and precipitated two common reactions. One was to avoid the house and its inhabitants for fear of contracting the dreaded influenza. The other produced a prime example in William Mawson, twenty years the family grocer, who had appeared on her doorstep within days, requesting settlement of the account. Laura distractedly gave him all the money she had available, and he retired, mollified. He was replaced within hours by an obsequious mantua-maker of her mother's, arriving with a handkerchief held to her nose. Laura asked her if there was anything within the house that she would find useful, and the visitor went away with a writing compendium, apparently content.

From then on, Laura had struggled with paying off servants and tradesmen by gradually emptying the home she had lived in so comfortably. Mr Davidson proved her greatest support, selling the property locally and the remaining furniture to a dealer from London. Once he had received the money, Mr Davidson was able to settle the remaining accounts and forward the brother and sister their half shares.

There's a saying that during times of adversity, you discover your true friends. Laura watched bitterly as sympathetic neighbours melted away but, in truth, almost nobody could understand her behaviour. They expected a young woman, prostrate with grief and despair, and would have dutifully consoled Laura and preached God's will. Yet here she was marching about stony-faced, haggling with creditors and daring anyone to pity her. Laura had taken such an active role because she knew how difficult it would be for her impoverished brother to leave a distant parish, organise a double funeral, and dispose of the assets speedily and efficiently. Certainly, Edmund had raced south in response to her letter and spoken with the solicitor, returning grim-lipped. He oversaw the obsequies and departed two days later, insisting he was required in his parish.

Laura guessed his problem. She had been surprised that her parents had left so little, but she pointed out his privileged position. 'Father gave you your inheritance when you married, and you should have been set for life. He told me so.'

'I am not discussing business affairs with a female,' retorted Edmund. 'There was a great amount to be done regarding our move to Tyneville and the repairs that were needed at the vicarage. Then there were our wedding costs and Emily's health problems, let alone the expenses attached to raising a family. And our villagers were suffering dreadfully from the drop in shipbuilding and the influx of refugees during the uprisings north of the border, let alone the rainy summer we endured last year. I supported our villagers in various ways.'

I hope not at the expense of your own family, fretted Laura. She could readily imagine how his capital would have dribbled through his fingers from constant little inroads. She considered arguing that the parish was supposed to support both its incumbent and its destitute but held her peace. Edmund took after their mother so there was little trace of the businessman in him. Father had once said he would need a wife with a head for figures. Father had also prophesied this scene they were enacting, Edmund's expectation that having spent his savings he would be granted more. However, with his doting mother deceased, the young parson no longer had anyone to cajole. Edmund's final admission that Laura seemed to be managing well was followed by orders to follow him as soon as the estate was wound up. He knew his duty when he saw it, and doubtless she could make herself useful. What a prospect to look forward to. Did Edmund expect her to be pleased with such a statement? Laura was no longer a minor, and recent experience had both strengthened and hardened her. Live in such a situation? Not while she had the money from her half-share to live on and the wits to earn an income.

Firstly, she wrote in hope to her old nurse to relay her news, but there was no return letter. Instead, there was the comforting, solid figure of Martha hammering on the front door a matter of days later. Laura was swept up in a pair of hefty arms and hugged until her ribs cracked. Martha was the only person to see her cry and told Laura stoutly it would do her good.

The house had already been sold to a florid businessman with ambitions, and with Laura living out of a trunk after disposing of her surplus clothing, there was nothing to do but pack the last few items and join this loyal friend at her home in Surbury. Martha and Ben proved staunch allies but even they, along with their neighbourhood, expected Laura to accept Edmund's offer of a home.

Laura did not fancy her reception in his overcrowded, underfunded vicarage near Newcastle, and for some days she searched for employment in Surbury without success. In desperation, she began advertising for and responding to positions as a governess or a companion. It was an interesting experience. 'Look, Martha, here's an offer to teach four little girls and "help around the home" for the princely sum of twenty pounds a year. Now wouldn't that be delightful. No? I agree with what you're thinking. I'll just have to resist it.'

On Sunday, she accompanied Martha to church. The day was fine, and the congregation gathered outside after the service, prior to dashing home to their belated breakfasts. Martha became engrossed in listening to a fat lady enlarge upon her health problems and Laura dropped back a little, bored. She discovered someone behind her was leaning forward to whisper in her ear. 'Mrs Tapper needs a housekeeper – my employment ends this Friday. Accept if you must, but the hours are twenty-four, the pay fifty pounds, the demands are endless, and there are five children. I'll visit and tell you more if you wish.'

Even as Laura looked around to see who had spoken, a middle-aged woman in black tipped her a nod and slid behind two men discussing wheat varieties. Martha bustled up, apologising for keeping her waiting and they walked home together, Laura looking regretfully around, before informing Martha of the circumspect stranger.

'That would be Polly Hendon. She is employed by the Tapper family who don't "know" me because Ben is in trade and Clive Tapper is an apothecary. I don't know any harm of Polly, just remember her words.' Laura was spared that expedient when the vicar's wife visited later, with gossip that Mrs Tapper had turned away her housekeeper. She had immediately hired two new maids for three pounds annually, live-out, bring your own food, and was supervising the house herself.

'I'm sure she always did so,' remarked Martha, and Laura continued searching for employment.

Letters plodded back and forwards, so expensive without a frank, but eventually Laura was successful. She was hired as governess to two little boys at nearby Monthrope for fifty-two pounds a year. Certainly, it was a long way from a worthy brother and his family, but not so far from her good friends, Martha and Ben. If she didn't find the home and family she wanted at Monthrope, she could be sure of a welcome at Surbury.

MOVING TO MONTHROPE

*T*he packing was done, and it was time to leave. Hefting a handle each, Martha and Laura walked her trunk down the road to the stout wooden doors of John Carter, the wagoner. Having a load to deliver in Monthrope, he was happy to offer her a lift and Laura was not at all too proud to save her shekels and travel on his wagon. While he stowed the trunk, she stroked his horses' velvety noses and satin necks. He helped her to a share of his driving seat, and it was time for Laura to say goodbye, tearing up as Martha's waving, stalwart figure receded.

They were soon clear of the township and had turned off the high road onto the well-kept lane leading to Monthrope village. John remaining silent, Laura recovered her poise and mused on her new appointment. It sounded well-to-do and the offered wage was slightly more than she had anticipated. Why?

'John, have you ever visited Monthrope Hall?'

'Aye,' he replied, with a light flick of his whip on a sluggish rump, 'that I have.'

'What sort of a place is it, John?'

'Ah, a dour old place, to be sure. They say it's belonged to the Hardacres from near the time of the Lionheart. It was going to rack and ruin but Augustus Hardacre married money, a Wilmott … Her father's a big merchant, owns a manufactory and a heap else.'

Dour it looked indeed on a day rapidly clouding over, as her last support vanished down the driveway. Laura thought the buildings were set a long way back from the entrance gates, not the sort of location designed to encourage casual visitors. She eyed its multiple storeys and towers, wondering what lay ahead of her, before crossing a porchway that darkened the entrance almost to invisibility and rapping on the door. A short, smart-looking butler answered her knock, responding to 'Laura Markham … I'm the new governess', with a nod.

He raised his voice. 'Luke, take Miss Markham up.'

A lad in fustian appeared, shouldered her trunk, and led the way across the hall and up several flights of stained oak. Laura, following, endeavoured to start a conversation. 'Have you worked here long, Luke?'

'Born here,' he retorted. 'And you? Wonder how long you'll last.'

Laura gave up trying to converse and was content to trail him up yet another flight to a room on the third floor, where he dumped the trunk at the foot of her bed.

'Ma Tillotson's the housekeeper. You'll find her there,' he said, nodding towards the appropriate wall. Laura thanked him and closed the door on his retreating form.

She thought it a fair room. There was a good four-poster piled high with puffy quilts, fresh linen and curtains, and a fire laid in the grate, ready for lighting. A peek through the window revealed a neighbouring tower and a pleasant view past lawns and ordered gardens, to a paddock where a groom was exercising a colt.

Laura tidied herself and knocked on the neighbouring door. Mrs Tillotson, elderly, in a white apron and cap, rose from a comfortable chair by her fireplace and greeted the newcomer politely. They returned to Laura's room where all the fittings were examined, and Laura's belongings stowed in a chest of drawers and a huge old clothes cupboard. When the housekeeper left, Laura felt that she had been quietly inspected and not found wanting. She sat plump on her comfortable bed and looked about her. This was surely better than Newcastle or even Surbury.

She was glad she'd made the change.

It suddenly occurred to her that Mr Davidson no longer knew her whereabouts and she had so much she wanted to discuss with him… *I meant to contact him weeks ago, but I was traipsing around Surbury looking for employment and forgot. Papa managed money well; I can't believe there's nothing left, and he was trying to tell me something when he died.* Her mind struggled with her last memory of her father as he lay gasping. 'Laura … there's … key … '

She walked across to a writing table and pulled its drawer open. Ah, such a nice packet of notepaper and headed too, and an ink bottle and goose-feather quill, much the best sort. She wrote busily then probed the drawer and, sure enough, there was a stick of sealing wax…

Mrs Tillotson returned. 'You can give that letter to Hocking, Miss Markham, he'll see it gets posted. In future, just leave them on the hall table. Now it's downstairs for luncheon today, everyone being away.'

They descended to the warmth and comfort of a huge old kitchen where plump Mrs Carson and Mary, her kitchenhand, good-naturedly welcomed her and made Laura feel at ease. Luke came in with a smart housemaid, introduced as Rosie. Presently, a fit young man in groom's attire entered along with Hocking. He eyed Laura appreciatively, and Mrs Carson, rather abruptly, introduced him as Bob Alston and told him to sit down. Disdaining the servant's hall, they sat in a comfortable group around the kitchen table while Hocking produced a jug of ale and Mrs Carson plied them with food. Within days, Laura would come to realise they had made her privy to a powerful little group, the beating heart of Monthrope Hall.

After their luncheon, Laura and Mrs Tillotson returned

up the back stairs to her bedchamber. Rosie arrived to light her fire but, before any chatter could spring up, Hocking entered. Lady Hardacre had returned and was available if Miss Markham cared to descend. Mrs Tillotson immediately led Laura down, curtseyed to her ladyship, and introduced the governess. A well-dressed woman turned from her writing desk, and she and Laura examined each other and exchanged greetings.

She eyed Laura consideringly. 'You're very young.'

'I'm twenty-one, Lady Hardacre.'

The indifferent gaze slid away, and Lady Hardacre turned back to her desk. 'Take Miss Markham up to the nursery, Tillotson.'

They climbed to a nursery wing where two little boys were seated at a table. Eugene, eight, was holding a book and six-year-old Michael a slate, while behind them Nurse stood guard. There were introductions, with the boys rising to utter 'Good afternoon, Miss Markham' before the two older ladies withdrew, leaving the new governess to her duties.

They could not be considered onerous. Laura wove some sums into a farm story full of strange animals and the boys happily worked them out and responded correctly. Each drew a picture while the other read aloud to her and answered questions. Their printing and handwriting needed attention and they appeared to know little history and geography, but they were obviously intelligent. Feeling they had been sitting for rather too long; Laura unearthed a drum and some clappers and taught them *The Grand Old Duke York*. They marched up and down singing, Nurse obligingly joining in on her return. Laura felt they had made a good start.

Just before five o'clock, Rosie brought up the nursery dinners. Laura was informed that she was expected in the dining room and hastened to her bedchamber to change. Mrs Tillotson arrived to approve her demure gown and shawl, neatly confined hair, and lack of ornament. Laura ascertained that the family met in an anteroom to the dining chamber and Mrs Tillotson returned to her own affairs.

Laura discovered Lady Hardacre standing by the fire, stately in silk with gold jewellery, talking to a neatly dressed young man. She introduced this gentleman as Mr Wakefield, his lordship's secretary. Wakefield shook Laura's hand and explained that he had visited Monthrope Major on business and was sorry to have been away when she arrived. Hocking circled with the drinks tray, but as a carriage could be heard outside, he exclaimed, 'Master's home', and vanished.

Lord Hardacre appeared at least ten years older than his wife, lean and observant. He greeted them all and stated that he would not detain them by changing his dress. He eyed Laura closely and averred that it was very nice to meet her, but the re-entrance of Hocking, to announce dinner, saved her from replying.

The meal was drawn-out and the conversation desultory. Lady Hardacre commented on each of the two removes and Lord Hardacre described an expedition to buy a racehorse. It appeared that his lordship's racing stable was a separate establishment to the Hall. He explained that he had been careful to take two mounted grooms to see his new acquisition safely to its quarters and would ride over tomorrow to ascertain how well it had settled. Laura contented herself with enjoying her meal and responding when spoken to, although she was amused to observe how adroitly Mr Wakefield fostered his employers' conversation.

At length, Laura followed Lady Hardacre to the drawing room where she seated herself by the fire and indicated a nearby chair for the governess. Her ladyship showed little desire for conversation, so Laura looked through some novels lying on a table and was told to help herself. Lady Hardacre, denying any personal musical talent, then invited Laura to try the pianoforte and she gladly occupied herself with the available music until the gentlemen entered. Hocking soon brought in the tea tray and Laura was directed to pour while Lady Hardacre discoursed on the merits of tea drinking. As soon as he had emptied his cup, Mr Wakefield rose to leave, and Laura decided it would be expedient to follow him.

RETURN OF A PRODIGAL?

*M*id-morning, around the time that Laura had been climbing down from the carter's wagon, Lady Ascot, at Monthrope Major, received the long-awaited letter from Bertram. She read it, at first with tears of joy and ardent prayers for a safe trip home from Calcutta, and then with growing concern, as she reached the final paragraph.

'I need not tell you, dear Mother and Father, of my growing intimacy with the exalted Patel family, which I have described previously. It has been such that I do not return alone. Her honourable father consented to my proposal, and Shreya and I were married before departure. The temple ceremony was most impressive, the generosity of her parents almost excessive and I return in triumph, but I will tell you more when we arrive. We shall travel first to Monthrope so that our separation be as short as possible.'

Lady Ascot waited until her husband returned from the barns where he had been supervising storage of the winter's grain and hay and listened patiently to his comments during luncheon. She saw him comfortably settled into his favourite afternoon nook before she announced that a letter had arrived from Calcutta. She presented what she thought of as 'the dire missive,' and left the room, knowing that he would need time to compose himself.

Lord Albert realised that the letter must be something quite out of the ordinary to explain such unusual behaviour. Mail from Calcutta had been the breath of life to Merle over the last four years and usually a cause of smiles and optimism. He took and read the epistle with misgiving. Like his spouse, he was at first elated to learn that, by this time, his only son was well on the way home. Like her, he was surprised, offended and shocked to read that he had married. Married, without his father's consent or intervention or support. Married in a temple to a woman named Patel. Lord Ascot's visage darkened as he read and reread his son's words.

Lady Ascot had gone in search of their daughter, Amelia. She found her standing by her father's writing desk, looking through Albert's register of employees, intent on some enquiry of her own. Lady Ascot eyed her with the rancour of long dissatisfaction and announced, 'I have some news for you – if you care to hear it.'

'Yes, what is your news?' Amelia replied in the disinterested voice that invariably infuriated her parent. The tone betrayed Amelia's boredom. (Was it the shortcomings of Lady Ascot's dresser or some deficiency in the kitchen or the flower arrangements?)

'Your brother has written that he is returning from India. He has married out there.'

There was silence while Amelia stared at nothing in particular and considered all that her mother's two sentences might convey.

'And the deficiency of one piece of news outweighs the joy of the other, I gather.'

'Yes. I have just given his letter to your father.'

'Oh, lord.'

Amelia said no more but left her mother and went in search of her father. His comfortable chair was vacant, but she could see him pacing up and down a pathway outside. Amelia studied him carefully. What were they to expect? He was noted for his lack of patience and sudden rages, and he looked troubled. Would her presence invoke an opportunity to express himself with his usual exaggeration and outrageousness, or not?

She stepped through the open French windows and walked up to him, the view it gave her of his face and his stance broke her heart. She put her arms around him and held him, and he clung to her, as to an anchor in a world gone astray.

ENTER TWO AGEING SPINSTERS

*T*o the surprise of the neighbourhood, Miss Carstairs and her friend, Miss Halbert, made a late entrance to Monthrope that memorable day, arriving just on dark at Sutton House. The gate stood wide, and the post-chaise drove straight to the porch, where the front door swung open, and Peggy Pelham approached and welcomed her employer. She had preceded the pair, and all was in readiness. They descended, carrying a single travel bag each, and the post boys departed, after relieving their feelings with a few terse remarks on the thriftiness of spinsters.

Peggy showed them into the front parlour where both fell into chairs, demanded tea and laced it with brandy, averring they were exhausted. Peggy supplied them with some biscuits as a further restorative, and they eventually found sufficient energy to explore their new domicile. It was adequately furnished, and they declared it would do; a nice quiet stay in the country was just what they needed after all the turmoil of packing and moving.

If you don't die of boredom, thought Peggy, wondering what on earth they would find to fill their days. Aloud, she opined that Monthrope was a pretty village, although perhaps a little small for their tastes. Miss Carstairs remarked that the lease was not a fixed one and they could take Monthrope day by day while they made up their minds.

They retired upstairs for the evening, since they both preferred to unpack their own bag, then came down to eat at the kitchen table, deciding it was too late to dress for dinner and oblige Peggy to wait on them. She filled them up with a hearty soup and toast, and they returned to their bedchambers and called it a day. Peggy cleared up after them, piled ashes over the fire in the ingle, hopeful that a few coals might last the night, and retired to her room next door. She had made herself at home there, appropriating a good firm bed for her own use, and she slept peacefully through the night while, upstairs, Miss Halbert crept into her friend's room and slid between the sheets with her.

A CRY IN THE NIGHT

*E*ven with a nor westerly howling and thumping the stonework, Laura found it delightful to leave the company of strangers and be free to relax in all the comfort of plump pillows and quilts. She shifted a branch of candles to her bedside table and settled contentedly with her novel just as Mrs Tillotson entered with a pan which she placed by the fire.

'It's a good night for a hot toddy,' she remarked, pouring Laura a glass. Laura, replete with dinner and cups of tea, thanked her, dutifully managed a few mouthfuls, and drifted off to sleep, her book abandoned on the eiderdown and all the curtains undrawn.

A scream jerked her awake midway through the night. She took a candle to the fireplace, lit it, and looked about her. A glow outside attracted her to the window and she discovered its source was the tower room opposite. Someone was frantically struggling with the tiny tower window, shouting, and causing the curtains to flap wildly. Snatching up her candleholder, Laura charged into the corridor and hastened to help, but the tower room she entered was strangely dark and empty, its flagstones icily chill underfoot. There were no curtains at all covering its window, and occasional flashes of sheet lightning startled her, providing glimpses of dusty stone walls. She shielded the precious flame with one hand and peered about. It seemed nobody had used this room in ages. Could that horrid shriek have come from higher in the tower? No. She had seen a face at this very window and hurried immediately from her bedchamber.

Dissatisfied and distressed, Laura returned to her room through a house heavy with silence and added wood to her fire. The little pan still rested on the hearth, and she crouched by the flames warming its contents. As she sipped, she suddenly remembered becoming sleepy after her first drink. She put the glass down and climbed into bed.

From the moment Rosie placed a tea tray on Laura's bedside table, the following day was a pattern of peaceful country life. Nobody mentioned noises in the night and, although anxious and concerned, Laura remained silent, dining alone in the breakfast room downstairs and partaking in the nursery nuncheon with her charges. The day passed in dutiful care and the children worked so consistently she took them into the wildwood.

She taught them the names of the leaves and flowers they collected and, on return to the nursery, showed them how to press their collections between sheets of blotting paper. They inserted these between some wooden covers unearthed from a cupboard and anchored them with weights retrieved from the kitchen. She taught the boys how to buttonhole-stitch pages together to make a scrapbook each to hold their future pressings, and they finished the day proud of their efforts.

The Hardacres dined out that evening and Laura shared a near-silent meal with Mr Wakefield under the supervision of Hocking. When the secretary headed for his office, Laura indulged in some much-needed pianoforte practice before retiring to her room. Retrieving her sewing kit, she repaired a hem torn that afternoon and was just completing it when Mrs Tillotson entered with hot chocolate. Laura thanked her but advised against spoiling the governess.

'Why, Miss Markham, think nothing of it. Don't you let that drink get cold,' responded the housekeeper, bustling out.

Laura carefully banked the fire and retired. She woke in the small hours and went to her window. Again, there was a light in the tower room and a distressed figure passing and repassing the window. Laura dragged on her dressing gown and returned to watch. Suddenly she heard a series of desperate cries, but Laura remained rigid at her post. She saw the tower window swing wide and a wraithlike figure struggling through the opening. Shocked, she stepped back as it tumbled untidily to earth. That night, a shaky Laura was glad to reheat and drink the hot chocolate, before sinking rapidly into slumber.

There was no comment from anybody next morning and, once again, Laura forbore to ask about the strange scenes she had witnessed. She was glad that the two lively little boys kept her fully occupied and that they appeared to find lessons preferable to loafing around the nursery. On this third day, they once again worked hard and, as a reward, she asked if they had a cricket set. It was unearthed and carried out to the back lawn. She was teaching Eugene the intricacies of bowling when Hocking arrived, rolling up his sleeves. He seemed almost genial and coached both the batsman and bowler while Laura fielded. Luke and Tom, the gardener's assistant, joyfully joined the group and the game became noisily lively.

The boys had been taking ten hits each and then swapping places but now everyone had a turn and Michael called out that Miss Markham should not be left out. Tom bowled and Laura happily whacked the ball into the rose garden, but as Eugene and Luke were searching for it, she suddenly noticed Lord Hardacre leaning against the garden door, slyly watching her. Discomfited, she decided to finish the game up, saying she feared she might be making the boys late for their dinner.

Lady Hardacre sent for Laura and the children just prior to the dressing bell. They arrived in her writing room, a boy hanging on each side. Were they nervous or just relaxed? Her ladyship kept them waiting a few minutes and then entered behind them. The children instantly dropped Laura's hands and straightened. Lady Hardacre eyed then sombrely. She deemed the boys sadly overtired by all their exercise, but both stoutly denied it, saying it had been just the best day. They endeavoured to launch into a description of all they'd done, but Lady Hardacre sent them back to the nursery and Laura hastened upstairs to dress.

She was teased at dinner. Mr Wakefield complained that nobody had invited him to show his prowess at cricket and hinted to be included in future games. He cited a famous headmaster, Richard Mulcaster, entirely unknown to Laura, on the virtues of sporting activities for the health and wellbeing of children. Lord Hardacre made a revoltingly sly reference to 'our young Amazon', leading Lady Hardacre to smother a yawn and enquire after the horses. Lord Hardacre took the hint and commandeered the conversation, discoursing on the merits of his new racehorse.

'You should ride with me to Monthrope Stud, Evadne, and see what your money paid for.' Judging by Lady Hardacre's expression, neither his words nor the suggestion they contained was welcome.

It had been a long day, following two broken nights. Laura excused herself from the dining room, prepared for bed and found her novel. 'I've made you another hot toddy,' explained Mrs Tillotson, entering quietly. Laura thanked her, but she fell asleep before she'd read a page or drunk anything.

Suddenly, she woke. Light shone from the tower room, and she got up and closed the curtains, feeling that a reprise of some stranger's agony was more than she could bear. Her room was lit by the fire and, as she bent to add a log, her attention was caught by the sight of her door opening. A lighted candleholder, held high, raked the room. It was Lord Hardacre. He's in the doorway, I can't get past him, thought Laura. I'll have to make a noise, a big one.

'Get out,' she yelled, hurling the piece of firewood at him as hard as she could. 'Get out, get out!'

An astonished Lord Hardacre ducked sideways as the missile cracked the wall beside his head. He overbalanced, dropping his candle as he reached out to steady himself. Doors could be heard above and below stairs, and the aggrieved voice of her ladyship rose from the second storey. 'What is going on? Is it burglars, Augustus? What is happening? Augustus, where are you?'

His lordship righted himself and Laura grabbed more wood, ready to throw it, but Lord Hardacre backed away and she followed him, yelling, 'Get out of here!' He blundered past Mrs Tillotson, shivering in nightcap and dressing gown in the corridor, shakily clutching her candle. Wakefield and Hocking came rushing along the hallway from the opposite wing. They all listened as Lord Hardacre stumbled downstairs in the dark, missed his footing, and crashed at his wife's feet, shrieking. Hocking and Wakefield hurried down to attend to his injuries, but Lady Hardacre, bearing a candlestick of her own, silently ascended to Laura's room, followed by Mrs Tillotson.

'What were you doing?' Lady Hardacre demanded.

'I was drawing the curtains against the light in the tower room,' Laura replied. 'I saw Lord Hardacre come in. I couldn't get past him, so I shouted.'

Mrs Tillotson stammered, 'There's his candle on the floor.' She picked it up, along with its candleholder. Lady Hardacre reached out and took it.

She announced, 'Tomorrow, Hocking will see that a bolt is fitted to Miss Markham's door,' and stalked downstairs.

Apparently, the governess was worth retaining.

'Well done, Miss Laura. That should do the trick,'

whispered Mrs Tillotson, restoring firewood to its basket.

'Why did you drug my drink?' demanded Laura, more than somewhat overwrought, and tired of mysteries.

'I wanted you to sleep through the noise in the tower and not run away like our previous governesses.'

'Dear Mrs Tillotson,' begged Laura. 'Who is the ghost in the tower room?'

'She was Minnie Harcourt, our very first governess. She appears whenever a new one arrives. I believe she is trying to warn them. I don't think she'll bother you again.'

After Mrs Tillotson had returned to her room, Laura got into bed and lay puzzling it over. How strange to be so nonchalant about a ghost in a tower room. From what Laura had seen, Minnie had chosen to squeeze through the tower window. It didn't look as if she had been pushed. Had the first governess committed suicide because Lord Hardacre assaulted her? If so, why would Lady Hardacre remain with such a man? Was it because of her sons or didn't she care? Laura lay there in the warm, thinking about the family she now worked for: the unappealing husband and his frosty wife, hardly the sort to allure any man to bed, and the two delightful children who lived so remotely in the big house.

Laura had returned to bed feeling like an overwound watch spring and hardly expecting to sleep at all, but the discussion with Mrs Tillotson acted as an effective distractor. Thinking about the poor soul haunting the tower room as a kindly spirit helped her unwind. Thinking about the children, rather than the family, continued the relief. Her narrow escape, her remaining fright over what might have happened, and the realisation that she had jeopardised her employment, gradually diminished sufficiently for Laura to have some confidence that she was now safe. Lady Hardacre had said that tomorrow a bolt would be fitted to her door. Laura took that as meaning Lady Hardacre had no intention of dismissing her. She wouldn't have to pack and move back to Surbury and start the soul-destroying search for employment all over again. She wouldn't be faced with any further demands from Edmund that she move to Newcastle. Minnie Harcourt's done me a kindness; she mused.

Laura gradually drifted off and slept until Rosie woke her as she opened the curtains and set the tea tray on her bedside table. It appeared that the Hall's servants had their own problems. Rosie announced it was raining fit to bust, and the laundry-maid, just come from Monthrope, was in a fair taking.

WHO ARE THESE PEOPLE?

*L*aura became readily accepted in Monthrope; the Hardacre's governess was polite, ladylike, and known to have lived in nearby Surbury – which came close to qualifying her as a local. The village's other new arrivals were considered a different kettle of fish, although of interest because they placed the local inhabitants on their mettle. It was inordinately difficult to find out anything about them, and even their arrival on the verge of dark was interpreted as a means of avoiding notice.

Enquiries ascertained that Mr Scott, an agent based in Monthrope Major, had arranged the rental of the late Mrs Sutton's furnished home on the edge of Monthrope. It appeared that the fees were high enough to appease any doubts felt by Claude Sutton about renting to strangers. The Suttons could report only that their tenants were a pair of old maids moving on from a neighbouring county.

The newcomers' arrival by post-chaise was considered a good sign, although there were only two horses and no great amount of baggage. It was acknowledged that not much could be observed, due to the time of day, and the house being so closely screened by its hedges. Of course, Peggy Pelham had preceded them, and the strange thing was that nobody recollected her arrival or what she had brought with her. She had emanated ghost-like, and emerged only to visit the shops, even when her employers were settled.

The couple fell in Monthrope's judgement when they failed to do their duty and acquire local servants. A married couple or a housemaid and yardman were what the two old dears needed, someone known to the village and likely to become a source of useful information. However, Monthrope was impressed by the strapping young woman who 'did' for them, and perhaps money was short. The village waited for further enlightenment and reserved judgement.

Miss Carstairs and Miss Halbert attended church once and thereafter, irregularly. Peggy Pelham had near-perfect attendance, but always arrived for the meagrely attended early service and left immediately afterwards. Such behaviour subverted village efforts to learn all it could about these fly-by-nights. Monthrope decided Peggy probably had so much to do, that early service was the only time that suited her. Only the sourest implied that it looked like everyone in the household was avoiding the neighbours.

ASCOTVALE ISSUES

*L*ord and Lady Ascot had decided, by common consent, to say nothing of the letter from Calcutta until they knew more about their son's situation and intentions. This was an entirely unheard-of resolution for two such outspoken people, but then it was considered the worst news they had ever received. Even Amelia's infuriating refusal, five years ago, to marry a viscount momentarily taken with her, couldn't compare.

The news was carefully kept from the servants, which meant that the butler, who delivered the envelope to her ladyship, and Lady Ascot's dresser who had seen her reading the letter and witnessed her consternation, smirked their way around the servants' hall to the fury of everyone under them. Lord Ascot abjured the barns for a few days rather than upset the field hands, but he handed out the stiffest sentences he had ever imposed as local magistrate to the usual assortment of petty thieves and poachers fronting him that week, and perhaps this did him some good.

Lady Ascot and Amelia remained silent on the matter. They were at war over another issue, Amelia's scorn of a possible match with Seth Barlow's son, after having the temerity to refuse every respectable and profitable offer previously arranged for her.

'Nigel Barlow! That moonling; what a great husband he'll make,' Amelia declared when she learned of a proposed approach to this member of the lesser farming families, and she erupted into a peal of laughter. To further lacerate her long-suffering parent, she devoted a few minutes to depicting life with a man who was likely to remain more devoted to his prize sows than he ever would to anyone else. Her mother listened and longed to slap her, but the justice of the claim prevented her from further pursuing the matter, and she informed her husband that she had decided that a Barlow just wouldn't do. Unfortunately, she didn't mention this to Amelia.

To overcome her exasperation, Amelia dragged a driving coat over her morning dress and strode off to the stables. Here, she was greeted with relative friendliness; Miss Ascot was always the person to be approached when help was needed. A chaise was harnessed up for her in short order and she departed on her drive.

Everyone assumed Amelia was visiting the village shops or a friend, but Amelia shopped only when something was needed, and she had no friends. Instead, she considered every estate she passed as to whether it was inhabited by somebody marriageable. She found Monthrope woefully deficient and was really becoming rather warm and bored when she saw someone walking purposefully down the lane ahead of her. It was an unknown female, dressed in grey with a wide-brimmed bonnet against the changeable weather, and apparently on her way to the village. Amelia drew up. 'Do hop in and save yourself walking along a puddly lane,' she invited.

'Thank you, I will.' A young and pretty face smiled back at her and then its owner climbed nimbly into the chaise, 'I'm Laura Markham, the new governess at Monthrope Hall,' she hastened to add, for she saw, that despite the thrown-together outfit, the voice and mien were those of a gentlewoman and she was unsure how long a governess would remain welcome.

'How lovely to meet someone new,' said Amelia and Laura observed that she was genuinely pleased. They drove into the village, not talking much just yet but looking forward to exchanging confidences if an opportunity should arise.

'Let's be very daring and ask for a drink at the Monthrope Arms,' Amelia suggested.

If Mrs Haldon, the innkeeper's wife, was surprised to find two young ladies on her doorstep that morning, she rose nobly to the occasion and established the pair on comfortable chairs under a grape arbour. It was a while before either of the girls realised that they had been seated in the Haldon family area near an orchard at the rear, and therefore out of sight. Nor were they aware that Mrs Haldon had limited their attendant to her own daughter, who bustled out with a selection of drinks, fruit and biscuits and waited on them in a pleasant but most unassuming manner.

'This is lovely, we must do this more often,' Amelia exclaimed. 'We'll start a trend.'

Comfortable under the trees, they soon began to talk more openly and personally. Laura relayed a description of how she came to be at Monthrope and explained that Lady Hardacre had taken both boys on a visit to her sister at Studley. Laura, with several free hours ahead of her, had time to walk into Monthrope to examine the shops. Amelia, with years of anxiety and rage to release, took Laura on trust and gave her rather a full view of life with two autocratic parents. Laura, who adored her own father, was amazed to meet someone who both pitied and despised her male parent and was commonly at loggerheads with her mother.

'I suppose I've got to marry,' Amelia complained. 'But who to? I'm twenty-two and Mama's been searching since I was seventeen.'

Restored by their break in the shade, they walked around the little row of village shops, made a few personal purchases, and then headed back to collect their transport from the ostler. Both marvelled internally at how comfortable she felt with the other. Laura couldn't see how it was possible for a governess to associate with the daughter of what appeared to be a leading family, unaware that Amelia was as strong-willed as her parents and delighted that she had made a friend. She insisted on driving Laura back to Monthrope Hall, and they parted with promises to meet again as soon as feasible. Amelia sailed light-heartedly home to her troublesome family, pleased that, having talked her problems out with Laura, she had come to a decision; it was high time she took her destiny into her own hands.

SURPRISES AND SECRETS

That afternoon, Laura was drawn away from daily routine in the nursery schoolroom when Hocking entered to inform her that Bob Alston was about to repair her wall and secure her bedchamber. Leaving Nurse to supervise the boys, she accompanied him downstairs and found Mrs Tillotson watching the groom screw a sizeable brass bolt to the inside of her door.

Laura couldn't understand Alston's position on the staff at all. Why was the groom, rather than a carpenter, attending to the job? He seemed to have nothing to do with the racing stable but a great deal of licence around the Hall. She stood by, watching him competently carry out his task and the thought came to her that his features markedly resembled those of Eugene and Michael – or even Lord Hardacre. Was it possible? Well, of course it was possible: look what had nearly happened during the night.

Alston's work was soon completed but Hocking then led him across the bedroom to Laura's clothes cupboard. She hurried after them to peer in astonishment when he leant inside and pulled a handle she had never noticed. It drew a door back against the inside, revealing a dark aperture. Hocking saw Laura was bursting with curiosity and motioned her to come closer.

'Take a look, Miss Markham.' She found she was peering down a cavity something like a chimney. Hocking walked across the bedroom to her candlestick and lit the stub. He brought it to her, and she held it over the space, to discover a ladder fastened against the wall and leading downwards but also passing upwards, beyond her room. Hocking explained that it provided an access way, from the ground floor library up through the master's bedchamber and her own room to Rosie's domicile in the attic. Laura was flabbergasted. She had no idea that her bedchamber was above Hardacre's, and she hardly dared imagine to what uses such a sneak might put his hidden pathway.

Mrs Tillotson was equally amazed. 'Why it explains everything,' she exclaimed. 'Rosie complains someone gets into her room at night even though she locks her door. Said he must have another key. I told her he couldn't open the door if her key was left in the lock, and I accused her of being no better than a strumpet, poor girl. The wretch!'

Alston gazed at Laura's horrified countenance and reassured her. 'I'll fix that for you, Miss Markham.' He delved into his leather workbag and produced a smaller brass bolt. 'I'll use two of these little fellows, one top and bottom.'

Laura returned to the nursery schoolroom feeling shaky and unable to settle. If she hadn't felt so well-supported by the staff, she would have rushed outdoors, and probably off the property. Once again, she had to tell herself that she had two delightful pupils, a place to live, and an income, so she had no need to panic. She told the boys to bring their books and music and led them downstairs to the pianoforte. She found that having to concentrate on giving one a music lesson while the other turned pages in his storybook, acted as a successful calmant. When they finished, she sat down on the settee and asked them to describe the stories they had read and what they thought of them and was able to praise their insight; they had done well.

'Now we'll have a treat.' She had some concerns about the boys' coordination and devised a march, watching their actions as they paraded, and encouraging them to step out strongly and swing their arms like soldiers. She then switched to a skip, but Michael couldn't manage it and she got up to show him how. 'See, hop on one leg, then hop on the other,' she demonstrated, and he practised beside her until suddenly it clicked, and they were all gaily prancing about the room, she and Eugene congratulating and encouraging the younger brother.

'Very neatly done,' said a voice at the door, and it was Alston. How long had he been watching?

The boys raced across yelling, 'Bob, Bob, can we go horse-riding?'

He ignored them and spoke to Laura. 'I came to tell you I've repaired your wall. Please leave it to dry and don't touch it.'

Laura thanked him, and he left. She returned to the piano and set the boys walking and jogging forwards and backwards. Nurse, arriving to see what her darlings were up to, was easily inveigled into joining them, her apron and skirts proving little hindrance. Afterwards, they all trooped upstairs to the nursery, the boys chattering excitedly. Internally, Laura was counting the hours till she could pounce on Mrs Tillotson.

She kept the boys gainfully occupied during the remainder of the afternoon, rewarding them with a race in hoods and pattens to the carpenter's workshop adjoining his cottage. He told them he had been busy all week making shelves for Mrs Carson so she could store extra apples and quinces through the winter, but he took time out and taught all three how to hammer nails. The boys mastered it quite rapidly although they laughed at Laura's because her first effort went all awry.

Not till she had endured dinner that evening was Laura free to join the housekeeper in her sanctum and sink gratefully into a comfortable chair. Mrs Tillotson, of course, knew all about everything and everyone and she warned Laura to be ready with explanations, even proof of the usefulness of what she was teaching the children. This was good advice and it left Laura somewhat puzzled about Mrs Tillotson. She enquired why the housekeeper had tried so carefully to make her fall asleep of a night. Why had she not just told her about Minnie Harcourt, instead?

'Laura, I've found myself thinking that very same thing ever since last night and feeling that I am just a very ignorant old woman. I must assure you that Mother Simmel, who gave it me, promised the oil would not harm you. Dear, your behaviour is so different to the other girls, the other governesses who came here. I won't mention any names but when they heard Minnie – because I don't think any of them saw her – they buried themselves under the bedclothes screeching like wildcats when my room was just next door and they could have run into me. Then, next morning, saying they were too sick to work, they'd be off, rushing out of the house and telling the most extravagant fantasies to anyone who would listen.

'That's not all that happened, Laura. We had bouts of hysterics and screaming and crying – let alone that they were so dreary with the boys. Nurse was in despair of her poor mites learning anything, although I must say the boys were very naughty. You are worth ten of those governesses and we all determined, that first day when you so nicely came and shared our luncheon, that we would do what we could to keep you here.'

Laura said that she understood, although she remained too irritated to thank Mrs Tillotson and, as soon as she could, switched the conversation to the scene in her bedroom. She was so glad that now she would be able to sleep soundly at night, so thoughtful of the mistress. How surprised she had been to find there was a secret link between the library and the garret.

Mrs Tillotson's gaze fastened on Laura momentarily, although she contented herself with agreeing that it was all very unsettling. She explained that she had apologised to Rosie for speaking so harshly and Rosie had then demanded a bolt on the hidden entrance to her own bedroom. 'And got it,' Mrs Tillotson added.

'Mr Alston closely resembles the two boys and Lord Hardacre.'

'Ah. So that's it.' The housekeeper settled back in her chair and appeared to consider what to say. After a few moments, she explained. 'Bob Alston's mother is Maisy Alston, who worked here as a housemaid. When she found herself with child, Lord Hardacre installed her in a cottage in the village and supported her until Bob was old enough to work here. Robert Alston is trapped in an invidious position.'

'So, he's half-brother to Eugene and Michael. Would that make him the heir, being older?'

'It's more complicated than that.' Mrs Tillotson paused again, and Laura deemed it best to wait while she made up her mind how much to relay.

'Lord Hardacre has taken advantage of many a servant here. It seems that Maisy is the only one who ever conceived. Certainly, Lady Hardacre never did over ten long years … not until she took a fancy to Bob Alston.'

Laura's expression revealed her astonishment but she decided to say nothing. I wish I'd never asked, she thought. She bid Mrs Tillotson good night and retired to her room to sit in bed, once again mulling over what she had learned and debating how much of it she dared believe. What a thing for a wife to do. How desperate or how attracted had she been? And what sort of man was the young groom? He appeared so capable and strong and personable, but he was the son of an unmarried housemaid and what she had learned tonight was horrible. It would obviously be her wisest course to avoid him.

What an odd family she worked for. From her personal experience, she believed Lord Hardacre insufferably self-absorbed, but it was more difficult to understand Lady Hardacre. Laura could no more picture her passionately attached to any man than she could imagine her scrubbing floors. Quite possibly, in fact, almost surely, she had cold-bloodedly wed an older man as a means of moving from affluent middle class into the aristocracy. She would have expected to raise a family. If it was essential to continue the line, she may have become desperate after finding herself barren for ten years. To provide an heir and spare, she had either succumbed or had ruthlessly chosen Alston as her solution. Talk about keeping it in the family.

Laura decided Lady Hardacre was certainly an original. Already, Laura could see that she had taken over the financial management of the house, running a very tight ship. Lord Hardacre apparently had no valet unless Hocking assisted him. There was no sign of a dresser for Lady Hardacre, although Laura suspected Rosie functioned as one. Mrs Tillotson and Rosie managed the housework and that meant many rooms must be under Holland covers. How else could they manage the workload? Nurse seemed to run the nursery wing by her own efforts. Hocking buttled, while Mrs Carson and Mary, the kitchenhand and scullery maid, cooked – where you might have expected a French chef, and something more than Luke as footman and yardman in such a household.

Outside, she had learned, there were several gardeners and a lad. Somewhere, there might be a farm or pigs and poultry or game and the appropriate people to tend them. She understood the racing stable was headed by Hardacre's groom, William Grimes, and a number of stableboys, while Alston headed the home stables with one groom and a stableboy. Really, the horses were the best cared-for of all the creatures at Monthrope Hall. Lady Hardacre may have married as a means of entering the aristocracy, but nobody could say she lived high.

Laura's mind darted away to another issue. If Lord Hardacre had assaulted female staff and lived with his wife for ten years without her or anybody else becoming *enceinte*, then Minnie Harcourt had acted far too hastily in throwing herself out of a tower room window. One pitied her and could imagine her panic and shame but how much better if she had waited. She could have had a bolt fitted to her door and kept any attack secret. Poor girl, her appalling death now appeared even more desperate and unnecessary than Laura had originally thought.

It was at this point that Laura took herself to task. Who was she to judge Minnie Harcourt or Bob Alston, or the Hardacres? How shocked she had been on finding that Hardacre had entered her room at all, let alone that he retained a secret access to it as well. She had been close to terrified. She had almost run away from the place, and she believed it was fortunate that she had recollected, in time, how difficult it had been to gain employment.

When she had accepted this position, it had never occurred to her that working at Monthrope Hall would put her in danger. And what would she have done if Hardacre had overpowered her last night, or if she had been turned away? She had successfully rebuffed him without losing her employment and she felt that was a double triumph, but she had taken a very big risk. And, if he had succeeded would she have waited calmly to discover what the result was? She doubted it. All she knew was that she would have fought him tooth and nail.

Would she have turned to Mr Davidson or to Edmund - no, because both would have swept her away from Monthrope for ever. Edmund and his tiresome wife would have rebuked her severely and rightfully for entering such a position, she recollected belatedly. They would probably have installed her as their own unpaid governess or even as a skivvy. After all, in the world's eyes, she would have become a pariah to be avoided. Thank goodness Hocking knew of the secret entry to her bedchamber.

Finally, Laura drifted off to sleep, glad that her room was now secure, and determined to remain governess at Monthrope Hall without ever again being trapped by the proprietor or anyone else. The only difference was that tonight Minnie in the tower room was singing sweetly, soothingly, gently. How strange.

EXPLORING

*T*here was one further event related to Lord Hardacre's intrusion, although Laura had no further issues with his lordship. Once he had recovered from his wrenched ankle and bruises, he absorbed himself in his racing stud and appeared to bear her no grudges.

Laura bided her time and when she saw Hocking crossing the hall alone as she approached the stairs, she paused and asked him how he knew about the secret entrance. He stopped and looked at her, and his face lit with a smile. 'It happened when I was first made butler here at the Hall. I was only a few months into the job, and I tell you, Laura, anyone watching what happened would have had a good laugh out of it.

'As you can see,' he said, gesturing, 'the library has a double door. It also has a smaller back door near the servants' hall, so his lordship can come in from the stables and go straight to his desk. Well, one day I tried the key in that back door to the library because it never seemed to be locked and to find out if the mechanism still worked. I was horrified when something in the lock caught and the door wouldn't open again. To make the situation worse, just at that moment Lord Hardacre did come in from the stables. He walked right past me, tried the door, cursed, and then stormed down the passage to the front of the house before I could explain what happened. I followed because I felt that I ought to tell him about testing the lock, but he was too quick for me. His lordship went through those double doors and shut them behind him. I thought, well I've still got to get it over with, so I opened the door and entered the library - and he wasn't there!

'Can you imagine, Laura, how I felt and how I looked about? I tried the back door and, of course, it still wouldn't open. His lordship hadn't come out past me, so where was he? I stared around the room and gradually it dawned that there must be a third door. But where?'

Laura enthused, 'Oh, how exciting. So, then you looked for it?'

'At the time, I didn't dare look. In fact, I waited until I was sure both Lord and Lady Hardacre were off the property before I did try to work it out.' As he spoke, Hocking opened the library door and they both peered in, checking the room was empty before stepping inside.

'It wasn't difficult. You can see the front wall here is all shelves and cupboards below the windows. There are no paintings to swing out of place anywhere in the room, and over by the fireplace seemed the likeliest area, with that lovely old panelling. If it wasn't that, then some of the bookshelves must be movable.'

They walked behind the desk and approached the panelling. Laura couldn't see any keyhole or handle, but Hocking pointed and then used his fingers to pull on the frame of one of the panels. It swung towards them and inside she could see the lowest rungs of the wooden ladder ascending upwards.

'Climbing that would be a real effort,' she commented, peering upwards.

Hocking said, 'I don't think I'd like to try it. There's no real landing on each floor and, if anyone lost their grip or slipped off a rung, they'd likely crash all the way to this library.' They returned companionably together to the foot of the staircase and returned to their own duties. There were no further incidents and Laura completed her first week steadily and happily.

On Sunday, she and the boys followed Lady Hardacre's barouche to the village to attend the local church service. Afterwards, with her ladyship apparently engrossed in conversation with a friend, Laura seized the opportunity to wander with her charges among the tombstones. She chatted with the boys while casually searching for Minnie Harcourt's headstone, but there were few recent grave sites, so she discovered nothing. They rejoined her employer who, like all of them, was now most anxious to return home and partake of breakfast.

Alston had responded to the children's earlier request for horse rides. He approached Laura before luncheon and asked if she rode.

'Oh, it's a long time since I was on a horse,' replied Laura.

'Have you got a riding outfit?

Well, yes, she had, thinking of her well-worn habit, long immured, and wondering if it still fitted her.

Alston stated that he would see her at the stables with Michael and Eugene after luncheon and walked off.

They duly arrived. Alston saw Michael into the saddle, watched him do a lap of the round yard, handed him over to a stableboy and directed them to the next yard. He repeated this with Eugene, spending longer because Eugene was more advanced. Laura stood watching, admiring his thoroughness, and remembering the competency he had shown at carpentry. When it was her turn, Grimes emerged from the stables, leading an aged gelding sporting a lady's saddle. He assisted Laura to mount the horse.

They walked to the round yard and Alston called out, 'Titus, you can take Michael up the lane. Jameson, you can take Eugene.' Laura praised heaven that there would be fewer witnesses to her first efforts.

The brothers were cantering gently but they were thrilled at the change, and both their grooms threatened to put their horses on a lead if they didn't quiet down. As they disappeared up the slope, Alston watched Laura ride laps walking and trotting, before moving her to the larger yard and repeating the laps, urging her to canter. She overcame her nerves, even turning the horse and riding figure of eights.

'Okay, up the lane with you,' he called. Grimes came out with a fine hack for Alston to ride and they joined the others in a gentle canter on rising ground.

On the return journey, Alston asked Laura if she drove. She began to say, 'Of course, I ... ' and stopped. Her face worked as she struggled with unbidden memories of riding and driving with a beloved father, and she turned her head away hoping Alston hadn't noticed. Regaining self-control, she replied, rather tersely, that she was used to handling a gig or a chaise. When she felt able to risk a look at her escort, she received a most understanding glance and was relieved that he had said nothing. Back at the stables, nobody wanted to dismount, but Alston was immovable. 'You'll be too stiff if you do any more today.'

A RURAL ROMANCE

*N*ew arrivals in Monthrope Village were rare and usually preceded by, or carried, letters of introduction. The misses Carstairs and Halbert appeared to belong to nobody and provided no opportunity for anyone to ask them where they came from or whom they knew. Peggy was more often encountered in the street than her employers, presenting with a smile and a bob if someone greeted her and then hurrying onward. The two misses, as they became known, seldom shopped and offered nothing beyond a bow or a 'good morning' to anyone met in passing.

The vicar visited when they arrived, but never called again, and although he spent twenty minutes on the premises, gave no clear report on the occasion. Monthrope gossips, lacking information as to whether this pair were suitable people to know, assumed otherwise and decided to leave them to their own resources. Surely there was something havy-cavy about them.

Miss Carstairs was small, with very feminine mannerisms, ('It's like watching a stage performance,' Lady Hardacre remarked), and always presented very well-dressed. Miss Halbert was taller and mannish and somewhat more awkward in her dressing and gait. The general feeling was that they were a snooty pair of old maids and not particularly interesting.

Among the eagle eyes studying the situation must be included Peter Jameson, one of the Hardacre grooms. The sight of the stout but sturdy Peggy appealed to him, and he quietly assimilated information on her habits, looking for an opportunity to strike up an acquaintance. This came as Peggy left the church just prior to seven o'clock one Sunday. Peter stepped forward from among the few stalwarts who had risen early and introduced himself. 'Good morning, Miss Pelham, may I walk you home? I'm Peter Jameson.'

Peggy looked up at the attractive young man and was smitten. She readily assented and neither of them hurried on their journey from the main square to Sutton House. Peggy learned that Peter was twenty-two and heard about his hopes of advancement in his employment. He learned that she was nearing twenty-four and had kept house for Miss Carstairs for seven years. No, they employed nobody local, she did everything needful. Peter questioned whether she found any of her duties too heavy for a woman, offering his support. He was thanked while she turned over in her mind whether finding something for him to do would provide a means to further meetings with him.

When they eventually reached the tall picket gate for pedestrians, set in the hedges surrounding Sutton House, Peter took his courage in both hands and asked Peggy if she would walk out with him. This was a recognised ritual for Monthrope's courting couples, and Peggy happily agreed to do so, their first outing to be that afternoon. A delighted Peter returned to Monthrope Hall, aware that Peggy was now loosely bound to him.

For his walk, Peter chose to take Peggy to his parents' home. Realising the importance of the occasion, they made her welcome. Beth Jameson sat them down to enjoy a bowl of bacon and vegetable soup, and her husband James rubbed up his workaday boots ready for the morrow while admiring Peggy's sturdiness. Like Peter, he thought her a lovely armful.

They found out from Peggy that her parents were dead, and she was one of five surviving children from a hamlet east of Surbury. She was less forthcoming about Miss Carstairs and Miss Halbert, saying only that her employer had moved around a lot. She asked about the Jameson family, proving a willing listener as Beth described Peter's older siblings and how they were faring, and explained that husband James was employed by Hugo, the village blacksmith.

The Jamesons were proud of their well-furnished cottage and showed Peggy around before leading her outside to inspect a truly outstanding vegetable garden. She was escorted down the yard to meet the pig, an important family member destined to a sybaritically brief life, and learned it was due to be replaced after Mick Olsen's sow's next farrowing.

Both Peggy and Peter felt that their fledgling courtship had been accepted by the family. It was apparent that Beth and James had decided that Peggy, hailing from nearby Surbury, was near enough a local. This piece of happenstance made her less doubtful than a newcomer might otherwise have been considered, and the young couple walked happily back through the village to Sutton House, aware that his parents approved and there was no obstacle to their achieving happiness.

LEARNING AND EARNING

*F*acing another dinner passed in silence with Mr Wakefield after her first riding lesson, Laura asked him whether her two pupils had any other relatives. This proved a happy choice.

'There are no living Hardacres other than Lord and Lady Hardacre and the children. Lady Hardacre has a sister who married a local gentleman and lives about five miles away. Lady Hardacre's father, the children's grandfather, is Julius Wilmott – the great entrepreneur. Wonderful man. I was his secretary, but when Evadne married Augustus, he placed me here to help with their finances. Once the repairs were complete on the house, it proved unnecessary because the household accounts rapidly became her ladyship's forte. I am useful, however, in softening the messages I am required to deliver, supervising how the money is spent up at the stud, and organising the farming program. I also provide a means of keeping Mr Wilmott up to date on the two beloved grandchildren he seldom sees.'

'I particularly want the boys to know men of good character. Are you able to invite him?'

'I will convey your words to him and then, I am sure, he'll invite himself. He usually comes alone; he seldom brings Beryl.'

'Is Beryl Mrs Wilmott? What is the difficulty?'

'You will see for yourself when you meet her. He says he owes her a great debt of gratitude: that owing to her financial management, he progressed to his current affluence. Certainly, she may have supported him in achieving a vast and growing fortune, but breadth of vision, wide respect, and trust – she had nothing to do with those aspects of his nature.' Laura had to be satisfied with that sudden burst of confidence.

The boys had their next riding lesson the following day although the weather was changeable. Laura found Grimes waiting for her with a horse and gig. She drove him around the farm and stable-yards, practising backing up and turning without incident. Then he directed her to drive around the house several times and finally down to the gates, where Laura was rather pleased with the neat circle she achieved at the entrance. By that time, Alston and his entourage were returning along a distant lane. He rode up to the gig and asked Laura's silent observer, 'How did she go?'

Grimes replied tersely, 'Good hands; light on the horse's mouth, knows what she's doing.'

Laura, sneaking a sly glance at Alston, thought he looked impressed and pleased. She had no inkling that he was already attracted to her or that her presence had led him to seriously consider his future. Laura returned to a quiet evening at the Hall while Bob Alston set off to locate a longstanding friend he had been promising to visit. He was surprised to see someone ahead of him in the lane. Aha, someone else from the Hall was also out for the evening. The figure looked back and waited for him to come up, and he discovered it was Peter Jameson.

'Going courting, Peter?' asked Alston, intending to engender a humorous note, and was somewhat jolted when Jameson replied smilingly, 'Aye, that I am.'

'So, who's the lucky lass?'

'Peggy Pelham.'

'Never heard of her. Thought I knew everyone in the village.'

'She's new hereabouts. It's taken time to get to meet

her, but it's been worth it. We're walking out,' Peter said proudly, and Bob dutifully made appreciative noises.

I never expected to envy Peter Jameson, thought Bob, as he headed off to cast an eye through the door of the Monthrope Arms, and was delighted to discover his friend had halted there on the way home from market. Mick Olsen was the son of a local farmer, now deceased, and both young men had attended Monthrope Major's Grammar School as boys.

Bob nursed a tankard of ale and listened to Mick prattle on about his livestock. Olsen had benefited from his father becoming a landowner after years of being a tenant, and then saving enough to increase his acreage. With only one son to provide for, he had passed on a goodly heritage to Mick, who doubtless had ambitions of his own. One thing was plain, Mick was currently secure in his acreage, and his heart and soul appeared bound to his land.

'You seem happy, Mick. I guess you're fairly well-to-do these days.'

'Aye, that I am.' He paused, indicating to Mrs Haldon that he would have one more, and added, 'I'm happy in the best way possible for a working man, Bob. Bess Kyle and I ha' been handfast since Eastertime and we'll be parents before the year is out. And it's a good life, Bob. We work hard but we eat well. Bess spins better nor most and Jock, the agent, makes it worth her while. You haven't been to us since we set up together. Come over soon. It might make you think about where you're going with your own life.'

'Lately, I think about it almost daily, Mick, but I will come. You can be sure of it.'

Bob became aware of someone pressing against his side and glanced round to see Nancy Nickol from the bawdyhouse leering up at him. She and he were the same age and she had been a relief to him in times past when the blood ran hot in his veins. Now he was reluctant to speak to her, but he was also concerned about her appearance.

'Tis years since you visited me, Bob. Found some'un else?'

'Maybe. You don't look too chipper on it, Nan.'

'Oh, I get by. Drop in on an old friend once 'n a while, Bob.'

Some of Bob's distaste and certainly his reluctance showed, and she unwisely sneered at him. 'Gone up in the world, are we?'

'Nan, what do you want?' interrupted Mrs Haldon from further along the counter, before Bob could retort.

'Bottle a mother's ruin, Missus.'

'You got the geldt?'

'Aye,' and she paid up and left without a backward glance.

'You avoid that one,' Mrs Haldon advised Bob. 'Never been the same since that ratty pedlar passed through last year.' He nodded.

Bob followed through on his promise and visited the Olsen farm the following Sunday, finding a great state of excitement. 'Come and see,' ordered Mick, almost dragging him inside. They were setting up a loom in what had previously been the sitting room. 'Ain't she a beauty? We'll still sell the agent some of our wool, but he pays even better for well-woven cloth.'

He remembered his manners and introduced Bess, rosy-cheeked and smiling, a picture of rural good health and attractively rotund in pregnancy. They left her to try her hand at warping up and headed off to inspect the barns. Bob stayed to supper and rode home thinking what a good life Mick had with his Bess, and how little he himself knew about farming.

The following day, Alston decreed that, while he took the boys riding, Grimes would accompany Laura to Monthrope in the chaise to find out if Miss Markham could be trusted with a carriage off the estate. It was a pleasant day for a drive but, just short of the village, the horse cast a shoe and Grimes walked it to the smithy. Laura headed for the churchyard and systematically scoured the graveyard, searching unsuccessfully for Minnie's tomb.

Laura decided that the following Sunday she would explore further, someone must know where Minnie was. That night, she stood looking across at the tower room, listening to a voice singing a tune that felt vaguely familiar and thinking, Minnie, where did they put you?

She was surprised and concerned that the tower window was once again lit. Did it signal another warning? Laura opened her own window and instantly the opposite one swung wide. No figure was visible, but a charming voice continued a well-known song, '

Down yonder green valley where streamlets meander…

Twas there in the twilight I pensively rove …

Or at the bright noontide in solitude wander, amid the dark shades of the leafy ash grove.'

Laura recollected that she knew the words and began to sing along with her. 'I'll find you, Minnie,' she called across and was answered by the glow fading in the tower room. Now she was certain that all the tower room noises were intended to transmit kindly messages. This one was certainly a message because she knew where she had seen a grove of ash trees. And one day soon she would investigate.

LOST AND FOUND

*W*eeks passed, each as little like another as an inventive teacher could organise, until the day, quite early, when Hocking knocked at Laura's bedchamber door and solemnly presented a salver supporting a solitary envelope.

It was from Mr Davidson. He begged Miss Markham's forgiveness for his belated reply but the pressures of business, et cetera. He admitted finding an unknown and unusual key among the late Mr Markham's personal papers. After receiving her letter, he had, with some difficulty, tracked it down to a famous bank in London. He had taken the first opportunity to visit this institution, now a rapidly rising star in a new commercial business, called savings banks. He had found documents and bonds showing that a substantial sum of money was held there in trust for her. The paperwork revealed an original amount of fifty thousand pounds had been deposited, but further additions and years of compound interest, plus the value of the bonds, had rounded her wealth up to almost eighty thousand pounds. He had informed the manager that he would escort Miss Markham to the premises when she needed the money. In the interim, he had arranged an improved interest rate with the institution and had given them her current address. He finished by saying, *Laura, I'll help you and support you all I can but be careful. Be careful who you tell and careful of your wealth, particularly of anyone who takes an undue interest in it.*

The flutter his letter aroused in Laura might have astonished the residents of Monthrope Hall, used to seeing a quiet, well-mannered young governess on the premises. For Laura, the feeling was overwhelming: a delicious compound of relief that she now had the power and security of money; gratitude to honest Mr Davidson for his painstaking efforts, and delight that a beloved father had not let her down. It led to a bout of laughter and tears, and she was glad there was nobody to witness any of it, her tears and excitement, or her frolics around her bedroom.

Laura wrote immediately to express her thanks and her pleasure to her trustee, leaving the letter, as usual, on the tray in the hall. She decided to tell nobody, except Martha when she next visited her, but she was excitedly aware that she was no longer obliged to be a governess.

Heeding Mr Davidson's warning, she thought through what her fortune might mean to others and decided that she would rather nobody knew about it. If she mentioned it here it might change too many things and most of them for the worse – some might be jealous, some greedy. Certainly, her position would become untenable. She must quietly look about and decide how to achieve a place and family of her own. In the interim, she was more than happy to stay where she was. Really, she was feeling like she belonged here.

Laura descended to the breakfast room, half inclined to inform Mr Wakefield because of his business acumen, but wary for fear that he would report the news elsewhere. In the end, she did nothing. As well as she could, Laura hid her excitement and settled into the day's work.

There was much to think about, and the inheritance occupied her mind well past that first day. She was astonished that her father had so secretly set aside such an enormous sum for her. After much thought, she attributed it to the fact that in financial matters, he trusted very few people. This might explain why Mr Davidson, rather than Edmund, was her trustee. Papa had possibly anticipated he might die or become incapacitated and had secured Laura's portion from being misused. Edmund was relatively honest but too self-absorbed to be sensible with money. Her mother, soft-hearted and doting on her only son, exacerbated his selfishness. Of course, Mr Davidson would have been Mama's trustee and Laura didn't know how persuadable the old lawyer was. Would Mama have felt that Edmund deserved more than he had already received, or would she have resisted any pressure to divert a portion of the bequest? Laura did not doubt the answer for a moment. Edmund was possibly the recipient of the money Mama acquired from selling her trinkets.

Laura knew she resembled her mama only in appearance although she appreciated the training her mother had given her, ensuring she was well-versed in the domestic arts. It was due to her example that Laura's manners and behaviour generally followed the dictates of society. Her father, however, had read Mary Wollstonecraft and he always talked to Laura as an equal and encouraged her to think, to read widely and learn. She had either inherited or developed an incisive mind, grounded in the thorough education he had given her at home, alongside a brother who was no slouch at his studies either. What foresight Papa had.

That momentous day was to herald two further events. Mid-morning there was a great noise of someone arriving, a hearty male voice causing both her pupils to look up from their slates and turn excitedly towards the door. Time passed. The visitor must be with Lady Hardacre. They settled back to work, but eventually their patience was rewarded. The door was flung wide, and an elderly man surged in. Julius Wilmott had arrived. In every way, he was an influence for good. He sat down, first by one boy, later by the other, and took part in the lesson. The boys worked hard to please him. He joined them for luncheon and Laura was astonished that Lady Hardacre did not either retrieve him or join them. Afterwards, he sent both boys off for their horse ride, telling Laura that he wanted to talk to her.

'You're as good as Charlie Wakefield said you were.'

'And so are you,' she cried. He loved that and his eyes twinkled.

'Now, I want to know all about you!' They each proved so easy to talk to and such a good listener that they rapidly established rapport and shared their stories. Laura learned of the development of his mercantile empire and told him about her earlier years, although she did not mention her inheritance. Instead, she told Wilmot about her quest for Minnie's grave.

'Well, let's go and see,' was his response.

He led the way downstairs, roaring for Hocking to fetch his carriage, he was taking a lady for a ride. Away they whisked to the village in his curricle. She led him across the graveyard and out the little back gate to a grove she had noticed. There, among a sprinkling of ash trees, was a grassy clearing where a simple mound indicated somebody's last resting place. It was peaceful and beautiful but appeared to Laura so lonely that her eyes teared up.

She was surprised when a gentle voice enquired what was so earnestly engaging her attention and looked around to find the vicar had joined them. She wiped her eyes and explained that she was searching for Minnie Harcourt. The kindly face clouded. 'It was a great sadness to me that she couldn't be interred among the brethren. She was very devout, a simple girl with little worldly experience. She strictly followed her parents' dictum, and, to her mind, there was only one solution to breaking their rules.'

When he saw her puzzlement, he added, 'You see, she killed herself, so she couldn't be laid in the churchyard.' They walked over for a closer look at the grass-covered mound where the governess reposed. 'I'm sad that she couldn't, but Verger found her this pretty spot and I hope

she sleeps in peace. I planted bluebells round this grove.'
The thought of bluebells among the ash trees heartened
Laura, but she was troubled that Minnie lacked even a
headstone.

Mr Wilmott came bustling up and voiced his own opinion.
'Dumped here to be forgotten, was she? Well, she
deserved better, but we can mark the site. I'll get a stone
for her at least.'

A GOVERNESS WITH PANACHE

*A*fter such a series of dramatic events, life settled back into normal routine. Laura was the recipient of an immediate response from Mr Davidson. He began by apologising. *'I was so delighted to be sending you good news, Miss Laura, that I came close to neglecting my most important duty, that of guarding your welfare. You are now wealthy and can decide where and how you want to live, although I would take strong measures if you looked like making an irrevocably bad choice. You are also vulnerable to predators. Fortunately, you are an intelligent woman and have undoubtedly thought through your new situation, but it is my duty to warn you that humans can be both greedy and lazy. Why would anyone toil for a living when he can marry money and then dictate how it is spent? While I will do all I can to protect you while you are single, do not forget that my guardianship ceases when you marry.'*

It was a letter designed to make Laura think and she wrote again to thank Mr Davison and reassure this kind trustee that, indeed, she had considered the issues he raised in his letter. Laura then informed him that she had decided on her immediate future. Until she made up her mind and was sure of what she wanted to do, she would stay right where she was. She tried to express how delightful it was to be loved and appreciated by her pupils, and her pride in discovering that she could be a successful teacher, instrumental in helping them progress. She felt well-accepted by her fellow employees and her employers. She summed it up by saying that she was comfortable, settled, and gainfully employed.

Laura knew now that she was the sort of person who could hardly spend even a day in idleness. She put the problem of her future to one side and concentrated on bringing the boys' education up to standard, working out progressions in the subjects she taught, always searching for ways of teaching them that might interest children.

Aware that she might be asked for proof of their progress, she kept samples of the boys' output by getting them to copy from their slates onto precious paper, building each boy a folio of his achievements. 'Look, these are your first sums, and these are the ones you are doing today; see how far you have come.' Laura felt as proud and delighted as either of the boys. Their stories and descriptions were stitched into booklets, and she was thrilled to sometimes discover a passing adult absorbed in reading one. It was her first insight into the interest that people take in their fellows and the hunger that the less educated have for learning.

Laura didn't realise how unusual a program based on her own education appeared to people brought up to consider scripture, Latin and handwriting as the only essentials. She leavened the heavier subjects she taught by introducing music, drama, art and literature. Geography and history became stories about real people, tracing explorers across the globe. Science remained mostly natural history, and their collections grew. She introduced French, soon to follow it with Latin, thankful that her parents had believed in female education. An introduction to Latin would help Eugene and Michael when they inevitably transferred to one of the great public schools and was essential if they ever wanted to enter university or any of the sciences.

Laura had an instinct that strong, healthy children learnt more easily and believed that well-developed coordination was in some unknown way allied to brain development. Being with the boys six days a week, she kept them busy with an incredible list of manual skills: drawing or cutting out shapes, colouring, modelling, playing spillikins, woodworking, practising piano, weaving, or plaiting. Nurse proved equally fascinated and readily acted as an unsolicited aide, even though she wondered why Laura introduced all these unheard-of activities.

As the summer slipped away into autumn, Laura set the boys running, jumping, and playing active games to develop their strength and stamina. She encouraged their riding and found that Sundancer, Lady Hardacre's beautiful riding hack, was now made available for her use – a change that allowed her to participate fully and enjoy increasing her own equestrian skills. On rainy days, Laura used the long first-floor gallery to exercise the children with a mixture of races, skittles, and ball games. She collared Mr Wakefield for team games and relays. Dividing the children between them, they particularly enjoyed playing 'Keep-it-off', with two participants throwing a cushion back and forth as they ran along the gallery while the other two endeavoured to intercept it mid-flight. Needless to say, Laura was no advocate of tight-lacing.

For games requiring more participants, she invited anyone handy to join in 'Dodge' or 'Drop-the-Kerchief'. Their bemused adult audience noticed that boys who were allowed to work off their energy and negativity were a lot more pleasant to be around. They were unaware that Laura strove to inculcate in her pupils the same politeness to underlings they normally reserved for their parents.

Occasionally, visiting children were embroiled in their activities. She included young Clarence Sutton in a nature walk to the river while his doting mother chatted with Lady Hardacre about Sutton House's strange new tenants. Clarence relished catching water creatures and examining them but was less keen to release them. She allowed him to bring a jar of pollywogs to show his mama who threw up her hands and recoiled.

'We'll look after them for you, Clarence,' Laura assured him, eventually managing to wrest the jar of lively tadpoles out of his grasp as he climbed into the Suttons' landau. He was still berating his parent as they drove away and Laura, passing the open door on her way back to the nursery, was astonished to see Lady Hardacre lying back in her chair, laughing. Was the woman human after all?

Study in the nursery schoolroom was interrupted another day by the arrival of relatives. Mrs Bright remained talking to Lady Hardacre in the drawing room, but the children and their father ran upstairs to the nursery. Sophie, Elinor, and Bethany Bright were nicely spaced at twelve, ten, and eight years old and indulged in a happy reunion with their cousins. All seemed to be chatter and excitement. Schoolwork stopped while the boys displayed their projects and described what they had been doing, and Laura was happy to let them show off their knowledge and enjoy this encounter. Mr Bright was standing watching, and he leaned down to her and whispered, 'Little bagpipes, all gabbling at once. I doubt a single one of them is listening.' It was uttered with such a pleasant conspiratorial smile that she was charmed. Was it personal magnetism or his manner of talking to her as though she was someone on his own level?

Her pleasure that Leonard Bright took an interest in his nephews, and the good impression she had formed of him was heightened when, after luncheon, they all walked in the gardens until the boys begged for cricket. A game was started on the lawns. Mr Wakefield and Leonard Bright joined the boys, their good humour acting as an encouragement to a fun time. Laura stood watching with the Bright daughters, and when one of the girls picked up the cricket ball and returned it to the bowler, she called out, 'Well thrown, Sophie!' This prompted the three girls to join in.

'We should encourage Miss Markham to play, she attacks the ball like a tigress,' Wakefield informed the world at large.

'Does she? We'll have to see that,' Mr Bright answered. Thankfully, Rosie came out with a tray of drinks, and

Laura was spared making a difficult decision. Afterwards, it was time for the visitors to leave, with many promises of returning as soon as they could.

62

TRUST AND APPROVAL

*L*aura was, necessarily, with the boys six days a week, guiding their table manners, introducing French phrases applicable to meals, and inculcating a team approach to nursery chores. Sundays she sat with the family during church service in Monthrope Village, then breakfasted before taking the rest of the day off. She felt a very small and unimportant member of the congregation and would have been amazed to discover that she was a source of considerable interest.

Practically everything that Laura did was observed by the Hardacres or their employees, and Laura was glad that Mrs Tillotson had warned her to be prepared for questions and able to justify her procedures. Lady Hardacre closely examined her methods, leaving Laura feeling nervous, until one day she was approached after church.

'Miss Markham, I've been told about your wonderful results. How well you have brought both children on. Great progress and no more recalcitrance.'

'Thank you, Lady Horton.'

'Miss Markham, I would be happy to offer you a place at Stedhall Horton if you should find it desirable to leave Monthrope.'

'You are very kind, Lady Horton, but I am quite well-suited at the moment.'

Riding back to Monthrope Hall in the second barouche with the boys, she wondered whether the servants had been gossiping around the village, but Lady Horton's Stedhall was a distant estate. The Hardacres had dined recently with the Ascots; perhaps the Hortons had too. Were the gentry as addicted to gossip as everyone else?

She debated riding to Surbury to visit Martha and Ben, but the weather was changeable, so she read a chapter of the Bible, then found a novel and happily relaxed by her fire. Lady Hardacre sent for her after luncheon.

'Lady Horton made herself known to you this morning.'

Really, the woman missed nothing. 'Yes, Lady Hardacre. She asked me if I would like to work for her.'

'And would you?'

'I've no idea. I told her I was satisfied at the moment.'

'Miss Markham, you will oblige me by seeing Mr Wakefield and enquiring into my instructions as regards yourself.'

'Certainly, Lady Hardacre.'

Her ladyship turned away and Laura departed. However, Sunday was also Mr Wakefield's day off and when Laura enquired for him, Hocking replied that he had ridden to Surbury. She had perforce to wait, but Sundays and the Hardacres' franking of her envelopes provided her with the time and opportunity to write letters.

Laura corresponded quite regularly with Martha and monthly with Edmund and Emily, taking care to couch her language in positive terms. It could not be said that her relatives reciprocated. Emily's letters were usually a paean of domestic woes, Edmund's epistles very much those of the big brother directing the inferior sister. His latest letter questioned her riding, 'racketing about all over the country with no feminine escort; most improper.' These ill-judged words put Laura in a temper, and she considered responding that she'd never met a female groom who could escort her, but over the week she had managed to achieve a wry smile on rereading his letter, and to answer him that she rode in a group of six people and that was safety enough.

The secretary knocked on her door prior to dinner time. 'You wished to see me, Miss Markham.' Mrs Tillotson is the only person who calls me Laura, mused that worthy rather wistfully.

Mr Wakefield was holding a ledger and had undoubtedly been primed, but she told him about the approach of Lady Horton, and her conversation with Lady Hardacre. 'Lady Hardacre said that I was to enquire what instructions she gave you as regards myself.'

He approached, seemed to recollect himself and said, 'I can hardly discuss this in your bedchamber, Miss Markham.'

'Just leave the door open, Mr Wakefield.' Really, his finicking pursuit of the proprieties was too boring.

He did so and set the book down on a table. 'Lady Hardacre initially set your salary at fifty-two pounds a year, to be reviewed. Normally, you would be remunerated quarterly but I followed the rule that holds here, of setting up a bank account for each staff member and I have placed four pounds in yours every four weeks so it could earn interest. After his lordship's unfortunate episode, Lady Hardacre amended your salary to one hundred and four pounds a year and I adjusted the payments. She has since required me to review it again and increased your salary to one hundred and fifty-six pounds per annum, so another adjustment will need to be made. You have not so far asked me for any spending money but, if you wish, I will set aside a designated amount each week or each month, whichever you prefer.'

Laura wanted time to consider all this, but she said, 'Thank you for explaining that, Mr Wakefield. Is there anything more I should know?'

'Yes, but we can talk on our way to the dining chamber if you are ready to go down.'

Laura immediately picked up her shawl and they headed downstairs.

'There are other items Lady Hardacre has, er, decreed. A riding horse is to be available at any time you wish to exercise. She has also placed the chaise or the gig at your disposal if you desire to visit Monthrope or Surbury, so there is no need for you to walk. She has paid for some personal expenses you booked up at Harling's Emporium and has informed me that such regular small expenses may come out of the housekeeping.'

Laura debated saying 'How kind' but she was sure that Lady Hardacre always had a practical reason for her gestures, and she wanted to consider this one. She said, 'I very much appreciate what she has arranged.'

His eyes twinkled, and he smiled at her, 'Well spoken, Miss Markham.'

'Does Mrs Tillotson know of these arrangements?'

'Indeed, she does. I believe it was through Mrs Tillotson that her ladyship learnt of your account at Harlings.'

Laura shook her head. She really preferred to run her own life.

'I understand you were in Surbury today, Mr Wakefield. Close friends of mine live in Surbury.'

'Yes.' He sighed and stopped at the foot of the stairs to add quietly, 'I visit my wife and family there every Sunday. I doubt that the Hardacres even know I am married. They have never asked, and I have never introduced the subject.'

'I cannot imagine why not, Mr Wakefield.'

'They think of me as a young man at their beck and call.

I think of them as a useful ladder to advancement. I am ambitious to rise as high as my abilities can take me.'

'You seem to be in the right place, Mr Wakefield. To achieve high ambitions, you would need support from a peer or a magnate and here you have access to both.'

'True. I worked for Mr Wilmott, but he set me here when Evadne married Augustus, to manage their financial affairs. I have done so, but she has changed from a seventeen-year-old youngster determined to marry well, to a woman whose intellect might better suit a moneylender. She has taken the household finances into her own hands and runs a tighter economy and less staff than I could ever introduce.'

'Have you explained all this to Mr Wilmott?'

'Yes, and he's dead proud of her, and of his grandchildren.'

'He should be so. They are fine boys. Michael is as interested in machinery and mechanisms as Mr Wilmott must be.'

They had reached the anteroom to the dining chamber and their conversation ceased. Mr Wakefield returned his ledger to his office. Lord Hardacre was waiting, and Lady Hardacre entered soon after.

SPREADING HER WINGS

*T*here were numerous outcomes to such a revelatory day. Her bank account book remained in Mr Wakefield's office safe, but Laura thoroughly enjoyed examining it every few months. She acknowledged that having experienced hardship had increased her respect for the security offered by capital. This little book held money that she had earned for herself in employment that she enjoyed, and she was proud of it, even if the amount was minuscule compared to the largesse her father had left her.

Laura was maturing fast and becoming more confident in herself, and her decisions. The latest letter from Newcastle was written by an aggrieved Emily. '*I managed to acquire a felted cloak to protect Edmund from the everlasting rain as he goes about his duties, and he is not at all grateful. He says I should have got Charlotte and Thomas something to cover their rags. I wish he would understand that he must be the priority. How would we three manage if he were to fall ill or die? I was tempted to tell him that the cloak was given to me by Widow Paterson, whose husband passed away a sennight ago, and cost me nothing, but I knew he would be more offended by my accepting a cast-off than worried about trying to pay for such a useful covering.*'

The letters Laura received from Newcastle had shown indirectly that Emily was a better manager than unworldly Edmund, so now Laura hid a sovereign under the wax seal of each reply and addressed the envelope to her sister-in-law.

One Sunday, she used the chaise to visit Martha and Ben in Surbury. They spent a pleasantly relaxed few hours relating the little events of Surbury life and discussing their home improvements. It was delightful to be with them, but Laura carefully confined the length of her visit and returned to Monthrope in good time. Was it by coincidence that the next day Lady Hardacre sent for her?

'Miss Markham, I find myself unable to visit the Monthrope pauper pensioners today. Am I asking too much for you to take the chaise and call on them for me?'

'Not at all, Lady Hardacre. What is required?'

'Mrs Carson will have put up some containers of soup or dried peas. Mrs Tillotson will have some lengths of cloth to distribute. Unfortunately, her lumbago makes it hard for Mrs Tillotson to get up and down from the chaise or I would ask her to go.'

Laura was delighted at the change of occupation and skipped off to call on Mrs Carson. Not only were the staples of peas, beans, flour and even a few raisins already neatly packed in a box, but she had added some paper twists containing precious tea leaves.

'Oh, how good of you,' exclaimed Laura, delighted.

Mrs Carson was most forthright. 'Don't you go giving them tea leaves to Mother Suckling or Snowy Widdeson. They'll just trade them away for gin.'

She visited Mrs Tillotson to ask for a list of people and directions where to go and was shown several neat piles of odds and ends. 'Those squares are for Nelly Johnson; she'll stitch them into a quilt for winter. These old sheets are for Mary Martin; she's got five childer and she'll make and mend and put them to good use. The rest are lengths of flannel and will make underclothes. This fustian shirt is for Kister Hyde and he's not to exchange it for anything, or he gets nothing more from Monthrope Hall. Be sure to tell him. Check the sores on Walter Smythe's toes and put this salve on them. There, put the things in this box and shift what you want into a basket before you get out of the chaise.'

Following luncheon, Laura donned her greatcoat and a close bonnet to shield against the wind and headed for the kitchen door. Bob Alston had loaded the boxes and was waiting by the horse's head. Was he intending to come? No, he merely asked her if she needed a groom, and when she denied any necessity, he strode off to take two excited little boys for their riding lesson.

Laura was amazed at the time it took to complete her rounds. The aged and indigent were delighted to see a new face, to welcome her into their antiquated cottages, and to tell or find out all they could. She rapidly learned the art of visiting and moving on without offending or she would have arrived home at midnight. As it was, the sun was noticeably low in the sky when she drew up behind the church and looked over her shoulder. And there it was, a new headstone standing tall among the little grove of ash trees, thanks to good Mr Wilmott. Clicking to the horse, she drove home contented and looking forward to returning.

That night, although she was curious enough to go and open her window, all was dark and silent in the tower room and there was no sense of Minnie at all. Was she at peace now and free to go where innocent simple souls went after this life? Or was it just that there was no longer any need for her to warn Laura?

DINING WITH THE ASCOTS

*L*ord and Lady Ascot paid a visit to Monthrope Hall, and Augustus immediately drove Albert to the horse stud to show off his equine treasures. Lady Hardacre, unaware that Lord Ascot was as horse mad as her husband, though his preference was hunters, filled in the time with her ladyship. She found it a long afternoon and, seeing Laura heading indoors, she pounced on her.

'Miss Markham, Lord Ascot has been so long with Augustus up at the stables, that I felt obliged to ask her ladyship if they will dine here. And she has accepted.'

Was there a hint of a sigh? Perhaps Lady Hardacre liked the Ascot parents as little as Laura did. This visit they had not been accompanied by their daughter. Laura wondered if it was due to some thoughtless imbecile remarking on their previous visit about how well the two girls had got along together. Were these top-lofty parents carefully keeping them separated?

'I will be quite satisfied to eat in the breakfast room, Lady Hardacre.'

'Nonsense, Miss Markham. You will support me through this.'

'Certainly, if that is your wish,' Laura replied, but Lady Hardacre was already heading for the butler's pantry.

Laura dressed for dinner with care, selecting one of her better gowns and perhaps something simple in the way of adornment. She eyed a gold crucifix presented to her on her fifteenth birthday by a misguided godparent and decided against it, descending unadorned.

The whole party was gathered in the anteroom. Had she kept them all waiting? No, Hocking had only just entered with the drinks, and she observed the entire group fell on their refreshments with gusto. They had barely time enough to finish before Hocking announced that dinner was served; perhaps he was miffed about the extra duties. They entered with the appropriate partner, Laura and Charles bringing up the rear. Lady Hardacre looked around complacently and remarked, 'Well, that's the only good thing about your lovely daughter being absent, the numbers at table are equal.'

'Oh, Amelia has developed a penchant for attending the church's Ladies Guild, and they meet of a Tuesday afternoon. She asked us to defer our visit here, and I expressed myself rather strongly on her presumption. Now I'll be able to tell her it was just as well she didn't come.'

Laura felt relieved that her suspicions regarding the Ascot parents appeared incorrect, and Lady Hardacre hastened to explain that the pleasure of a visit from Amelia far outweighed the disadvantages of an unequal number at the dinner table. They all settled, and Laura was intrigued to notice that Hocking had reduced the table so that conversation was possible as a group. Had Evadne arranged that?

Sitting in the centre, opposite Charles Wakefield, Laura quietly worked her way through the two removes and carefully turned an interested face to each end of the table in turn. It was hard not to laugh: Lord Ascot was discussing horses, particularly those most suitable for hunting – horses being a subject Lady Hardacre faced every night with stern endurance. Lady Ascot was regretting her lack of grandchildren, and Laura could imagine how exciting Augustus Hardacre found that topic. 'There really is no one available for Amelia. Bert was going to speak to Barlow about his youngest son. Nigel is single at thirty, although the age difference is not great. Of course, they are farmers, but something might have been done for the boy. However, Amelia pointed out that he really wasn't suitable.'

Lady Hardacre spoke. 'What news have you received from your son in India, Lady Ascot? Has he written recently?'

There was a moment's pause and Laura saw Lady Ascot visibly straighten and shoulder some burden. 'Oh, we have such exciting news of him, Evadne. By now he will be on his way home from Calcutta.' She took a breath and added, 'I should say "they will be on their way home". Bertram has married.'

Everyone stared at Lady Ascot, who turned red, then paled when she caught her husband's expression. Laura had immediately glanced at Lord Ascot and thought if looks could kill, his wife would be lying stone dead on the floor.

Lady Ascot, with a lioness's courage in defence of her young, leaned towards her spouse and stated, 'The marriage is a fact, Bert, and we must support our boy.'

Lady Hardacre said, somewhat at random, 'I gather Bertram's bride is no one that you know, Merle.'

Lord Ascot burst out, 'I never thought a son of mine would marry a native. Just think, Evadne, my grandchildren will be some shade of black or brown, mulattos I suppose.' His fist came down on the table, silently but clenched.

It was too much for Laura.

'I don't believe we should judge his wife sight unseen. She may be acceptable, and you may find you are proud of her. Have you learned anything of her background?'

'Well, he's mentioned the family, said that she's some nabob's daughter. That caused me to think, in fact, I expected her father was someone like Julius, but it can't be. He wrote that they were married in a Hindu temple.' He subsided but it was apparent that he was overwhelmed with anxiety and bursting to say more.

Lady Hardacre decided to take the easy way out. She looked at her visitor and Laura and asked if they were ready to remove. Both were only too eager to oblige, and they walked along the corridor to the vast acreage of the drawing room. Lady Ascot withdrew briefly, and Evadne turned to Laura and surprised her. 'Well spoken, Miss Markham. I wish I had uttered your words.'

The gentlemen did not keep them waiting long. Laura played the piano and Lady Ascot stood beside her and sang and Laura heard genuine enthusiasm in the applause that followed. The others joined them around the instrument, and they worked their way through several airs selected in the hope they would appeal to his lordship. Hocking entered with the tea trolley and the party broke up soon after, in order that the Ascots could travel home before it became really dark. Lord and Lady Hardacre returned from escorting the visitors to their coach to find Laura on her own at the trolley, collecting and stacking teacups.

'That didn't go too badly,' Evadne remarked, but Augustus interpolated, 'Poor fellow, no wonder he's in a heat.'

Neither of the women commented.

PETER AND PEGGY PROGRESS

*P*eter Jameson was just twenty-two and had worked for the Hardacre's for seven years, yet he approached Laura before risking his reputation on any of the stable staff or his master.

'Miss Markham, can I ask you something?'

'Certainly, Peter, ask me now before we all head off for our ride.'

'Do you think I should ask Grimes or Bob or Mr Wakefield if his lordship's got a spare cottage here?'

'Definitely ask Lord Hardacre himself. The others can only recommend you.'

'How would I go about that?'

'When is Lord Hardacre easiest to get along with? When can you see him alone?'

Peter was inclined to answer 'never' to both questions. He had noticed that lately, old Gus seemed quite shitty with Will Grimes, and therefore with everyone. This had led him to take Peter on his morning tour of the racing stables all week, which had put Grimes in bad skin. He didn't know what to answer.

Laura said, 'Next time you see Lord Augustus, ask him straight out and tell him why.'

It turned out to be surprisingly good advice. Lord Hardacre heard Peter out in silence, as the young groom explained his coming marriage and his need for accommodation. Until his lordship responded, Peter was unaware that his request was almost a godsend to his master, and that evening he could hardly wait to call on his intended and tell her the result.

Peter and Peggy met regularly, and a family visit always occurred somewhere during their outing, particularly if it was raining. In fine weather, they strolled, chatting, around the houses and nearby lanes, absorbed in each other and unaware of the village's pleasure in seeing a Monthrope son so happy with his choice.

Peter began this outing by asking Peggy how her employers were reacting to her walking out with him.

'Oh, I haven't told them much about us, Peter, just Miss Carstairs and she doesn't mind.' She continued, 'I was glad because I thought she wouldn't approve of my going out with anyone. They generally prefer we should keep to ourselves.'

Peter wanted to investigate this, but he was bursting with his own news and decided to find out the details later. 'Peggy, things are happening up at the Hall and I'm fair busting to tell you about them. I asked Gus if he had a cottage available for a married stable hand, and it turned out that I asked just at the right time. Gus found the lads up at the stud are playing merry-go-lightly when they're left on their own at night. So he decided to put an end to that and he's turning an old cottage into a house. It will mean that the stableboys won't be sleeping above the horses anymore, so it should be better for them as well. He wants a married couple in the new quarters to see the lads are properly fed and cared for and to put an end to their mischief.

'Of course, Grimes should be the one to go but he's single and he don't want to marry. I suppose somebody must have let him down once because he seems real sour on females. Hardacre told him he can head the home stables, and I can be head groom at the stud and he at the Hall. He don't like that either, but there's nothing he can do about it. Now, sweetheart, what do you think? To me, it looks like time for us to marry.'

'That's absolutely the best news you could bring me, Peter. Things are happening at Sutton House, too. They're argifying and rowing something shocking. I don't see it lasting much longer.'

'You don't see what lasting much longer?'

'Them being together. I've had enough of it, I tell you. I'll be glad to be out of it and settled here in Monthrope. I'm fed up with the noise and I've had enough of being ordered around and niggled at by Miss Halbert.'

This was happy news for Peter, and he told her so before going back to the story of his promotion, how he had been too nervous to ask Grimes or Bob and had approached Laura. Peggy asked who Laura was and he told her about the governess and how right she had been. They both wondered what Bob Alston's future was going to be if Grimes was heading the Hall stables. Gus must have something in mind for him; he always looked out for his boy.

They walked back along the lanes to Sutton House, and for the first time, Peter followed Peggy in through the kitchen door. Her bedchamber was on the ground floor, its door situated near the ingle, where Peggy halted. She stoked up the fire and put a kettle on the grille, and Peter stood beside her watching the flames. Above their heads, they heard footsteps and a door closing, and Miss Halbert descended the wooden stairway to the kitchen.

'Oh, so this is how you spend your evenings, is it?'

'It's my free time. I please myself,' retorted Peggy, looking her straight in the eye.

'Don't you talk to me that way, you cheeky snirp. I don't

take lip from anyone.'

Peggy put a hand on Peter's arm, knowing that only Miss Halbert's attire kept him from retaliation. 'You don't tell me anything, Miss Halbert. You are not my employer. Miss Carstairs has no objection to how I spend my free time.'

'So, you've told her, have you?'

'That I have. And proud to do so.'

Miss Halbert strode off upstairs and irate voices drifted down to the young couple enjoying their supper and smiling at the warfare above their heads.

JULIUS AND BERYL

*L*aura discovered that Mr Wakefield discussed almost every issue with Mr Wilmott, particularly those likely to affect the grandchildren. Julius visited Monthrope Hall regularly now and stayed for days. Although he had long sessions with his daughter, explored everywhere, chatted, and listened to everyone, some of his time was spent with Eugene and Michael, and therefore with Laura.

In Laura's circumscribed social circle, his visits were of great interest. Although Lady Hardacre continued her own activities, and Augustus appeared in awe of him and was seldom present, Mr Wilmott took a lively interest in his grandsons. The boys called him Pa which was apparently what Lady Hardacre called him privately. His invasion of the nursery and his pleasure in their erudition were a great encouragement to their perseverance. He said he hadn't much education himself and had done alright, but he would have loved to have had the opportunities available to them.

'New developments are occurring daily in every field,' he told them. 'Likely you boys will be making your own mark in the world one day.'

All the staff, except Mr Wakefield, quaked when they heard him, perhaps because of his size, but Laura liked him and was not frightened by his loud voice. She realised he was uneasy about mixing with the gentry and he particularly disliked supercilious servants, masking it with bluntness and occasionally humour. She decided the only approach with him was to tell the truth, to be bold, and was greatly helped by the two boys intuitively adopting the same approach. Mr Wilmott thrived on this, and his hearty laughter was heard so often in the nursery that the staff half-suspected Laura of setting her cap at him. She was not. Her affections had been placed elsewhere.

Julius accompanied them on a natural history expedition to the river and turned it into a picnic by bringing along a lunch hamper. He waded in the water with the boys as they pored over their nets and stored their catches of water beetles, tadpoles, and tiny fish in jars. It was a great success.

After enjoying their luncheon, the boys explored the area and climbed trees, while Laura and Mr Wilmott sat on the grass and watched. She stared in astonishment when he looked at her and said, 'You're utterly unaware of how attractive you look, aren't you? And of its effect. If you ever tire of this "governessing" lark let me know.'

Laura could think of no answer. She got to her feet and stood looking for the boys.

Wilmott apparently realised that he needed to explain further, for he added, 'Beryl, my wife, gave me two daughters and I decided I wasn't producing an academy of females in the hope of getting a boy, so I stopped right there. But my life is good. I found me a lass who accommodates my personal needs very well and she's been my mistress for many years. Hers is a place where I can relax and be comfortable. My youngest daughter has produced two excellent grandsons and they will one day occupy corners of my business empire. I'm not breeding up idle aristocrats to waste my hard-earned money. Aah, here come the little tykes now. It's time we went back, is it?'

'Yes. The hard part will be getting them to put the creatures back in the water.'

That was the right approach, she thought. Let his words pass over and not read too much into them – not wonder if Mr Wilmott wanted another mistress, or how he intended to help her if she tired of this so-called "governessing" lark. Did he mean anything by that; was he astute enough to realise she wasn't dependent on a governess's income?

Mrs Wilmott visited rarely, declaring the country was boring and she preferred to be at home. Mr Wakefield whispered to Laura that, at home, she complained no one took her anywhere. Laura at first thought her the most colourless individual on the planet: a pale complexion surmounting muted muslin and shawls hung about with tassels. But there was no frailty to her comments which were often personal and always acidic. If Lord Hardacre presented as one of the ghosts of Monthrope Hall, coming and going silently for the most part, Mrs Wilmott sometimes reminded Laura of Macbeth's three witches.

How Mrs Wilmott passed the hours she spent in her room Laura had no idea, but she occupied the visible part wandering around finding fault. In short order, she upset the gardener, the cook and all the junior staff. Foreseeing disaster, Evadne increased salaries and insisted her mother keep out of the kitchen. Previous experience apparently deterred Lady Hardacre from including this tiresome parent in her round of social visits, except for those made to her sister, Mrs Bright.

Their meals were farcically repetitive. 'Will you try a slice of this lamb, (beef, venison,) Beryl?' Lord Hardacre, armed with the carving knife and fork, would patiently ask each evening.

'Oh, I think not. It looks tough. Isn't it underdone? (Overdone, too dry?) Well, I'll try a morsel, no, not with root vegetables, I thank you. Isn't there any asparagus? McPherson (her old enemy, the gardener) will be dining well tonight. There were three lovely spears just fit to be picked this morning.'

'I'll thank you to keep out of the gardener's way,' Evadne advised.

'What words to use to your mother. You ought to be

ashamed.'

Julius distracted her by proffering a bowl with a pretty arrangement of carrot and parsnip and chuckling when she refused it. Mrs Wilmott generally ate slices of thin bread and butter and drank soup. On the occasions when she enjoyed a dish, she reported next morning that it had kept her awake all night, and her unrepentant husband would claim that was just terrible, but hadn't he heard her snoring?

Laura wondered if Beryl Wilmott had found a means of repaying years of neglect, but why would she persist in something so self-defeating? For reasons unknown, she never entered the nursery and Laura made no effort to include her. She was relieved to encounter her only at the meal table, always double-checked that she herself was neatly presented and not over-dressed, and was in this difficult visitor's good books simply because she once helped her with a recalcitrant chair.

For Laura, being in Mrs Wilmott's good books meant not being spoken to or about, but the chair event provided Mrs Wilmott with a recurrent source of complaint. She was able to abuse both the butler and Luke, who was acting as footman, decry the manners of everyone else present, and criticise the furnishings. Mr Wilmott remarked to Laura afterwards, that Beryl got full value from her chair mishap.

HOME AT LAST: BERTRAM RETURNS

*S*unday morning, with the service over and fine weather tempting people to dawdle, the sociable were making the most of their chance to share a few words with the neighbours. It had been a busy time of the year, with limited opportunities to meet, so almost the entire village was present to witness the entourage that passed before its delighted eyes.

At the head of it rode a sizeable escort of superbly accoutred outriders mounted on splendid horses. These were followed by a coach and four, the coachman and assistant in uniform, two grooms behind, ditto. After them came coaches of servants, and a baggage train of covered wagons hauled by draught horses, splendid in harness.

Some of the parishioners spotted the arms on the panels of the lead coach and called out excitedly, 'It must be Bertram Ascot,' but Laura had already guessed that by the riders' dark complexions and elegant turbans with coloured flashes. They passed on without a sideways glance, headed for Monthrope Major.

What excitement. What a buzz as Monthrope village collected to conjecture. At least five ladies decided then and there that a visit to the Ascots was imperative; just give the family a day or two to adjust, first.

He must have done that deliberately, thought Laura. He knows how the English will react to a foreign wife, so he is going to prove she is something out of the ordinary. They won't dare to slight her after such an entrance. Others had surmised similarly and everyone was eager to head home and spread the news.

The Ascots became a seven-day wonder throughout several counties, the road to Ascotvale was ground to powder by the flow of carriages, the bustle was never-ending, and an exhilarated Lady Ascot welcomed all who arrived.

Lady Hardacre was an early visitor and she found Lord Ascot much heartened to discover his daughter-in-law was the equivalent of a princess, her dowry immense and her father's wealth apparently bottomless. It appeared that her parent had been to school in both France and England and understood this country's ways. He liked stately, formal ceremonies and he got them at Monthrope Major, although, as soon as he was reassured that his daughter and son-in-law were being treated with suitable distinction, he proceeded to London.

Laura encountered Lord Ascot on one of her outings and he stopped to express his feelings on the subject.

'Well, Bertram will never make a farmer. It's fortunate that he appears to have other plans,' blustered his father, torn between pride in his only son and heartbreak that the boy would never settle to the family's traditional lifestyle. 'And you wouldn't believe the hullaballoo in the kitchens at home. Thank God, I had the sense to put in two stoves when we did them up. The nearest Shreya comes to good British food is beans and peas or eggs. She's a Hindu and they go through mountains of rice. Bertram says he's developed a taste for their food.' He screwed up his mouth at the thought.

'I can see you are as proud as punch of him,' demurred Laura. 'He's plainly done very well in India, and to top it off he has come home hale and hearty. So many of our merchants and soldiers don't.'

She paused a moment for him to absorb her words and added, 'You have an extremely capable daughter in Amelia, and she will be the saviour of your property whether married or single.'

She observed him take her words on board and decide

that he did indeed feel proud, but he remained aggrieved at no longer having everything his own way. Bertram was showing far too much taste for independence, let alone Amelia who was merely a female. They really had better bestir themselves and find someone to take her off their hands. He had been petrified all week that she would be swayed by any one of the rajah's handsome entourage.

Laura was genuinely pleased when Amelia drove over that afternoon. She had no qualms about discussing the home situation and Laura was surprised at the topics she touched on. It was astonishing to find she had spent much of the week out in the fields with the agent and the farmhands, apparently planning the next season's cropping. She heard much more about Lord Ascot's unsuccessful efforts to interest Bertram in running the estate than any other subject, and Amelia admitted that something was afoot, but doubtless she would find out what it was one day. When Laura asked her how she liked her new sister, Amelia said openly that she was surprised at how well Shreya spoke English. She had the most beautiful clothes, saris, that Amelia had ever seen, and appeared fit and well on her strange diet.

Laura replied, 'I'm glad you like her.'

Amelia looked at her quickly. 'How do you know that?'

'I just felt it,' replied her friend quietly.

'You're quite right,' Amelia answered. 'And very insightful.'

CELEBRATIONS

*I*n September, both the Wilmotts arrived two days before Michaelmas, and Julius helped Laura and the boys brighten the passageways with vases of autumn leaves. The Brights arrived the next day, but there were no school lessons, just games and drawing and reading, so Laura was not greatly burdened. That night, the entire family gathered in a drawing room decorated with chrysanthemums to play party games and sing while Laura played the piano. They roasted chestnuts by the fireside and munched happily. Laura found it all very pleasant and different from her earlier years when Michaelmas had provided a time for quiet reflection.

On the evening of the twenty-ninth itself, the family, including the children, gathered for a superb dinner of goose and other goodies. Another dinner was held for the staff in the servant's hall, which was later cleared, so that hired musicians could play for a servants' dance. Mrs Carson and Mary provided 'a bite of supper' afterwards. The children were returned to Nurse's care while the adults came down to observe the dancing and gradually join in. Mr Bright and Mr Wilmott danced with their wives, before both ladies retired to their bedchambers, saying they were exhausted. Laura was happily watching the revelry when a voice spoke at her side. It was Mr Bright, inviting her to dance. She accepted and enjoyed a country dance with him, and a second with Hocking, the butler. Ben Alston asked her for the next dance and there was an energy to his dancing that roused Laura, and they held the attention of the room each time they spiritedly ducked under the arched arms of the lead couple and returned up the length of the set.

Laura needed a break and a glass of fruit punch before she was ready to try again, and Leonard Bright sat and chatted to her while they watched the staff enjoying themselves. Mr Wilmott chose her for the last dance and proved surprisingly graceful waltzing, and Laura knew they made an elegant couple. Since the Hall lacked European servants, few of the staff knew the steps, but she was delighted to see that several found themselves partners and earnestly endeavoured to follow the master.

The next morning, Laura left to spend the day with Martha and Ben in relaxation, idleness, and peace. During this time, she confided in Martha about her inheritance and the difficulties attached to changing her lifestyle, even with Mr Davidson's guidance. She felt that living among the gentry in Monthrope had shown her that the higher up the ladder you rose, the more restricted and formal your behaviour had to be. Like her father, she could see no point to an existence free of work; humans were meant to employ their brains. As such, she had no desire to enter fashionable society or try climbing the social ladder; nor was she an intellectual who could seek out fellow bluestockings. She didn't want to travel; she wanted to settle somewhere, but she dreaded having to acquire a companion if she set up her own house. She had seen them in other people's houses, and they were to be pitied. As for herself, she neither needed nor wanted a watchdog. She wanted to marry but knew she would now be pursued for her money. She wouldn't have anyone know about her good fortune for the world because she had seen how mercenary people could be. Until she decided which of these was the lesser evil, she was more than happy to stay where she was. Really, she was feeling quite at home. If Martha suspected her of having another reason, she was content to remain in ignorance until Laura decided to say more.

FRIENDSHIP

*M*onthrope's recipients of 'Poor Relief' were paupers further assisted by the benevolence of four notable landowners whose wives or retainers paid a regular visit to their hovels, and Laura became accustomed to making the rounds each month on behalf of Lady Hardacre. She found the outing was always interesting, although occasionally the weather made dashing from chaise to cottage and back unpleasant.

'You really need something to do with your time,' she announced one afternoon, straightening her back after cleaning and bandaging Walter Smythe's blackened toe. The old man chuckled, reached around in his chair and hauled a bag from under the table. From it, he took a piece of wood and handed it to Laura. It was a sheep, lovingly carved from a piece of scrap timber.

'Thath how I spend me days,' he lisped through the remnants of his teeth.

Laura turned it over in her hands. It was more than a faithful representation of the ovine. It somehow embodied everything that sheep meant to an old man who had once herded them, shorn them, watched over them, and possibly even helped his late wife card the fleece that she spun. Laura sat stroking the beautiful result, spellbound.

'Yer can have it, Miss Markham.'

'It's too good to give away, Walter. What do you usually do with them?'

'I makes little sets for the childer to play with. Lady Horton is dubbing me a sixpenny bit a beast and I've been making a farmyard full for her younkers.' He chuckled complacently; he obviously felt he was earning a fortune.

'Well, I'll give you sixpence for this one, if you are sure that you can spare it.'

'You're welcome.'

'I'll bring the money as soon as I can and then I'll collect my sheep. See if you can get about on those feet a bit more, Walter. Wiggle your toes while you work. But now I've got to go.'

She headed out of the cottage, still quite mesmerised by meeting beauty in such surroundings, and observed that a woman was sitting outside the neighbouring cottage, enjoying a burst of sunshine, and singing under her breath as she spun fleece. Laura couldn't help comparing her home to some of those she visited. It was pin-neat and glowing, with the flowers fronting a fine show of vegetables. She was seated on a stool at her wheel, her hands feeding carded fleece to it from a basket while one foot gently beat time with the treadle. Laura paused to watch her.

'Come ye and try it,' the unknown called. Laura walked across and the woman rose and fetched another stool. Laura watched the spinner draw the fleece out and build it up into a thread around her bobbin. She was persuaded to try for herself and it was by no means easy. The result of her attempt was uneven and she rose to go, thanking the spinner.

She looked for the woman on her next visit and again she tried the spinning wheel, and though she felt she did better, it still felt awkward. There was something about the voice of the wheel, its homeliness, which entranced her. She would have liked to have immersed herself in its gentle rhythm and created her own homely tune while she magicked thread out of wool.

She introduced herself and her hostess said, 'Oh, I know your name. Everybody knows who you are. My boy told me about you.'

'Why, who are you?' demanded Laura, tired of waiting for an introduction.

'I'm Maisy Alston, that's who I be. Come and have a cup of cha with me.'

'Thank you, I will, but I can't stay very long.' Laura followed her into the cottage. She found it a museum piece of the home-made, everything done carefully and thoroughly.

'Now, where be you from?' asked Maisy, determined to find out how much of a foreigner Laura was.

'I'm from Surbury,' replied Laura, for want of a better answer. 'Have you always lived in Monthrope?' She got up as she spoke and walked about, admiring the spotless room with its dresser and scrubbed table, while Maisy encouraged a kettle on the grille over the fire in the ingle. A snowy curtain covered a window with its shutters fastened back against the outside wall, and heavy winter drapes hooked back on the inside. All was cosy, clean and homely. How little we require to keep ourselves happy, thought Laura.

Maisy opened a cupboard door to get out two mugs, and there were her jams and pickles lined up above the shelf of crockery. 'A place for everything and everything in its place,' commented Laura, admiringly. They sat in good fellowship, looking out at the sunny garden and enjoying their break. The contentedness of her new acquaintance provided Laura with subject matter for her next letter to Newcastle.

Laura was driving peacefully homeward that evening when she saw a couple loitering along the laneway. The young man's arm was around his love, but he straightened when they heard the chaise and they both moved onto the grass lining the hedgerow. Laura realised it was Peter Jameson, the groom, and she called out a friendly greeting, 'Hello, Peter. Nice evening for a stroll.'

'Why, hello, Miss Markham,' said Peter, smiling serenely up at her. 'You just heading home? This is my girl Peggy, Peggy Pelham.'

'Lovely to meet you, Peggy, I'm Laura Markham. Do you live in Monthrope?'

'Aye, that I do. I does for Miss Carstairs.'

'Oh, so you've not been in Monthrope long; where did you come from?'

'I was brought up in Little Surbury, as they call it locally. All me family live there. Me Ma and Da are buried there.'

'My parents have died, too. I'm glad you've found someone nice, it's lonely on one's own.'

Peggy smiled up at her and Peter immediately added, 'We're getting married soon, Miss Laura. Will you come to our wedding? I'm to be the new head groom up at the stud. Gus wants a married man and Grimes ain't the marrying type.'

'Of course, I will come to your wedding. Thank you for inviting me. Goodbye, for now. I hope to see you again soon, Peggy. Bye, Peter.' Laura drove on.

Two weeks later, the important event was a town meeting. The four great landowners had decided something needed to be done about the wattle and daub cottages of the poor in Monthrope village, due to the lowering effect of their appearance on the hamlet. The plan was to provide new buildings, starting with five terrace houses. The original group of worthies was enlarged by the inclusion of the vicar, a hopeful mason, and a lawyer. They joined other landholders around a table at the Monthrope Arms to decide where, when and how an improvement was to be introduced. Since they were meeting in a public venue, the populace considered themselves invited. Among the crowd, Laura attended with Evadne, one of the few women to show a face, although Mrs Haldon and two barmaids were kept profitably busy all evening. It intrigued Laura that none of the pensioners were in attendance or even expected.

At first, it appeared that rivalry between the two largest landholders would neutralise the evening but, thanks to Claude Sutton being appointed chairman, the belligerent few were kept on task and on track. The presence of the vicar also proved salutary when old grudges raised their heads. Lord Ascot, as a local justice of the peace intimately acquainted with Snowy Widdeson, averred that he would desert the project if 'that old scoundrel' was given a house, but was placated by learning that there were currently ten pauper families, and the current plan was to build five houses.

Several attendees, and Laura suspected Evadne agreed with them, suggested that all pauper pensioners should be moved to the Monthrope Major workhouse, but the vicar spoke so straightforwardly about the conditions there – the separation of families, the overcrowding in the dormitories, the heart and body-breaking working conditions, and the taint the whole idea of it brought to the township – that the tight-fisted abandoned their argument. Not a soul in Monthrope but feared being reduced to entering the county's most dreaded building.

Agreement was eventually reached that, those who could, would donate ten pounds; the lawyer was appointed to complete the paperwork and all necessary approvals, and the mason builder was approved. The vicar ended the evening with a prayer of thanks and gratitude, suggestive that heaven was attainable for all who contributed.

Julius listened to Evadne and Laura's separate descriptions of the plan and deemed Monthrope village's response cheeseparing. His gift of one hundred pounds set the donations off to a flying start and led to the lane eventually being named Wilmott Close. Laura suffered, due to a self-created problem. She donated ten pounds, asserting to the vicar who was acting as secretary, that she wanted it to be an anonymous donation, never dreaming it would become public knowledge.

Laura's earnest entreaty unwittingly helped the committee recollect that a certain amount of pride is usually attached to having carried out a charitable act. They decided to ensure and encourage the miserly to open their purses wider, by listing and prominently displaying the names and contributions of all donors. If a little governess was prepared to wring out ten pounds, more shame to those above her. They proceeded, hoping her gift would be a salutary spur to the population. Of course, no one could comprehend a governess proffering such an amount, and it aroused an undue amount of gossip. Fortunately, someone started a rumour that her employers, for their own unguessable reasons, had supplied the money. After a week of regretting she had unwittingly exposed herself, Laura breathed again, and life went on.

'I suppose you think you were very grand, making such an addition to the building fund,' sneered Mrs Wilmott. 'It's caused a lot of talk and serves you right for trying to ape your betters.'

'I just thought how much I would dislike having to move to the workhouse,' said Laura. She toyed with the idea of asking Mrs Wilmott if she was intending to donate but decided not to descend to the old harridan's tactics. Thereafter, she bore peaceably with occasionally being twitted about her donation by Mrs Wilmott, who remained determined not to let Laura get above herself.

EASY COME, EASY GO

One evening Peter and Peggy strolled down to the village for a chat with the vicar. He was willing to marry them for his standard five-shilling fee, and he would announce the banns three Sundays in a row and then perform the office. They paid the half-amount for the calling of the banns and Mr Greenaway fetched his wife to join them for a celebratory glass of wine. Neither Peter nor Peggy was a drinker, but they appreciated the vicar's kindness and enjoyed the experience. They departed, smiling to think of the villagers' surprise when the banns were read at church next Sunday, unaware that their unnoticed observer-protectors had predicted almost the date of it.

Feeling that they had celebrated suitably, the young couple returned to Sutton House and sat down in the kitchen. Peggy put a kettle on to boil and Peter fetched in some sticks from the wood box outside the kitchen door. They began to discuss the furnishings they would need so that they could set up in their future domicile, trying to estimate what the Hall would supply for them and what their family would have to provide, when they were interrupted by the sound of a door banging and footsteps on the stairs above.

It was Miss Halbert. Quite possibly, both their faces revealed that, if it had to be one of the ladies, it had best be Miss Carstairs. She came slowly down the staircase and Peggy, who was facing her way, saw how critically she looked at the scene below.

'Quite comfortable, are we?' asked Miss Halbert, strolling around the kitchen and looking them up and down as she went, and they both replied in the affirmative. With nothing further to keep her there, she walked back to the stairs and began to mount again. Peter thought she appeared bored with life and had hoped to create some excitement by stirring them up. Their response of silence, while patiently waiting for her to leave, had apparently outmanoeuvred her.

She stopped and turned in their direction when she had mounted a few steps, and they both wondered what her game was. Peter stiffened as he realised that Miss Halbert was eyeing him over. She examined what she could see of him sitting at the table on Peggy's right, with an avidity that made his skin crawl. Good lord, the woman was hot for him. He straightened against his chair and sent her a look that made his rejection and disgust apparent and was amazed to see that this heightened Miss Halbert's interest. Watching him, she moved and twitched from side to side, smirking and showing herself off. Talk about a cat toying with a mouse. Only the need to stay, to stand by Peggy, prevented Peter from rushing outside.

And then he noticed something else, something she was teasingly demonstrating: a bulge apparent behind the drapes of Miss Halbert's gown. Surely that was ... good grief, she wasn't a woman. She was a man and rampant. Miss Halbert interpreted his gaze correctly and she responded by posing on the step, reading his reactions in his face, and delighting in his astonishment. She leant back a little, moving and repositioning herself so that she flaunted what was hidden. Peter had heard about men who for some reason liked men; a man who dressed as a woman and appeared to like both was way beyond his experience and his imagination.

Peggy said, quite roughly, 'Get back upstairs where you ought to be and leave us alone.'

And the creature left. She ascended in stately fashion, turning at the landing, possibly pausing to make one last statement, verbal or physical, but her plan foundered. She saw two strapping youngsters she would have bedded with glee and realised that in their youth and inexperience, they saw an atrocity.

Years of disdain from society had taught Miss Halbert how to read minds for her own safety, and what she read in their young faces struck through to the remaining dregs of her soul. Peggy saw a debauched old hag, Peter some incomprehensible male-female abomination. She turned and ran from them, stumbling up the second flight, and rushed into Miss Carstairs's bedchamber. Sounds of an agitated and angry voice poured forth, to be returned with laughter and derision.

Peggy turned to Peter and said, 'Now you know what life can be like in this house.'

He grabbed her hands and held them tight. 'I'm taking you home to Ma. You're not staying here a moment longer.'

'Don't get mifty Peter, I'm not in any danger.'

They were interrupted by the increasing noise from upstairs. They heard Miss Halbert stamp off to her own room and slam the door. Peggy sighed; this was how it usually ended. She made more tea and set out bread and cheese and some fruit.

Peter remained seated, but his attention was turned upwards as he mulled over the fact that Miss Halbert was a man. 'He must be in hiding from the law. Fancy him living here disguised as a woman and nobody twigging it. Maybe he killed his man in a duel and he's on the run… hiding for his life. Or maybe he was a highwayman. Why else would he try to pass for a woman?'

'He's being himself, Peter. I imagine he's always been like it, except that he's gotten nastier. He wound himself around Miss Carstairs 'cause she's the one with the money. Her family pay her a regular allowance to stay out of sight and she's kept him for months now. Halbert's family have thrown him off, and I imagine he's lived by his wits for years. He's been with Miss since we came here and he's getting worse – or else she is. One thing's for sure, country life don't suit him at all. Miss would be quite happy here if she had something to do.'

'I suppose Miss Carstairs needs a man's help ... a man's support to get rid of him, she's only tiny.'

This seemed to amuse Peggy, although she replied, 'You could say that, but she's a sure hand at picking wrong'uns.'

Their refreshment had cooled enough to be drinkable, and they both turned their attention to their meal. Time ticked by until their peace was interrupted by Miss Halbert coming downstairs. She bore a travelling bag and was now dressed as a man with a beaver hat and greatcoat. Her long hair was tied at the nape of her neck in the style that only grandfathers used these days, and she looked a sight better. Male attire suited her.

'I've had enough. I'm out of here,' she said and was gone. Neither of them asked where she was going or how she intended to get there.

'Good riddance,' opined Peggy as soon as Miss Halbert was beyond hearing. They had finished eating but Peter was loath to go. A weak voice drifted down to them, calling feebly for Peggy. She went upstairs and Peter could hear her explaining events.

The voice wailed, 'Oh dear, what will I do? How can I cope?'

'You will cope, one step at a time,' he heard Peggy announce firmly. 'Like you did last time and all the previous times. What do you want to do? Are you going to stay here, or are you moving?'

'I'm going. I'm not happy here. I'll move to Bath. I know people who are kinder in Bath and there's more to do there. More fun.'

'Well, some of them are kinder but you'll have to be

watchful. You'll need to be real careful, or the traps will be after you. You sleep on it tonight and see how you feel on the morrow. If you still want to move, I'll help you pack, and I'll stay and clear up when you've gone.'

'And then you'll come to me?'

'I will not. I like it here. You know that. You know what my plans are.'

Frantic wails greeted this. Peggy left her to it and descended the stairs. Peter listened to the noise, appalled. 'The poor thing. She must really care for you, or else she must have really cared for him.'

'It's like I told you. She picks 'em. But she's no angel, Peter. And, by the way, it's not 'her' or 'she', it's 'he'. They're both men.'

Peter's expression at this news was too much for Peggy, and after struggling valiantly to maintain a straight face, she began to giggle until it sank in that he was truly shocked.

'Well, what are you doing here with them? Are you one of them?'

'Not at all, not ever. And they've never laid a finger on me, either of them. I knew how to handle Halbert so that he kept his distance. Carstairs' tastes lie another way. I've kept house for Miss, seven years now, without any problem except picking up the pieces and helping her, him, move. We've moved times almost beyond counting, but it's better than seeing him fined, whipped, or even hanged.'

'Peggy, why on earth did you stay with him. Did you love him?'

'Love him? No. Far from it. But I couldn't help but feel compassion for him, Peter. I've heard him called an abomination, but this was how he was born, this is how

God made him and everywhere he goes he's mocked and pointed at. Everywhere he tries to settle, he is shoved out, pushed off.' She looked at Peter. 'I don't fancy him or his life at all. It's not a good life, and it's not a fair life, but he's not as featherbrained as he makes out to be. Between his choice of friends and his personal habits, he gets mistreated everywhere. It's a pity he's never found someone who liked him for himself.'

'It's a pity he was ever born. Why do you work for him?'

'I was seventeen when I began keeping house for him because I was sick of being bullied by an innkeeper's wife in Surbury. This job has paid me well, very well indeed. I live at his expense, and I've saved every bit of my earnings. In return, I've kept my mouth shut about anything I heard and tried to take good care never to see too much. And that's real hard to do, with a couple of regular show-offs in the house.'

Peter remained silent and she tried again. 'I gave him a bit of steadiness… stability you might call it … in his racketing to and fro. That's all, Peter. But I must admit, it shocked me the one time I saw the pair of them naked.'

'Well, it's fair taken my breath away, I tell you. But I've got to be up at six, Peggy. I must go, but I feel like I ought to stay.'

'You get back to the Hall, Peter, and don't worry. Come and see me tomorrow night.'

LOVE MOVES IN STRANGE WAYS

*I*t was a measure of Peter's faith in Peggy's strength and determination that he left her without a great deal of further worrying about her personal safety. The critical adjustment he made to the most astonishing news he had ever heard was that he mentioned it to nobody because it was not his secret. Also, the thought of how the village might react if they ever heard the facts, frightened him. He felt that anyone associated with such strange people as Carstairs and Halbert might be deemed tainted, and not for the world would he have done anything to undermine his fiancée's standing.

It was, therefore, astonishing when William Grimes bailed him up barely a day later with a bold question. 'What's this I'm hearing down at the inn, about one of the ladies taking off? Abandoned her friend, and your missus too, I suppose, and left the town.'

'She was nothing to do with my Peggy. Nothing at all. She was Miss Carstairs's friend and no friend of mine.'

Grimes looked at him long and silently. 'So, you don't follow the same interests as those two…um…ladies?'

Did Grimes know what he was implying? Peter felt his insides go all shaky with fright. He took a moment to consider and then said, 'No. Not me, not at all. And nor does Peggy.' He waited, holding his breath.

It was Grimes's turn to be careful. 'I thought not. But you knew about them, and you were kind. You didn't report them to the vicar or the village constable?'

Peter began to relax a little. 'As Peggy says, they are how God made them. Well, Miss Carstairs is. I still think there was something real nasty about the one who left.' He took another chance and added, 'Why? Do you follow the same interests?'

'It's a plumb dangerous thing to say out loud; you work it out,' said Grimes. 'But I think I might go and console that so-called "Miss" Carstairs this evening.'

Grimes was as good as his word, appearing at the kitchen door of Sutton House and asking for Miss Carstairs. Peggy sat him on a chair and fetched her employer down to meet him. Miss Carstairs eyed her unexpected visitor very nervously when he took her hand and said, 'This need not be a sad time for you, my dear. You have suffered and perhaps it's a little early to offer you a new start, but you need to know I'm your friend and that you are not alone in this village. If you are seeking a new home, I can offer you a place in my cottage.'

(At this, both listeners were sure he thought she was a woman.)

'And if you need employment, Hocking will take you on at the Hall as a footman. I've asked him about it and he says he's happy to have the extra help.'

Peggy saw Miss Carstairs's face light up with joy and she felt it was safe enough to leave them to discuss their future and walked outside to the garden to stand staring at nothing and thinking that the world was full of kindly people in the strangest of guises. When she returned, Grimes was sitting alone and he said, 'Theo's gone up to change and to pack up. He's moving into my place and going back to being himself.' Peggy told him how glad she was to hear this, how fortunate it appeared for her employer, and how greatly they both appreciated Grimes's gentle kindness. William Grimes turned quite pink with pleasure and assured Peggy that he would take good care of her friend.

Peter had walked away from Will in a state not far from shock, but he wasn't surprised when the stableboys informed him that now Miss Carstairs had also left town.

Nor was he perplexed a day later, when Titus relayed the news that some middle-aged fellow, name of Theo Glover, had moved into Grimes's cottage and, what's more, taken a job as footman. He knew Peggy would fill in the details when he next saw her, and they both hoped that this time, Theo might have made his best choice.

PREPARATIONS FOR AN EVENT

*L*ady Hardacre, a woman who closely considered the expenditure of every farthing before parting with it, was planning a dinner party. She said that she was ashamed of the number of county families she owed, and an effort must be made. There was nothing nipcheese about her plans, although how much she was influenced by Julius, Laura was unaware.

Maids draped sheets over hearths throughout the house as chimney sweeps scrambled onto the roof and stirred the soot of ages. Daily, the house rang with clatter and chatter as ladders and buckets and brooms were unearthed so that Mrs Tillotson and a gaggle of village women could uncover and clean the smoking room, card room, library, saloons, drawing rooms, and not forgetting the withdrawing rooms. Windows and mirrors were polished, curtains and carpets beaten or shaken. Village women and farmers' daughters could be seen wielding massive irons in the laundry and, outside, men with scythes shaved the grass while a team of rustics transformed the driveway. The gardeners exerted themselves and the stable crew refurbished the farm and horse yards. Supplies of everything imaginable were ordered in.

Charles Wakefield hid in his office, Augustus fled to the horse stud, and Lady Hardacre inspected each completed room, calling back any miscreants who had failed to adequately wash and polish the crystal lustres, hang the curtains straight, or dared alter the mantel arrangements. At first, Eugene and Michael were agog with excitement, so Laura allowed them to beat carpets if they would continue till their allotted task was completed. By this means, they discovered for themselves how hot and dirty and tiring the job was. It rapidly lost its novelty, and they were glad to wash their hands and faces, swallow a cool drink, and return to normal duties.

Once the main rooms were completed, bedrooms throughout the house were turned out because not all guests could be expected to drive home, and they were likely to arrive with servants who must also be housed. The bustle seemed endless, but everyone appeared excited and enthused, and nobody complained about the extra work.

Mr Wilmott collected the boys and took them on a visit to London which kept them out of the way for the rest of the week, and Laura continued only her role of visiting the needy. She returned to find footmen, housemaids, and kitchen maids had been hired and uniformed, while the crowning glory was the appointment of a French chef, dominating the kitchen.

After one stormy meeting related to the antiquity of the furnishings, the kitchenware and the food, an exasperated Lady Hardacre promoted Laura to the role of mediator because Wakefield spoke no French. Laura listened and soothed both parties and everyone settled in. Only Laura knew what time and effort it had taken to flatter Monsieur Dupres into accepting his situation in this obsolete outpost of the aristocracy, and then to find the time and words to hear out and mollify Mrs Carson, Mary the kitchen maid, and Hocking – all of whom had their noses thoroughly and apparently permanently out of joint.

She helped Lady Hardacre write invitations on gilt-edged cards in perfect copperplate and Lady Hardacre personally delivered them to the chosen families. Most were returned within days and Lady Hardacre had the pleasure of finding every response was an acceptance, meaning that eleven couples would grace the dining table over which she and Augustus presided.

In spite of her arctic calm, her ladyship must have felt some excitement because, looking up from reading her governess a particularly flattering reply, she informed Laura that she had purchased a new outfit for the evening. She added that she had also bought a new outfit for receiving any visitor with the temerity to turn up early. What was Laura going to wear?

Laura froze on her chair and stared at her employer in shock.

'I never dreamt I would attend. In fact, I believe I should not attend; it would be most inappropriate.'

'Don't you want to come?'

'No, but only because a governess would be so out of place.'

'If you don't attend, we won't need Charles, then. Very well, I won't insist that you attend, except in one instance. If we should be a lady short, will you fill in?'

'Yes, of course. I would see it as necessary and therefore the right thing to do. I might be of assistance somewhere or able to help any lady who needed it.'

'Well, thank you, Laura. Make sure you hold yourself ready. Usually, we need an extra man and Charles fills in, but the Ascots' daughter is not attending. Still, I have a funny feeling about this party, and I suspect you will be needed.'

Laura didn't answer. The realisation that this was the first time Lady Hardacre had used her given name, had distracted her.

Lady Hardacre proved right. The following day brought a letter requesting that the Cockrams be permitted to bring their newly arrived guest, Mr Lang, rather than leave him on his own for the evening. There was only one possible answer, and in addition, Mr Lang was a well-known Scottish industrialist and, therefore, almost guaranteed to add distinction to the evening. Lady Hardacre hastened to respond by means of the footman who carried over the original note, that the Cockrams' guest would be most welcome. She left the problem of how to seat an extra couple at the table to Hocking and sat turning over in her mind the problem of who was to fill the remaining place. Should she insist on Amelia? No, she already had one risky guest. In the end, she went in desperation to Laura.

'Lord and Lady Cockram are bringing Colin Lang. I can't refuse such a celebrity, Laura. I've racked my brains for some female to make up the numbers. There is no one else, so will you join us?'

'Certainly, Lady Hardacre. You have enough to worry about, so I will attend and be what use I can.' She received a 'thank you' and a grateful look as Lady Hardacre hurried off to consult with her butler.

THE DINNER PARTY

*L*ike everything at Monthrope Hall, the dinner party had its extraordinary moments. For Laura, they began on the evening prior to the big event, soon after the Wilmotts arrived. While Hocking and Tillotson saw the Wilmotts' dresser and valet up the back stairs to suitable rooms, and Julius joined Augustus in the library, Mrs Wilmott began her solitary inspection. She examined everywhere but without gaining much ascendancy over her daughter for, when she complained that she had found dust on one windowsill in the little morning room, Lady Hardacre merely looked up from her writing desk and snapped, 'Then wipe it off.'

Beryl stated loftily that she wasn't a servant and picked up the guest list, holding it at arm's length so she could read it clearly and query half the names listed on it. Receiving no answer, she then asked why Evadne had failed to invite Leonard and Elizabeth Bright, her own relatives. Evadne somewhat impatiently explained that the Brights had dined at Hardacre expense numerous times without being able to return the favour due to her sister's health. Unfortunately, Laura walked in with a vase of flowers at that moment, just as Mrs Wilmott discovered her name at the bottom of the guest list.

'Why on earth would you invite a governess to a dinner party?' Mrs Wilmott turned to Laura, admonishing her. 'It is no good you trying to inch your way in; nobody will talk to you and it's totally inappropriate for you to be present. You'll just look and be utterly out of place.'

Laura had sent an appalled, 'I-told-you-so' glance at Lady Hardacre and turned to this noisome guest, wondering why her ladyship would risk her mother's presence ruining the evening. She then realised that, of course, Lady Hardacre wanted her father to attend and so she had felt obliged to invite the other parent.

Lady Hardacre responded before she could open her mouth. 'Laura is attending at my express invitation. Now, Mother, you had best retire to your room and rest before the festivities start.' Surprisingly enough, Mrs Wilmott stalked out. Evadne turned to Laura and one of those strange instances occurred: they both opened their mouths and said, 'Please don't let it worry you.' Relishing the synchronicity, they both laughed.

The following evening, Laura arrayed herself in the least antiquated of her evening gowns and shawls and fastened the crucifix around her neck, feeling she needed every support she could get. She stayed upstairs until the noise level suggested that a great many people were conversing in the red saloon. Thinking she could safely hide among the crowd, she proceeded downstairs.

The Ascots were just handing their evening cloaks to a footman and Lady Ascot approached, saying she was glad to see Laura attending, and introduced her son, Bertram and his wife, Shreya. Laura found herself greeting an impeccably dressed young man and a doe-eyed Indian lady in an exquisite sari. They walked into the saloon together, enjoying the burst of colour from all the elegant outfits and the sight of Hocking and two waiters weaving in and out of the throng, proffering drinks.

Laura noticed a mousy little woman sitting in a corner and walked across and introduced herself, asking if she could fetch her ladyship something to drink. The mouse refused the drink, but she invited Laura to occupy a neighbouring chair and introduced herself as Lady Cockram.

So, this was the person with the notable guest. Laura was really interested. Rather than wait for her social superior to lead the way, she asked Lady Cockram where she lived and then what family she had, and her ladyship smiled and chattered amiably. When she eventually ran out of words, Laura ventured again. 'So, you have Mr Lang as a guest?'

'Yes, isn't it exciting? I grew up near Aberdeen and Colin was the boy genius of our village. I think we all knew he would do something extraordinary in life. He and Thomas, my husband, have developed a pump and are expecting great things of it.'

Their chat was interrupted by Hocking, who was standing by the dining room door and sonorously intoning, 'Ladies and gentlemen, dinner is served.' As the guests prepared to move to the dining room, Laura stood aside and was the last to enter, partnered by Mr Ainsley, whom she hardly knew. She noticed Bertram and his wife were seated facing each other, higher up the table and thought it a good move. Her own seat, in the middle of the long dining table, was opposite Mrs Wilmott and Laura decided she would have a more relaxed meal if she confined her attention to her plate and the gentlemen on either side of her.

Fortunately, it turned out that Philip Ainsley's estate was quite near Horton, where he was master of hounds. He wasn't above talking to a governess and remarked that he believed he recognised her face – hadn't he seen her tooling a gig or a chaise about the village? Laura answered in the affirmative and explained that she now regularly visited the poor for Lady Hardacre. From discussing this, he was easily encouraged to talk about his horses and hounds, and it was just as easy for Laura to slant her answers to show that she knew something of horse-riding.

The gentleman on her left introduced himself as John Tuppen and said he lived at Monthrope Major. Laura confessed to never having visited there, which gave him the chance to describe the many excellent features of his pretty market town. He went on to talk about his own property, adding, 'We are satisfied to produce good English lamb and mutton – none of these French kickshaws at our table.' This comment was overheard by his wife who was sitting one up from Mrs Wilmott, and she looked up and smiled across the table at Laura.

The meal was almost over when Bertram Ascot stood up and announced that he would like to say a few words. There was instant silence. 'I want to thank you all for welcoming me and my wife, the Rani Shreya Patel, back to the country of my birth, and for taking us to your hearts. It grieves us both to inform you that we are required to leave this delightful locality, but we are not going far. I have been appointed to the diplomatic service and will be based in London, although we anticipate occasional trips abroad, particularly to India. The rajah, my father-in-law, has by this time finished adapting a suitable residence in the city to our requirements, and I hope to see you there whenever you visit London. I drink to the health and wellbeing of every person present.'

His words caused immense excitement. It had suddenly become obvious that young Bertram was no mere son of a local bigwig, but a person who moved in circles well above theirs. Many of his audience wondered if they would ever have the nerve to take him up on his offer to visit him in London, and a few hardy souls even resolved to do so.

The ladies soon left the men to enjoy their port and removed to the drawing room, Laura seizing a moment to ask Hocking how he had fitted everybody in. 'Moved some furniture out and found another leaf for the table,' he responded with a twinkle. She smiled her approbation and followed the crowd along the hallway. She was pleased and relieved to see Mrs Wilmott heading upstairs and wondered if she was retiring for the night. It seemed almost too much to hope for.

She found the guests had gathered in groups on and around the drawing room settees, some chatting, some gushingly praising each other's attire and head ornaments, while Lady Shreya's sari was almost swooned over. Lady Hardacre was circulating in a relaxed way that showed she was attending to her guests without experiencing any problems. Laura sat next to Mrs Tuppen who immediately asked her who she was. She did not seem at all put out by finding Laura was the governess and said, 'Wasn't John funny at dinner? Fancy him sitting there, criticising French kickshaws when he was stuffing himself with them.'

It was simple to get her talking about her family and soon Mrs Sutton came up and said, 'This is the intrepid governess my son begs me for; all because she taught him how to catch pollywogs.' She sat down beside them, and they began happily comparing children and their funny ways.

Laura looked up and saw Evadne signalling her. She immediately walked across the room and her employer whispered, 'The men are approaching and will be here in a moment. Will you start the ball rolling by playing the pianoforte; perhaps some songs they can sing will be appreciated. Then I can ask John Tuppen if he'll take the floor – he's got an amazing voice.'

Laura forced herself to quietly respond in the affirmative, but she felt understandably nervous. I just hope nobody here is a real proficient, she fretted. She looked around the group and reasoned that it was a fair sample of the local gentry and lesser aristocracy and decided that they were out for an evening of enjoyment, not attending a sophisticated London soiree.

These calming thoughts had their effect. She played relaxedly, choosing well-known songs, and saw the guests gradually converging around the instrument. John Tuppen turned out to possess a heartbreakingly melodious tenor and played extremely well, and everyone joined in happily. Laura returned briefly but soon yielded her seat to a series of ladies who were now eager to demonstrate their proficiency. As soon as she sat down, Lord Ascot came and joined her.

'When Bertram broke the news to me this morning, I

remembered your words. They were very true, Laura. I am as proud as punch, as proud as any father can or has a right to be. It appears he has done some very good work mending relationships in one Indian state. Sometime, in weeks to come, I will let the neighbours know that he rejoices in an increase in rank and salary as well. It doesn't pay to arouse jealousy in one's neighbourhood, but it would be just as offensive to act as if they were not worth talking to.'

Laura smiled and sat back to watch the throng, thinking that she had found it a most enjoyable party. The people she knew were really the heart of the countryside and tonight they had made her feel welcome. No wonder she was satisfied to remain in Monthrope for the moment. Soon Hocking and the footmen entered with the tea and coffee services and a trolley of French delicacies, as though they hadn't all eaten a huge meal an hour or two ago. Laura assisted Lady Hardacre with dispensing the cups and then took her own and found a chair somewhat apart. She was feeling tired. Colin Lang, who had been chatting with Julius, strolled up, smiled, and sat down beside her.

'I understand your name is Markham.' She replied that he was correct. He then asked, 'Was your father's given name Andrew?' Again, she replied that it was. He sat quietly for a while, enjoying his drink, before rising with his empty cup. 'I knew him well, prior to his retirement. I can't understand why you are a governess.'

Laura paled, realising her cover was about to be blown. She looked up at his face, wondering in what way she could silence him.

He continued. 'Do you need to work as a governess?'

She replied, 'Not at all.'

'You have fallen out with your family?'

'No, my parents have died.'

'When my inquisitive hostess, Lady Cockram asks me what we are talking about, I shall say that I queried your whim of working for a living when you don't need to.'

'I would much rather that you say nothing at all.'

'Now I am even more puzzled.'

'It's too long a story for tonight. I found employment I enjoy and, until I think of something else that I would like to do, I shall remain here.' She suddenly remembered how observant Lady Hardacre was and rose to leave.

Colin Lang stood, looking at her earnestly and said, 'I look forward to discovering what your next venture will be. I suspect you have all your father's strength and courage and, whatever it is, it will be something well worth doing.'

Grateful, but unused to such open praise, Laura replied rather incoherently, 'Being thrown upon the world an orphan, even though I was an adult, has been of considerable assistance to growing up quickly.'

Colin Lang ignored this statement. He waited, watching her discomfort for a long moment, then said, 'You don't need to fear me, Miss Markham. You can keep your secret and I'll say nothing about your history.' He walked away.

Laura helped with collecting the cups, then discreetly headed out the door. As she passed, Lady Ascot smiled and leant forward to whisper her thanks for the impromptu concert. 'Bert says it's the best evening out he's had in ages.' It was obvious that Sir Albert was the authority in the Ascot household and Laura left the room, smiling at the oddities of humanity but pleased that a guest's evening had passed pleasantly.

Lady Hardacre was equally forthright. She entered the

nursery the following morning for the first time since Laura had arrived at Monthrope and thanked Laura for her assistance. The Wilmotts had remained at the Hall and that night, Evadne had a shot at her mother by commending Laura at the dining table. 'I don't know what we would have done without Laura last night. Firstly, she finds Lady Cockram, of all people, sitting alone and has her chatting as if they've known each other their entire lives. Then she keeps the two biggest bores in Christendom happily occupied throughout dinner and still has the energy to play the pianoforte for half an hour. Everyone is praising her manners and her poise. She is such an asset.' 'I'd no idea you were so good on the piano, Miss Markham,' added Augustus. 'Sutton asked me, and I said I didn't even know you could play.'

'You must spend your evenings asleep on the sofa, Gus,' snapped Mrs Wilmott.

Lady Hardacre then astonished everybody. 'And you were very good, Mother. I asked you to keep your opinions to yourself and you did. I asked you to go up to your bedchamber after dinner and you did. That's the first social evening you've attended that I haven't had to apologise for you. Thank you.'

Beryl Wilmott gave her daughter a look that shouted, 'I'll get you back for that, one day.' but Lady Hardacre, basking in the light of the evening's social success, was not daunted. Laura had to admire her courage.

Helen BeDe

AMELIA SETTLES HER FUTURE

*A*melia Ascot was looking at a list of names. It was quite short, three only, and she had crossed out all but the last one. She had undergone a busy week with surreptitious visits to the other two.

The first, Vernon Watson, she had located on a distant farm in the hills near Surbury and they had a long and extremely interesting discussion on cropping after she found his fields flourishing with a considerable variety of beet plants destined for winter fodder. Her father, Albert, had adopted the growing of turnips at Ascotvale as a means of getting his livestock through winter but without trying anything else.

Amelia then asked Watson for a drink of water, hoping for a look at the house, but he called out and a woman came running from inside, listened to his requirement and brought them a can. Watson had roared, 'You don't offer a lady a tramp's mite,' hurled the can over the fence into the lavender bushes, and the female scuttled indoors again. She didn't reappear, and Amelia mounted her horse and rode off without explanation. She had seen that the woman's eye socket and cheek were yellow with an old bruise, and there were more on her arms.

She visited the Barlow farm, nominally to order some weaners for Ascotvale and she had an informative half hour with Barlow senior and son, while they earnestly and thoroughly discussed the care and management of pigs. This was probably seeing the menage at its best. Mrs Barlow bustled out and would have her come and take tea with them. This made Amelia wonder how far her mother had gone in sounding out Nigel as a prospective husband. She accepted the proffered refreshment in the cosiness of the kitchen, but the pervasive smell of pig was too much for her and she was glad to leave.

The remaining name on her list was her last chance, locally.

If this man proved unworthy, she would either be forced to find some stratagem that wrested the management and then the inheritance of the estate from her father and brother, or else tour the city relatives, using their homes as a base while examining who was available for matrimony. She was now almost twenty-four, and throughout the county, she saw attractive young ladies launching into society everywhere. She knew the latter part of her plan was a tall order.

Richard Lukin was the remaining option, and Lukin was a respected county name. Why wasn't such a man married? When she examined further, she found he was an only surviving child, and both his parents were already settled in the family tomb in Monthrope churchyard. Single men were fair game for ambitious parents on the hunt. How come this one had not been bagged and carried off in triumph by some local?

For someone so independently minded, Amelia was surprisingly nervous about making verbal enquiries because everyone assumed what she preferred to keep private: that she was looking for a partner. She had begun attending the Church Ladies Guild and keeping her ears open and had gradually ascertained that Richard Lukin was bookish, which was a positive for Amelia.

Mrs Greenaway, the vicar's wife, seeing Amelia glance up from her stitchery at the mention of him, commented, 'He'd be a good match for you, Amelia. Trouble is, he's very shy. He hardly ever goes out.'

What none of them knew, of course, was that Richard Lukin had a nice little arrangement with a tradesman's wife in Surbury and visited her regularly. He was content to potter around his acreage of a morning, garden of an afternoon, and relax with a book at night or whenever the weather turned nasty. Each evening, his household help, Mrs Potter, left him a substantial dinner on the side of a stove he'd seen installed, before ambling home along the lane to her husband, a Lukin tenant farmer. Life was peaceful, untroubled, and likely to continue so forever.

When Amelia, pleased with the fine old house and garden, walked in unannounced because Mrs Potter had gone out for the afternoon, Richard Lukin was seated in the sunshine afforded by his favourite window. Perhaps the eroticism of the Classical author he was reading influenced his view when he looked up. He saw a sturdy, well-dressed young woman, certainly younger than he was and in prime good health. He mused that she was examining both him and his home with considerable interest. Not with the fascinated irritation that he eyed garden pests under a magnifying glass, but as one hopeful and desirous of learning. Finding all this intriguing, he rose and walked towards her. They were both much of a height and they appraised each other with a certain satisfaction.

Amelia decided to get it over with. If she was going to make a fool of herself, then let it be done and she would cope afterwards as best she could. After all, shouldn't any man be flattered that some woman thought he was worth marrying? Well, she was about to find out.

She said, 'Hello, I'm Amelia Ascot,' and Richard introduced himself and indicated a nearby settee, asking if she would care to sit down. She sat and he joined her on the couch, studying each other across the gap that separated them.

'How can I help you, Miss Ascot?'

Amelia liked his voice and smiled. She didn't know it, but that smile made a lot of difference.

'It's difficult to explain. You know my family, I think.'

'I believe the Ascots to be the most prominent family in Monthrope, and I used to be a friend of your brother when we were quite small. We attended school together, two country youngsters barely old enough to be thrown to the lions. We were glad to find each other.'

Amelia was visibly relieved by these words, having suspected that he lived in such seclusion he knew or was known by no one.

'Mr Lukin, I understand you are single. Would you care to marry?'

'Yes, I am single. I imagine I would marry – if I met the right young lady.'

'I am hoping you might find me suitable. I want to marry.'

'Are you proposing to me, Miss Ascot?'

'Yes, I am.' Her voice shook and, witnessing her embarrassment, he reached across the intervening space and took her hand. Her kid glove felt soft and sensual under his fingers, and she lightly returned his clasp, which he liked.

He said gently, 'It seems a fortunate idea. Let us get to know each other a little.'

He began to describe his life and occupation and she responded in kind. He was delighted to see her relaxing because her words implied more than she said aloud. It was through watching her expression that he sensed her unhappiness, and through an allusion, the desperation of her mother to push her off onto any man who would have her. She mentioned that she took an active interest in the farming side of Ascotvale.

Richard listened to her peacefully and Amelia wished his face told her what he thought about her preposterous offer. She had unequivocally refused the few previous claimants for her hand and was aware that this had been misinterpreted locally as someone who thought herself too high for her company, a female equivalent of her autocratic father. She referred briefly to her brother who was doing so brilliantly but was taken up with his own interests.

Richard contented himself with saying, 'Come and have a look around the house and garden,' and they toured in amity, gradually changing to first names.

It took some time to explore their surroundings because the Lukin property, Nirvana, was huge enough to be self-supporting. There was a delightfully informal flower garden, and every imaginable herb, medicinal or culinary; but it turned out that their joint interest was in the vegetables, the greenhouses, and the orchard. Richard was pleased to find that this young woman, once previously encountered as a withdrawn little girl, was a keen gardener. It was delightful to show her around, to gently steer her in and out of doorways and gates, and to progress from taking her arm to taking her hand. Finished with the home gardens, they walked across to the farming centre with its rows of barns and byres and yards, and she was amazed at the extent of the enterprise.

They were both in need of a break when they returned to the house and the welcome coolness of the sitting room now that the sun had moved off it. Amelia picked up his book, and, to Richard's surprise, translated a few sentences. He smiled when she blushed and quickly put it down. Well, it shows he's a proper man, she thought, glancing up at his rueful grin.

He asked what she would like to drink, and she opted for tea, and they went to the kitchen and prepared it together, Richard explaining the absence of Mrs Potter to do the honours. While the kettle came to the boil, he led her around the house from the attics to the cellars before they returned and settled at the kitchen table. Richard set out plates and bread and butter, while his visitor made the tea. After so much exercise, they enjoyed their light meal and

Amelia avowed Mrs Potter's bread was the best she'd ever tasted.

Afterwards, they packed the dishes into a basin, and Richard led Amelia back into the centre of the sitting room and turned towards her. He picked up both her hands and said, 'I have utterly enjoyed our first meeting, Amelia. Let's make it the first of many because we have such a lot in common. Will you marry me?'

How easily it had all come about. She replied, 'Yes. I, too, have enjoyed meeting and getting to know you,' and her face was radiant with genuine pleasure.

Richard was still holding her hands and he slid his own up her arms and pulled her close. 'Then let's seal our union.'

Almost nobody, and certainly no man, had ever kissed Amelia and she was unprepared for the effect on her love-starved self, while Richard, who perhaps should have been prepared, was swept away by the trust and warmth and excitement of her response. They held each other firmly and stood there, alternately kissing, embracing, and gazing at each other for some time. Richard led her back to the settee and they sat down to decide when, where and how they were to marry. He escorted her out to her chaise, and she reluctantly drove away. She really wanted to skip the proprieties and every coming formality and just stay. She could not remember a time when she had ever felt happier.

A BRIGHT-EYED OBSERVER

The few guests who had stayed overnight at Monthrope gradually withdrew during the morning, and the Wilmotts were gone by the following evening. The French chef and his entourage vanished, and it appeared that life was about to return to normal when new visitors arrived. It was the Bright family and they had not come to chew over the success of Lady Hardacre's dinner party.

Elizabeth Bright, Lady Hardacre's sister, was married to Leonard, a respectable but untitled gentleman, living in the neighbourhood of Studley. Laura had gradually discovered that Lady Hardacre's regular absences were largely devoted to visiting her sister. This was a side of her employer she had never encountered before, but it was not till the Bright family's abrupt arrival at Monthrope that she learned that Mrs Bright was seriously ill. In fact, this was their return journey after a trip to London, where she had been examined by a renowned physician. Having confirmed the worst prognostications of her local practitioner, they had come to report and confer, to be consoled and to plan.

Laura, returning to the nursery after a horticultural expedition among the greenhouses with two little boys and three gardeners in tow, heard the news from Nurse. Shortly afterwards, a knock heralded the entrance of an attractive young redhead with Sophie, Elinor, and Bethany Bright hanging on her skirts. She introduced herself as Grace Fuller, their governess.

The Brights stayed for three days and the first was an ordeal for Laura. None of the children created any problems; the girls were full of admiration and leapt gladly into Laura's ways of doing things. Grace Fuller was unwell and spent much of the time in her room, leaving Laura to teach five instead of two. Laura was happy to do so because, when Grace was present, her commonest remark was an uncomprehendingly puzzled, 'Why?' Laura discovered it was possible to become tired of explaining one's methods and reasoning with a person who avowed that some beneficial and enjoyable activity was either too much effort or far too unladylike.

The mediating factor proved to be Leonard Bright, the girls' father. He poked his head around the nursery door during the morning and found everyone collecting and binding and sorting a huge pile of spillikins into bundles of ones and tens and hundreds. He happily joined in, and they began making numbers by arranging the little packs. Mr Bright, copying their efforts with some spillikin bundles he had appropriated, rather cleverly got his arrangement wrong when Laura asked one of the children to make the number 251.

'You made 215,' shrieked the children and they rushed to show an adult how to line the bundles up correctly. He demanded to know why he couldn't put the poor little one in the middle, it looked so sad hanging on the end all by itself; and, of course, the children swallowed the bait and patiently 'taught' him place value.

They went on to show him all sorts of numbers and how to make sums with them. Mr Bright looked up at Laura above their heads and smiled. And that did it. She felt they were in a partnership to help the children. What a jewel he was, keeping five lively small fry engrossed for so long, adding and taking away from the sets of spillikins.

Leonard Bright stayed nearly all morning. During that evening, around the tea trolley in the drawing room, he asked Laura about her methods and showed he understood the procedures she was following.

'These are excellent ideas that cover a wide range of benefits for the learner. No wonder Evadne is so glad to have you.' Laura glowed. He was speaking in front of probably the most important audience in her world and was heard by all present, servants and family. She felt appreciated and respected.

The three days of the Brights' visit went far too quickly for Laura. Leonard was quiet, gentle, fun, and full of admiration and, at games, he was athletic and supportive. He was, it seemed, the epitome of everything a man should be. She liked being near him and she also sensed the danger of doing so.

On the morning of the fourth day, the Brights' coach and accompanying chaise were about to leave when the girls began screaming that their folios were still in the nursery and Grace dragged up the stairs to collect the work completed by her three charges. Laura, sitting beside Eugene and concentrating on his writing lesson, merely indicated the shelf where the folders waited. As Grace reached to pick them up Laura realised the governess's appearance had changed. Puzzled, she looked quickly at Nurse who frowned a warning. Everyone returned to their activities and Grace walked away. Nurse remained silent while Laura continued with the calligraphy lesson.

The Brights returned home but from then on, only short visits back and forward were made as Mrs Bright's condition worsened.

If the family received less visits from Studley there were more from the Wilmotts, and Laura experienced the combined pleasure and wry amusement of seeing Mrs Wilmott trying to improve her demeanour. Her efforts had all the awkwardness arising from novelty and Laura noticed that Evadne was usually braced to step in and smooth the conversational pathway.

'That's quite a nice gown you're wearing tonight, Laura. That repair at the hem hardly shows at all.'

'Do you find wool your best material for winter, Mrs Wilmott?' replied Laura, snatching at the first distractor she could think of. 'I find it terribly itchy-scratchy and have had to line the sleeves of my winter gowns.'

'Yes, isn't wool scratchy?' commented Evadne. 'It doesn't bother me, but the boys can hardly stand it.'

From the way the menfolk joined in it was obvious everyone was trying to encourage Mrs Wilmott. Julius took his wife's arm to lead her to the dining table and smiled down at her, and she smiled back at him.

Later that evening, Laura was turning over music in the drawing room when Mr Wilmott brought her a branch of candles so she could see better. Laura whispered, 'You and Mrs Wilmott seem so much happier together and that makes us all happy.'

He smiled. 'We are indeed, but I'll shock you if I tell you why.'

'Well, in return, I shall be polite and not ask. And I'll pretend I'm not agog with curiosity.'

'Guess.'

'You bought her a present, something that she loves or has always wanted.'

'No.'

'Perhaps, it's like the boys when they're out of sorts. You doubled her ration of cuddles and hugs. That always seems to work.'

'You are nearly right. Well done, Laura.'

He could see her, one hand poised above the music books, head tipped slightly to one side, debating his words, and decided to spell it out. 'I've been doing my husbandly duty, Laura. Beryl told me one day, quite unexpectedly, that she is too old now and unable to have more children, and I took it as a hint that she was available. Remember my words, Laura: when a woman gets cranky for no reason, direct a male to remedy the situation.'

Laura managed a smile, but he was right about one thing; she was shocked at his broaching such a subject until she recollected the loving, tender relationship her parents had experienced.

Later that night she exonerated him. Sitting up in bed, once again considering, and more kindly assessing the people who employed her, Laura acknowledged that Mr Wilmott had treated her as a close friend, and he had treated her as an adult. Nothing could alter the fact that such a subject was verboten in general male and female conversation, but within a family, it was surely permissible. Did this mean that she now had a family? It was an interesting thought.

She couldn't imagine Edmund broaching such a topic. His latest letter rebuked her for visiting the paupers because they would only try to draw her in with their sly and crafty ways. What a comment to come from a man promoting the Christian faith. Laura felt real gratitude that the extra task of almsgiving had become hers. It took her out into the world and added interest to the daily round. She decided to tell him so in her next letter.

DECISIONS

*T*he following week was particularly fine for the time of year, and the Brights ventured over so that Elizabeth could chat with her relatives. They came without the children, but Leonard visited the schoolroom and showed his usual interest in the boys' activities. They begged for another cricket game but since it was so late in the season Laura suggested shuttlecock. Permission being granted, the brothers raced off to locate the equipment and choose a space to play in, while Leonard immediately turned to Laura and drew her close.

'I never thought I'd be granted such an opportunity, lovely Laura,' he said and kissed her.

Laura tingled but she drew away at once and hastened after the boys. He was a married man and downstairs his ailing wife was seated peacefully talking to her sister, hopefully unaware of his behaviour. She could not, and must not, condone Leonard. She disliked deceit, and he was placing her at terrible risk of losing her reputation and possibly her employment. She was also troubled by the unspoken implication that she would welcome his advances. Who was he to imply that she was automatically available whenever he deigned to approach her?

She made sure he had no further opportunities for breaching propriety by keeping her distance – knowing full well who would be blamed if anyone observed them, but the incident affected her. Laura found herself daydreaming about Leonard Bright and gradually built up a favourite fantasy: in some not-too-distant future, poor Mrs Bright passed away peacefully and gently. By that time, Eugene and Michael had aged enough to move to one of the great public schools, and Grace Fuller had departed the Bright household. Rather than having to seek employment further afield, Laura was hired as governess to the three pretty daughters, where her devotion attracted Leonard's affection and the desire of the whole family that they should marry.

Laura knew it was a pleasant, unlikely dream and endeavoured to reason herself back to normality. On considering the matter calmly, she decided she only knew Leonard from several brief and irregular visits to Monthrope. There were times when his charm seemed somewhat too contrived for her taste, although their conversations were normally based on the school activity of the moment. She felt sickened by the slyness of this latest approach, with his assumption that she approved of it – when he was, above all else, a married man.

The next great event was the Christmas season, with extra attendances at church and special days when they celebrated with good food and wassail. On these days, the children joined the family in the dining room before gathering in the lounge for games and gift-giving. Mr Wilmott handed around little parcels and Laura was delighted to receive a pretty vase. Mrs Tillotson organised and handed out presents from Lady Hardacre for the employees, mostly new uniforms, or handkerchiefs.

Determined to shake free of her previous illusion that Leonard really cared for her, Laura endeavoured to think sensibly. She acknowledged that perhaps she was approaching the time when she needed to move – to live in circumstances that would allow her to attend assemblies and meet eligible men. She felt comfortable, quite settled and at home here, but as a governess, her behaviour was expected to be modest and self-effacing.

Another reason it was time to set up her own establishment was that living within the boundaries of Monthrope Hall and the village gave her almost no opportunity to meet anybody. She considered the few single local men who were available and dismissed them contemptuously. This one was too young, that one too old, all of them too hound and hunting mad, too addicted to port, or as stupidly bovine as their cattle. For a moment the thought flashed into her mind, what a pity it was that an athletic young man with the personal appeal of Robert Alston should be unacceptable. He was capable, understanding, and attractive. She shook her head to dismiss this image, and decided she was really becoming a sad case.

If Laura had been told how much she occupied Bob Alston's thoughts, she probably would have replied along the lines of, 'Poor fellow, he seems to cope very well but, as Mrs Tillotson said, he's in an invidious position with little opportunity to better himself.'

Laura did occupy his thoughts. At first sight, Bob found the new governess utterly attractive but assumed that she would follow her predecessors and flee the place within days. This was succeeded by a reluctant acknowledgement that Lord Hardacre would certainly pursue her. When Laura surmounted both these problems, Alston was full of admiration, and this was maintained by her skills in handling small boys and horses. He hoped she was aware of his interest, but her manner remained cool, quiet, and polite, so he adopted a similar pose. For Bob, the riding lessons combined delight and agony. For an hour or more, he could associate with a woman he esteemed but without being able to display his growing affection. He knew that not even someone as low on the social scale as a governess, would accept a man without property and the son of an unmarried woman. He was doubly handicapped.

Bob Alston could see that Laura and Mr Wakefield were nothing to each other. After an initial concern over her delight in Mr Wilmott's company, he realised that the pair had simply formed a good friendship. When Laura was charmed by Leonard Bright, he recognised real competition from a practised adversary. As Alston saw it, Mrs Bright had not long to live, and Laura would be available, in the right place and the right time, to step into her shoes.

Not that he really expected Bright to marry her. Unlike Laura, Alston suspected Bright was a silkier version of his brother-in-law. However, Laura was so attractive and so beloved by the Bright daughters, that she just might bring it off.

On one of their riding lessons, Bob took his courage in both hands and asked Laura if she would go with him to Mick and Bessie's wedding.

'I can't do that. I don't know them, Bob.'

'Not knowing them can be amended. I'm happy to take you to meet them and I think you will like them.'

'That's not really the problem, Bob. I'm the governess. I'm supposed to lead a quiet, retiring life and avoid entanglements. Can you imagine how much will be read into a simple outing to a friend's nuptials if I turn up with a single man?'

'Are you saying I'm not good enough?'

'That's a separate issue. I'm saying that in this quiet little village, so much will be made of my attending the wedding with any man, that my position will become untenable. The nicer-natured people will say we're walking out, engaged or about to be married. The remainder will pronounce me a strumpet, you a philanderer, and decide we're having an affair. It'll be a seven days wonder.'

They rode on in silence. Bob was chewing over her response to his asking if she thought he was not good enough. He felt that she had made it plain he was not, but she had carefully kept the conversation on topic, so the underlying issue could not be discussed. Not for the first time, Bob Alston experienced a sense of entrapment. He made an excuse and cantered after Michael to direct his horsemanship, leaving Laura to herself.

Laura watched him go and wanted to say she was sorry for refusing to go to his friend's wedding with him, but she felt it was safest not to. She reminded herself that soon after arriving at Monthrope, she had decided it would be wise to avoid Bob Alston. She debated whether to give up taking part in the riding lessons and then deferred the decision. Really, riding was a great help to her wellbeing; to get away from the house for a while on a beautiful animal and gallop the frets out of her system was good for her. She proceeded to do so.

Lord Hardacre had sent Bob Alston to a good local grammar school; he was capable and strong and fit. Bob had considered careers in the army and navy and the business world but realised that his interests were country-oriented; now he sought in vain for a way to raise his status in the eyes of the world.

He visited his friends, Mick and Bess Olsen, and applauded their progress. Mick was moving towards sheep, with wool and meat both selling well. Bess was delivered of a sturdy boy, the image of his father, and Bob stood godfather to the child whom they named Tobias Robert. He felt he had two pictures of rural wellbeing to guide him. One was his mother, contentedly busy in her cottage, and the other, this young couple whose lives remained happy, healthy, and profitable on what they produced. I really don't want much more, he thought. I just want to have a job and a home of my own, pay my way and marry a woman who matters to me, but how? How could he establish himself; how to find employment and income that would provide and support him in sustaining a home and family?

Mr Wilmott's increased presence at Monthrope meant that he saw more of all its occupants. He approved of Alston's neat and capable appearance and appreciated the man-to-man way in which they conversed. He recognised that Alston was at a loose end and looking for something more fulfilling than what he was currently occupying at the Hall. His bluff good humour and tolerance gradually overrode Alston's awe, and the young groom decided that if he made no progress by his own efforts, he would approach the great man and ask his advice.

131

THE SWEET-SOUR TASTE OF HAPPINESS

When it was time for Amelia to leave, Richard Lukin determined to visit her father the following day, but she asked him to wait until she had gauged her parents' reaction to their engagement. It was as well that she did. Amelia found that her father was absent on some unannounced expedition of his own. Lord Ascot's failure to inform his spouse had upset her mother. Lady Ascot was, consequently, not in any state of mind, considering the pressure she had previously applied to her daughter, to immediately hear her news with acclaim.

Richard had made it possible for Amelia to fudge the truth and say that he had proposed to her, but she opted against it. When she arrived home and had safely turned the chaise over to a stableboy, she walked nonchalantly into the house. As she had expected, her mother came bustling out to greet her.

'Where have you been, Amelia?' she demanded. 'Mrs Sutton dropped in to say you had not attended the Ladies Guild this afternoon, which you have never missed. She dreaded that you were ill or had an accident driving, lord knows where, without a word to anybody. You make me ashamed when I am obliged to tell someone that I don't know where on earth you are. You don't care how much worry you cause other people.'

'I visited Nirvana, Richard Lukin's home.'

If Amelia had waited a moment, her mother's eagerness to be rid of her would have led to her instantly fastening on the idea of Richard Lukin as a possible spouse, but it was not to be. Amelia, impatient with her parent's tone, could never spare herself the pleasure of rattling her mother's nerves, and she continued. 'I asked him if he would marry me. We had a long discussion, (here, she momentarily smiled), and we are now engaged.'

Merle Ascot was shocked. 'You drove alone to the home of an unmarried man. And doubtless, you were alone with him there.' Amelia nodded. 'And you had the gall, the impertinence, to propose to him?' She tottered to the nearest chair and stood, hanging on to the headrest as if it was her only support.

Amelia thought it was absolutely one of her mother's best performances and stood turning over retorts guaranteed to inflame the situation. Fortunately, she realised before creating an irreparable hiatus, that this would work against her own interests and remained silent for a few moments before answering. 'Steel yourself for the inevitable, mother. Richard is a gentleman. I suspect he has a considerable landholding and, remember, he and Bertram were once friends.' She walked away, thinking that she had let her mother off lightly.

'You can tell your father yourself,' her mother called after her.

'Certainly. Where is he?'

Merle, irritated at having to admit that another family member had departed without a word of his destination, was obliged to confess that she didn't know, and Amelia was forced to wait.

It was not to be supposed that Amelia Ascot expected a heroine's welcome in honour of her success in finding a prospective husband, or that her mother would cease to upbraid her. Amelia's explanations were listened to with horror. Merle was only reconciled to a daughter behaving so outrageously by the knowledge that the Lukin family had lived in their back corner of the county for centuries and were utterly respected. Amelia had planned to emphasise that Richard was shy until she realised that, in her mother's eyes, this was a fault in a man almost as undesirable as a daughter proposing marriage to anyone.

Unable to contain his curiosity, Lord Ascot had travelled to London to see for himself how much truth there was in Bertram's assertion that he was entering the diplomatic service. He returned two days later, highly elated: rank and emoluments confirmed, an awe-inspiring mansion in the right part of town, hordes of servants racing to obey his every whim; definitely, a son to be proud of. Albert had attended a soiree where a multitude of ambassadors, politicians, and aristocrats condescended to nod to him, and he had wished his dress suit was newer while reassuring himself that nobody could see it in the crush anyhow. Shreya's parent, the rajah, had returned to his homeland, but Albert decided to make an effort to approve his son's spouse, and her beauty and charm won him over, despite his preconceptions. Consequently, he returned in fine fettle and handled Amelia's news better than his wife.

'He did propose to her, and she accepted,' he insisted, in the face of Merle's animadversions on their daughter's conduct in even driving to a single man's domicile, let alone proposing to him. He decided to request a large settlement in return for the equally large dowry he would be handing over, and Amelia fought Richard's battle on this front, acceding to some of her father's demands for carriages and allowances, and achieving the inheritance of the Ascot property in return.

Amelia coped with family pressure by increasing the amount of time she spent at Nirvana. She arrived for her second visit on horseback, and Richard used the opportunity to saddle up and escort her over his beloved acres. They rode out to the main gateway where a well-kept lane ran down between neat fields, each headed by its farm cottage and methodical rows of barns and byres.

While Amelia struggled not to gape in amazement, he described the acreages and activities. Ascotvale was an extensive property, but she realised Nirvana was on a different scale altogether. 'This is the original farming property, Amelia. My father increased and enclosed the acreage and there are ten tenant farmers settled on hundred acre lots. Each of them pays me a tenth of their income. This leaves them ample money to improve their animals and acreage. I joke with them about my share, calling it my tithe. Should I buy a surplice? But I want to show you my own land, so let's head back.'

He led her back up the lane again, past the farm buildings, heading steadily uphill and running through rows of fields where she saw evidence there had been a wide variety of crops. Around them, farmhands were busily carting out and spreading the ordure from the middens, city soil carts were unloading, and teams of horses and field hands were turning over some of the ground prior to winter. Soon they were cantering across pasture and Richard continued the upward trend so that she could see along the length of the escarpment. A shepherd was strolling, followed by his peacefully feeding flock with two sheepdogs acting as rear escort. Amelia could have named every breed of animal currently inhabiting Ascotvale, but she failed to recognise either the dogs or the sheep, and she eagerly enquired what they were.

'The sheep are Lincoln Long Wool, wait until you see and feel their fleece. It is so long and crimped and soft. Clothiers love it, and they pay well for all they can get. They're a large breed but I am trying to increase their size and numbers so that we get more returns. You'll find the dogs interesting, too. They are Border collies, and I went all the way to Yorkshire and further north for their parents and have bred from them. They are the most useful sheepdogs I've encountered, and all their pups are in high demand.'

They rode down to the shepherd, Joshua, who was pleased to have company. The sheep grazed placidly, the two dogs supervised, and their master leant on his crook and described his activities. 'I'm on m' way down to the sheepfold now, the flock will get there nigh dark. Ben will come up noontime and watch till we lock 'em up and I'll go down and spread the straw this afternoon, but I half expect he's done that already; he's a good worker. We don't leave the sheep outside now it's cold and no moon. Gives us both a good night's sleep.' He pointed down the valley. 'In summer, we fold them in that there stone corner on the far boundary, but we need to watch sharp all night for foxes and dogs. It would be a great help to have another barn in that there corner.' Richard said he would give some thought to such a practical idea.

They left the shepherd to it and rode down to the barn. In front of it was a long sheep trough which their horses immediately headed for. It was pleasant to dismount. They found Ben piling up a midden behind the building and he explained that they did this daily. 'It's a lot o' work but it keeps the fleece cleaner and that makes the sheep easier to wash and pleases the agent when he makes his rounds.'

Richard unpacked a saddle bag and Amelia discovered he had brought bread, cheese and meat for the shepherds. There were two huts nearby and she saw a woman sweeping her doorway and went up to speak to her. She introduced herself as Ben's wife, and she said Joshua's wife wouldn't come and live so far from the village, so he dwelt alone, except for the dogs. Amelia determined to visit her as regularly as she could, as it was obvious that she relished the chance to talk to one of her own kind. It was also plain that she was handy with the sheep.

Richard found Amelia's knowledge of farm management considerable and her interest in stock and crop improvement genuine. She told him excitedly about the varieties of beet she had seen on a farm not so far from Nirvana and he decided to visit for a talk with the owner. She also described some of the Barlow theories on pigs, but he referred her to his pig-herd saying the fellow was another porcine enthusiast, while he wasn't. Pigs were just too clever for their own good. Through their discussion of stock and crops, Richard had begun to suspect that Amelia was the genius behind the Ascotvale success at stud. He thought Albert would only realise this and miss her greatly once she was gone.

They returned to the house and Mrs Potter set up a small table in the living room, where they ate together peacefully. Amelia carried the dishes back to the kitchen and Mrs Potter remarked over the washbasin that now her Horace would 'have to shut his trap'.

'He gives me stick and I give it him back,' she announced. 'Every time, he wants to know why, if I'm even five minutes late home. And now you've come, he's had to let up. It's a blessing.' On a later visit, when she and Amelia had spent the morning companionably turning out cupboards, Mrs Potter commented to her employer that it was nice having someone to chat to while she worked. Amelia wondered how much talking went on in the Potter household.

After luncheon, Richard liked to work in his vegetable garden while his team of gardeners occupied themselves nearby. Amelia had been delighted to discover that, like herself, Richard enjoyed eating a wide range of vegetables and disbelieved the stories that they were bad for you. Neither were chatterers and they worked happily in silence until one or the other found something new and interesting to discuss or thought of some useful development for the future. After their daily gardening exercise, they scrubbed up and retired to the living room where they settled with books, slaughtered each other at chess or backgammon, and cuddled in comfort. This delightful, resting, touching, caressing, and gentle exploring meant they were both looking forward to consummating their relationship.

The effect on the Ascot parents when they demanded to know where Amelia had been and what she had been doing, now amused her, where it would have once infuriated. They were almost agape after her second and subsequent visits, silenced by their daughter's indefensible behaviour. If she wouldn't act like a lady, it was either a case of locking her up or getting her married off as soon as possible, and they sensibly settled for the latter. Amelia continued to make her daily escape to Nirvana and the Monthrope vicar was instructed to call the banns.

Since neither parent had warmed to the match because they found their daughter's behaviour unspeakably independent, Amelia took up pen and paper to write to her brother. *'Bertram, can you calm Mama and make Papa see reason about my engagement? Yes, I am engaged to Richard Lukin. At the moment we are likely on the road to complete disruption.'*

She was delighted when Bertram arrived at Nirvana within days and listened to her description of her mother's rancour and her father's grudging acceptance, and how she had met Richard. She rode home as usual, but Bertram stayed overnight, the two men sitting chatting long into the night, enjoying renewing their acquaintance. Bertram had seen for himself how happy his sister was and rejoiced. She had chosen well, there was an increase in wealth and assets, and he was delighted that, at last, someone appreciated her.

Next morning, he drove to Ascotvale and was, of course, welcomed with open arms by two delighted parents, although they both expressed astonishment at his sudden appearance when he was known to be occupied with State business.

'Oh, I had to come. Amelia wrote to me of her engagement, and it hardly seemed to do either of them justice to pen a few lines when I felt like writing pages. She has made the match of the season, and he has captured a female of the highest calibre. I wanted to tell them of my joy and hardly knew which to congratulate first. Do you remember, Mama, what friends Richard and I used to be? What a pity we drew apart. I shall take care not to let it happen again.'

'You approve of the engagement, then?' enquired Albert, more in wonder than any other emotion.

'I celebrate it. Surely you are aware of Richard Lukin's standing, living so near as he does.' And observing their bemused gaze, he explained. 'Richard has become the major landholder in this county. His father enclosed his acreage as soon as it became possible. He watched the aristocrats snatching up everyone's land when enclosures started and began extending his own. Richard has quietly continued doing so. He told me what his annual income is; it's enormous and growing. He'll end up another Julius Wilmott because he's always on the lookout for ways of making his money work harder for him.'

Bertram leaned back in his chair and watched his parents consider his words. Already his father's chest was beginning to puff out a little; he'd always held a soft spot for his daughter. His mother was silent, her focus had always been on him. She said sharply, 'Well, I find it hard to forgive Amelia for the way she went about it. Did she tell you about that? How could she so demean herself and shame us? I've hardly shown my face around Monthrope for weeks for fear someone should ask me about her.'

'Amelia didn't demean herself at all. Truly, I believe she has the courage of a lion. And Richard made it possible for her to say he proposed to her. It will pay you to keep your mouth shut, Mama. She is the perfect wife for Richard. Papa, she has quietly run this estate for years without ever being given credit for it. I think you will miss her influence.'

'She has stood over me to make the estate over to her on my death,' snapped Albert, glad to bring up the issue he felt most keenly.

'Excellent. You know I haven't a farming bone in my body. There's too much in farming you can't control; look at the weather you've had for years or the instability of market prices. And as for stock breeding, it bores me witless. Leave it to her, Papa, and know it remains in good hands.'

'Since you feel that way, yes. I hope you never regret it.'

'Strictly in confidence, Father, Richard is putting out feelers for the land lying between his estate and ours. What do you wager he succeeds and Ascotvale will be joined with Nirvana?'

Bertram was pleased to see that his words were taking effect. He moved back into his old room and spent the day following his parents in their various occupations and allowing them to talk of whatever they wanted. Of course, they reverted intermittently to the engagement and the imminent wedding, but he had the pleasure of hearing them gradually change their tone.

His mother felt that entertaining an esteemed son without dinner guests was unthinkable, and she sent out invitations to everybody local. It rather nauseated Bertram, that night, to see his father strutting around, boasting of Amelia's engagement, and adopting his son's views as his own, but it was better than a family break. His mother was calmed by the fact that nobody had heard of what she had previously described as her daughter's 'disastrous visit to Nirvana,' and began to relax. Bertram was glad to return to London the following day and be free of them both, but he was pleased at his success and Amelia wrote soon afterwards to thank him.

TEMPIS FUGIT

When Laura decided to remain at Monthrope Hall while she considered how and where she wanted to continue her life, she had no idea that she would stay two years. Each week, either at church or attached to a visiting parent with children, she observed other governesses and occasionally a tutor. They were models of rectitude, humble and apparently barely above the servants, judging by the way they were treated. Laura compared their existence to the privileged life she led and to her feeling of being in the right place.

Occasionally, a chance remark gave her insight into a particular case. Mrs Tillotson referred one day to Miss Jones, an ageing governess surrounded by her employer's four lively daughters. 'Poor thing, fancy having to bear with all that insolence and energy for forty pounds a year. The Lawtons are so nipcheese. Having four bouncing girls to control exhausts Miss Jones, but she tells me she is petrified Mrs Lawton will dismiss her and find someone better able to manage them. And then what will she do?' Laura shuddered and considered herself fortunate to be differently situated.

Laura didn't realise that her own manner contributed significantly to the way she was treated. From the start, she had spoken to Lady Hardacre with common politeness and no desire to ingratiate herself. With adults, she remained on her best behaviour, careful to do nothing that could be construed as encroaching or likely to encourage gossip. With the boys, she was interested, thorough, and patient, allowing them to calm down prior to reasoning them out of any sudden bursts of temper. She left their mothering to Nurse and regretted that their parents were missing out on so much. The boys' adoration of Laura gradually grew into a warm and appropriate friendship.

With the servants, Laura remained kindly and polite, and

careful to cause them as little extra work as possible. When she found Rosie leaning on a broom while she spelled out the words of Eugene's latest story, Laura first remarked on how lively his writing was, didn't Rosie think so? She could see the housemaid chew this over and agree that it was well-written for a boy aged ten. She offered Rosie a loan of her copy of one of Mrs Radcliffe's novels. Rosie was elated but returned the book a week later, saying she hadn't finished it. It had scared her nigh witless, and she feared it would give her nightmares. And she'd never heard of a real person fainting so readily.

When Laura learned of her inheritance, she gained confidence. It meant that she was more relaxed because she appreciated the bulwark it provided. She was reluctant to leave the area while the man she admired was unavailable, but soon the Hardacres would be moving the boys to a public school. One Sunday, seeking some new experience, Laura abandoned Monthrope and drove to the hamlet of Horton. Its attractive church interested her, and she left the chaise at a local inn and walked across the square to the lych-gate. Once inside the building, she found the morning service was over and a group of boys were buzzing around the walls like so many blue bottles, excitedly locating and translating the Latin inscriptions on the wall plaques. Their progress was being watched by a benign gentleman, plump and white-whiskered, and his trim little wife. Having noticed her interest, the stranger said, 'It's not often they can put their Latin to use.'

'They're enjoying the exercise,' she responded, a little unsure whether she meant the rushing about the church or the translation, but willing to humour the old man.

'I'm their preceptor,' he explained. 'Let me introduce myself.'

She discovered she was talking to Dr and Mrs Humphries and that he eked out a clerical position by taking in such students as these boys. 'I've found eight Latin inscriptions in this edifice and have challenged the lads to locate them all.'

The boys never did find more than half a dozen but they obviously enjoyed the activity. When he suspected that their enthusiasm was waning, Dr Humphries called a halt. Picking up a sizeable hamper resting on a pew, he invited Laura to join them for lunch. Two of the lads relieved him of his burden, the professor offered an arm to each of the ladies, and they strolled down to the riverside and found a picnic spot. They were obviously used to doing this, for Mrs Humphries opened a capacious satchel and extracted a rug for them to sit on while they enjoyed their meal. The boys ate, ran about, explored, and were eventually retrieved before the little party walked Laura back to her chaise.

Eugene would soon be eleven and his parents and grandparents were discussing his future schooling. Laura had a major interest in this, both for her own sake and for the boys'. She thought it abominable that two country children should be thrown into a huge academy far from Monthrope, particularly if Eugene had to go first on his own. How would he cope, who would protect him, one among hundreds, without any family support? As far as she knew, he had never slept away from home a night in his life; she had never even heard of them staying with the Wilmotts or the Brights.

In Dr and Mrs Humphries, she suspected she had found an interim solution. First Eugene and then Michael could have the benefit of his tuition and get used to mixing with other students and adapt to boarding away from home. Eugene would pave the way for Michael and protect him, and then the two boys could progress to Eton or Harrow or wherever and, again, Eugene would be there to support his younger brother.

She took a Saturday absence from Monthrope the following week to visit the Humphries and observe all that she could of the accommodation and educational situation. She was made unaffectedly welcome, and it was mid-afternoon before she returned, deeply satisfied. In every way, Horton seemed the best, the most sensible solution.

For the first time in nearly two years, Laura requested to speak with Lady Hardacre. Her ladyship was once again sitting at her writing desk, and she turned to survey Laura keenly. Was there a trace of anxiety in her expression? It was hard to tell, but she listened as Laura quietly explained her idea, the program, and the living conditions at Horton Academy, followed by how she had come to meet Dr Humphries.

It took her quite some time and she summed up by saying, 'I see boarding at Horton as a useful first step towards public school and university. Living there will lessen the shock of being away from Monthrope Hall because Horton is close enough for Eugene to come home for a few days each week. Dr and Mrs Humphries appear most satisfactory – so far as a single visit to their establishment can show. If it should prove a happy choice, Michael could join him there.'

Lady Hardacre straightened the paper in front of her and spoke from the heart.

'Laura, you have been the instigator of the boys' proficiency. It seems to me almost inevitable that you should be the one to have hit upon the best next step in their progress. I will investigate further.'

IN THE PICTURE

*I*t was enough. It was more than enough. Lady Hardacre had supported her when she resisted his lordship, and thanked and praised her after the dinner party, but rarely had Lady Hardacre spoken in so moved and sincere a voice.

Laura walked back to her bedchamber, divided between pleasure at her success and pain at the coming parting. Of course, there was a chance that another plan might work out: that the Brights would seek her services, and a certain daydream become a reality. Or possibly she could really act like an adult should and come to a decision about where and how she wanted to live. After musing over her choices, she picked up a book.

Laura was relaxing, reading her novel by the fireside when Bob Alston walked in. She raised her eyebrows and snapped the book shut. 'What do you want?'

'The apple picking will be full on tomorrow. Are you and the boys taking part?'

'I hadn't heard about it. Possibly, we could join in for a while.'

'If it is in the afternoon and means no riding lessons, can you let me know? It will save a mort of work currying horses.'

'It will certainly be during the afternoon, but the boys won't want to miss their ride, so any apple picking needs to follow their riding lesson.'

Alston nodded and turned to go. He stopped at the door and asked, 'Why are you looking so cross?'

'You shouldn't enter a lady's bedchamber without an

invitation.'

He gazed at her for a long moment. 'Are you assuming I'd take advantage?'

Laura turned scarlet and didn't know what to say.

'I try not to imitate Augustus in anything.'

Laura shook her head and mumbled that she was sorry. Alston walked across the room and picked up the chair by her writing table. He set it down at a respectable distance, seated himself and gazed at her steadily.

'What sort of person do you think I am?'

'I've no idea. I know little about you.'

'I'm glad you realise that. Do you believe I had a love affair with her ladyship?'

Laura bit the bullet and said, 'That is what I was told.'

Alston made a gesture revealing his frustration.

'See if you can picture this, Miss Laura Markham: a boy barely eighteen, working in the stables, groom to her ladyship. One day, as she dismounts from her hack, she flings a backward word, "Come to the house at two of the clock." She tells me to make sure I'm washed and clean. I think she's going to turn me into a footman or something. At two, I go to the garden door and there's Hocking waiting. He tells me to take off my riding boots and go up the backstairs in my stockings. Nothing makes any sense to me, but I do it. At the top of the stairs he says, "Last door on the left" and heads down again. I'm nervous, and curious, but I do what I'm told. Lady Hardacre comes out in the hallway and takes me into a room – her bedroom. I'd never seen anything like it, I'm all agape. She's wearing what she calls a peignoir, and she reaches up and starts helping me out of my clothes.'

At this point, Laura knew it was imperative that she halt this unfortunate discourse and inform Bob Alston she didn't need to hear any more of it. She took a preparatory breath and, although she wondered at herself, then decided that what he was trying to convey appeared to be so important to the speaker, she could see it was best that her mouth remain shut for the moment.

'I began to realise what was wanted but I was new to it, although once I was over the surprise, I was dead keen. She took me into bed and helped me and, afterwards, she told me to visit again … same time next day. I did, and from then on, she began to teach me how to please a woman. My head was a-whirl for days: proud and elated one moment, terrified of being caught out the next. What if Augustus had walked in? In fairness to her ladyship, after those first moments, I was always hot to the chase. I wish I could say that she felt the same, but she's too hard-headed. Not much more than a week later, she told me I need not go there anymore. I asked if I had displeased her, and she said not at all, but she had achieved her goal. Nine months later, she had Eugene. During that time, I was a misery. I knew I had done something wrong, and I knew that I had let down the one person who supported my mother and me. And I had become used to having a woman. Her ladyship had nothing more to do with me for almost two years, but I was just as hot for it when we went through it all again for the same outcome. She has taken no notice of me since. If it has benefited Gus, I am glad to have it so.'

Here, Bob took a long overdue breath and then added, 'And I've one final message for you: I don't pursue the servants like her husband does.'

He ceased talking and sat eyeing her steadily. Laura, in a sad whirl, endeavoured to hide her shock at his broaching such a topic, to look wise and understanding beyond her years, and to gather her thoughts into some reasonable imitation of a sensible reply. Alston waited, watching her.

When she felt able to speak, Laura used his name for the first time. 'Bob, this is none of my business. I thank you for talking to me about such a private matter and I promise you I will keep it private. Even though it's been a shock, I admire your honesty and courage in telling me. I don't know whether it's been any relief to you to unburden yourself, but you've given me a better understanding of what happened, and I do feel that I know you better.'

'Well, that's all to the good then,' he answered, rising and replacing the chair. He gave her one earnest look and walked out.

Laura sat back; her novel forgotten. What was that all about? I fired up at the arrogant way he walked in. No, arrogant is too strong a word, the confident way he walked in; that was all, wasn't it? I didn't really think he'd assault me or seduce me. Why did he become so upset? I wonder if people throw it up at him that he 'had an affair' with the mistress? Of course, at least some of those who work in the house must know about what happened between Bob and her ladyship, and perhaps someone does chip him about it. Lord, he was plain-spoken about what happened. Eighteen! He would have been almost overwhelmed at that age by her approach and then, I suppose, swept up in the thrill of it. But fancy him broaching such a topic with me. It's outrageous.

Of course, on the other issue, I am at fault. I assumed he was like Hardacre, but all the time I've lived here, no one has ever suggested anything of the sort. He appears liked and respected. I should have apologised properly for implying that he is a lecher. She got up and walked restlessly to and fro, but the facts were staring her in the face. She had assumed Alston was a predator on little more than the fact that, from her first day at Monthrope, he had looked at her admiringly. She had listened to Mrs Tillotson's story about him fathering Michael and Eugene, without questioning the housekeeper as to how she thought it came about – whether it was a longstanding relationship, or who had instigated it. She had been shocked and thought only of her own protection, based upon assumptions that were wrong.

The following afternoon, Laura ignored the need for fruit pickers and made sure she accompanied the boys to the stables. Hurdles had been erected in the large exercise yard and they practised jumping the horses over them, before going for a canter up the lane and across the hills beyond Monthrope's boundary. The boys rode ahead with the stable lads, allowing Alston to monitor their behaviour. Laura was mounted on Lady Hardacre's Sundancer, and she enjoyed the pace, the fine day, and the open spaces after being indoors.

Eventually, they dropped down a hillside where water burbled out of a spring. The leading horses put their noses down to drink and the remainder waited their turn. Laura, seeing Eugene and his groom move off and Michael and his supervisor move up to let their mounts refresh, decided to make the most of the opportunity. She turned to Bob Alston.

'Mr Alston, (so hard to be formal today) I apologise for all my mistaken ideas about you when they were based on gossip. There were no grounds for such thinking and I should have apologised properly yesterday.'

He looked at her briefly and thanked her. Laura felt quite disappointed and didn't know why. They walked their horses to the spring and smiled at the eagerness with which their mounts drank, then cantered to catch up with the others. Well, at least I got the apology over with, she thought discontentedly.

At the stables, they both dismounted and Alston approached to lead away her horse. Shielded by its bulk, he looked at her and said, 'It really pleased me yesterday when you called me Bob.'

Laura hastened to say, 'When we are both on duty, I think we need to speak more formally.'

She saw his lips twitching and the smile in his eyes as he responded, 'Yes. We mustn't shock Sundancer or Thunderer.' Laura laughed and walked off. She felt relieved, light at heart: a nice feeling.

A GOOD SOUSING: VILLAGE PAYBACK

Visiting the paupers in place of Lady Hardacre had become Laura's regular duty and she came to know them well and was received by them with pleasure. She recognised that for these poor souls, her welcome was due to more than the food supplies from Monthrope Hall that she delivered, or the cast-off clothes, or applying salve to a sore foot. It was more than the fact that she didn't condescend to the villagers or preach Christian resignation to one's lot in life, as she heard others did. It was the chance to see a different face and talk to someone new that sparked up the everyday sameness of their lives.

Although Maisy Alston was not a pensioner, Laura also managed each month to call by her cottage, feeling that visiting a person so content with her existence did her good. The discovery that humans don't require a whole fortune to be happy inevitably rose to her mind every visit. On this particular afternoon, she received a huge surprise at Maisy's home, when she arrived to find Augustus Hardacre present. Not the racehorse-mad Lord Augustus of Monthrope Hall, but a relaxed and contentedly busy man in his shirt sleeves, carefully setting a window glass back into place.

'A bird flew smack into it,' he informed Laura casually, continuing with his self-imposed task as though it was the most usual thing in the world for a peer to be doing. She remembered that Julius Wilmott had once described one of the many benefits of visiting his mistress was being in a place where he could relax; and on this occasion, she recognised Maisy's cottage as Augustus's retreat. Not only did Maisy bring out the best in him, but the time he spent in her cottage was arguably more restorative than in his mansion a mile away. Laura had no idea how long he'd been there or how often he visited Maisy, nor did he stay. As soon as his repair was complete, Augustus retrieved his horse from Maisy's old cowshed and rode back to the Hall, leaving Laura and her hostess to chat.

Parting from Maisy later than she intended, Laura walked across to where her horse and chaise were tethered and thought, one more visit to make, and sighed, for this last one was to Snowy Widdeson. Snowy was barely tolerated around the village, and because his end of the row cottage was so isolated, he rarely interacted with the community. She drove slowly, and Maisy, standing watching after her, observed Laura's slumped shoulders and silently followed her down the cart track between the hedgerows, fearing trouble.

Laura had been told not to enter Snowy's cottage. Having tethered the pony, she tiredly picked up the box of supplies, intending to deposit its contents on his doorstep and leave. This evening, as she walked the few steps towards the door, it was smartly opened because Snowy had been watching for her through the musty pane of his window.

'Why, thank you kindly, Miss, just pop it on the table,' he greeted Laura briskly and she unthinkingly straightened and complied.

The space she entered was quite small. A wooden peg in the wattle and daub supported an aged straw hat, and an ingle with a fire, and spare firewood drying on a shelf above it, occupied the side wall nearest her. A bed strewn with a few old clothes and some sacking for bedding sagged against the wall opposite the entry. Between it and Laura on the side facing the ingle, stood a board table sprouting three active legs, and a solid wooden stool that looked somewhat out of place. It was impossible not to wonder how Snowy had come by it.

Widdeson followed Laura the two steps it took to reach his table where she put down the box and turned to go. Neither of them noticed that Maisy Alston had arrived and was standing outside in the dusk, bending forward to peer through the doorway.

'Ah, it's a fair treat to have a pretty girl visit me,' he said, catching Laura's arm and dragging her away from the furniture.

Laura swung round, disgusted by the feel of his paw, and shoved him as hard as she could. Snowy rocked back on his heel from Laura's push, bumping the nearest wall but quickly steadying himself, and Laura suddenly noticed his face had turned pale and focused. With a growl that was hardly human, he sprang at her and Laura, having no place at all to move, snatched up the stool by one leg and reflexively leapt towards him with a wide, strong swing of her arm. She connected with the whole weight of her body assisting the stool, and Snowy crashed backwards against the edge of the ingle and slid down to the floor.

Laura, overwhelmed by fear and fury, ran right past Maisy, not noticing her in the twilight. She untied the horse, scrambled into the chaise, and snatched up the reins, desperate to get away. Clipping the patient animal with a smart flick of the whip, she drove off.

'Springing that poor nag,' muttered Maisy, as she peered out from Snowy's doorway. She turned around and discovered him still sitting, legs akimbo, on the floor. He was conscious and feeling the back of his head where an egg was developing. He was obviously sore, if not sorry.

'You old besom,' growled Maisy to herself, but she bound the least filthy rag she could find round his head and told him to rest, before walking back to her own cottage.

The trip home in near-darkness forced Laura to slow down and concentrate on managing the horse, and it also allowed her some necessary time to calm herself and consider what she had done. The first thing she realised was that she should not have left Snowy's cottage without ascertaining whether he was injured or even alive. At the same time, she had no inclination to return, in fact, she dreaded it. The trouble was that she remembered all too clearly the cracking sound when he hit the wall beside the ingle, unfortunately, the only solid area in the wattle and daub cottage. She wondered how much damage she had caused, and it seemed possible, even likely, that she had killed him.

Appalled, and increasingly terrified about what she might have done, it was a wan figure that halted the chaise in the Monthrope stable yard and shakily descended. Work was over for the day, and all was quiet, except that Bob Alston, who had been wondering why she was late, had delayed his own departure by grooming Thunderer and then led him out on a halter to the horse-trough. He took one sharp-eyed look at Laura's dismal arrival and strode across to her.

'What happened?'

'Snowy Widdeson grabbed me, and I hit him.' She paused while she struggled ineffectively to steady both her voice and her face, before muttering, 'I think I might have killed him.' Oh God, she thought, I'm going to cry. Not now, not here, she abjured herself silently.

'You didn't stop to have a look?'

'I was in a temper, and I was frightened and just ran out.' She suddenly remembered a forgotten detail and wailed helplessly. 'Oh no! I've left Mrs Carson's box there.'

Alston forbore to smile at this absurdity and yelled for Titus, who rushed out of the tack room. 'Put the chaise away, Titus, and feed the horse.' He looked down at the unhappy creature in front of him and said, 'I'll go have a look and find out.'

She glanced up, deeply grateful, but she could barely manage to utter a thank you.

Alston added, 'I can see that you badly need a hug, but I don't want to end up in the horse-trough, so I'll save it for another time.' This produced a wobbly chuckle and he slid onto Thunderer's bare back, saying, 'It's probably nothing serious. I'll let you know whether I find everything is alright.'

She watched him canter off and turned to go, reaching for the remaining storage boxes.

'Miss, don't you touch them boxes,' Titus called. 'I'll take them to Mrs Carson afterwards.' She thanked him and headed for the house.

Laura ate in the kitchen with Mrs Carson that evening, realising that she was too upset to risk sitting through an interminable meal with the Hardacres. Afterwards, she retired to her room but couldn't settle, pacing the floor or sitting sunk in thought, feeling chilled despite the warmth from the fire in the hearth. She was still in shock. Her stomach churned, revolted by memories of Snowy luring her inside, grabbing her arm, losing his temper and attacking her. Why had she been so stupid as to walk in there? Her anger rose again, and she could only be glad that the stool was handy. Yet, what if she had seriously hurt him, what if she had killed him? Emotions teetering back and forth, she paced and sat. With not even a cheering sound from the tower room to boost her morale, she felt she must be the unhappiest creature in the world.

Meanwhile, Bob Alston, having reached the village, decided to leave Thunderer in his mother's cowshed since he was only on a halter, and walk the brief distance to Snowy's hovel. This proved a valuable move because Maisy was able to describe all that she had seen and done that evening.

He left her watching from her doorway and walked the short distance to Snowy's hut, entering without knocking. Snowy was lying on the heap of oddments he called his bed, facing towards the wall, but he clambered to his feet when he heard Bob and asked, 'Whatta yer wanting?'

'How are you?' his visitor asked peaceably.

'None so good. Yer wanting something?'

'I'm just letting you know there'll be no more calls on you from Monthrope Hall, seeing as we are not liking the way you treat our people.'

Snowy arced up at once. 'An' I don't like being hit fair in the chest with me stool. Fell plumb against the inglenook n' bust me head. Had ta bind it up.'

'I thought my mam did that.'

'Well, yeah, so she did, sort of,' said Snowy, agreeing grudgingly, since he'd been found out.

'Learn from this, Snowy Widdeson, or I'll learn you myself. Do you understand me?'

'I does, I does. I don't want no trouble.'

Alston walked out the door, and it was probably as well for them both, that he couldn't see Widdeson's expression. He collected his horse and Maisy naturally enquired what had happened.

'He's alright. Spelt a few things out to him.'

'That's good enough. You kept your fists to yourself,' she commented. 'I wonder how long before he ventures down to the Monthrope Arms. And what sort of yarn he'll spin when he's had a few.'

'You think he'd do that it? It could put him in worse trouble.'

'It's sure as the sun rising the morrow. Snowy Widdeson

likes his bit of excitement; loves having' em crowd round him.'

'Then I think I might take a look in later. I have to go, Mam.'

Laura heard no more that evening until the sound of a horse cantering home along the driveway awoke at first hope, and then dread, when she realised it had pulled up by the kitchen door. She sat beside her fire, head in hands, her original worry as to whether she had murdered someone overtaken by a new and irritating thought. How am I going to live this down?

Whatever the outcome, she didn't want the news to get around. She liked visiting the paupers and this event might mean Lady Hardacre would stop her. Her mind made yet another switch. It was the second time she had acted violently in self-defence. What would her parents have thought of her? Her father might have understood. Her brother never. She eventually decided she could think of nothing more effectual that she could have done to save herself from a creature like Snowy Widdeson.

When Alston entered the Hall, he sought out Hocking, the butler, and asked him to tell Miss Markham that her latest victim had recovered. The curiosity this aroused led Hocking to discard his air of distant politeness and suggest they should both drop by the Monthrope Arms that night and wet their whistle. He then headed off to relay the message to its recipient, and was rewarded by the sight of the Hall's pretty governess glowing with relief and gratitude.

Later that evening, the two men ventured forth to discover an unusual scene at the Monthrope Arms. Snowy Widdeson had arrived before them. He had entered the inn all braggadocio, spouting a story about how he had been attacked in his own home and fought the beggars off barehanded. The locals, knowing him well, encouraged him to keep talking, some kidding him along and pretending to be impressed, others using ridicule as a spur to greater effort, but all of them hopeful that he might eventually disclose something probable or provable.

'So, who were these big blokes, trying to rob your home?'

'I dunno, maybe tramps, prob'ly some'un passing through.'

One of his listeners uttered slowly and thoughtfully, 'Yers, robbers would select your place, wouldn't they Snowy? It'd have the best pickings in the village, being such a well-to-do fellow as you be.'

Widdeson looked at the speaker slit-eyed but, before he could spit out a rejoinder, someone else butted in.

'I'll wager it was Ascot's gamekeeper and one of his mates; they're that fed up with you poaching his pheasants and rabbits.'

The sight of Hocking and Alston walking in the door caused Widdeson to quiver inside and out, recollecting Alston's earlier visit. He had not enjoyed Alston's terse message and, having confessed that it was Maisy who had bound up his head, he knew Alston must have heard his mother's version of events. He noticed Hocking and Alston greeted everybody with smiles or head nods except himself.

'Hey Bob,' called out Hugo Sampson, the blacksmith. 'Snowy here says he's been attacked by a couple of robbers. Did you ever hear the like?'

Snowy subsided onto a bench, listening to his fellows repeating his story and their own responses to these new arrivals, and watching Alston's reaction. Alston, thinking Snowy's version was pretty much what he had expected from him, observed the sceptical twist to Hocking's lips and realised he had made the connection. No fool, our butler.

'What actually happened?' Hocking eventually asked

sideways.

Alston leant closer to his ear. 'Widdeson lured Laura in and grabbed her when she arrived with the food-box. She thumped him a beauty – me mam saw it all. Said she had noticed Laura was loath to go to Snowy's house and followed her there in case something bad happened. What a creature it is, with all this robber yarn. But I think he'll keep his trap shut; I've had a word with him.'

The evening would probably have ended smoothly if Snowy had been out of money, but a recent sale of several hares had provided him with the means to swallow gin, rather than his usual small ale. Sick of being belittled and with his tongue unhelpfully loosened, he plumped down on a settle and told the nearest thing he had to a friend. 'Would yer believe that governess slut up at the Hall pasted me one for touching her arm?'

'What, only for touching yer arm?' scoffed the alleged friend.

'Yers.'

'Nah, don't believe it. Hey maties, hear this.' And he made Widdeson repeat his words, which he did as belligerently as he could, but he dared not look at Alston while he spoke. His tale induced a chorus of derision, the village wit calling out, 'Making up to you was she, Snowy?'

Buff Haldon, the Monthrope Arms landlord, took it differently. He walked around the end of the bar and, in measured tones, confronted the slowly deflating braggart.

'Are you telling we-all that nice little governess, who is so appreciated up at the Hall, assaulted you?'

'Yers.' Well, it's true enough, Snowy thought, justifying it to himself. Alston can't argue with that.

Surprisingly enough, it was a silent little yeoman in the background who stood up and announced, 'I dunna believe a word of it. Pass her in the lane many a time; always got the time of day for a workingman 'n' it don't sound like her at all, at all. She be a proper lady.'

There was a murmur of agreement, swelling to a dissatisfied rumble throughout the snug.

'She does a lot of good, giving out food 'n stuff round the village,' opined someone in the background.

'I tell you what. Yer a lying bloody toad, Snowy Widdeson,' said Hugo. His regular visits to the Hardacre stables made him more cognisant of the workers there, and he joined Buff in front of the culprit. They made a formidable couple and Snowy's main thought changed from a burning desire to thump his so-called best mate, to the more serious one of how to get out of the bar with a whole skin.

And then to cap it all, Maisy walked in as nonchalantly as though females were an everyday occurrence in the Monthrope Arms, and the way Widdeson blanched and began to edge out of sight almost told his story before she did.

Maisy was in no hurry and began by relating how the reluctant governess forced herself to visit Snowy, her own arrival there and overhearing Snowy's unwelcome instruction to enter. 'She were just putting the box on his step, and he says, "Just pop it on the table if you please, Miss", all friendly like.'

She spoke into an absolute silence and Snowy tried again to vanish quietly, except that somehow Hugo and Hardacre's damn butler kept hedging him in. Certainly, when Maisy got to the part where Snowy grabbed Laura's arm and jerked her away from the table, there was a stir, but not a word was uttered for fear of missing the next bit.

Maisy, proud to hold the centre of attention, then began to act it out, pointing at him with a finger each time she wanted to indicate Widdeson. First, Laura's full-bodied push, miming the disgust with which she did it, then indicating the culprit stumbling backwards before righting himself. Suddenly, she gave the most unimaginable roar of rage (Snowy should have been proud of it) and leapt. But almost instantly she swung round. Holding her audience's mesmerised gaze, she morphed into a slip of a girl seeing a monster springing at her, grabbing up the stool and gathering her terrified self. In an exact duplicate of Laura's preposterous leap, she swung upwards, following through, flung down the stool and pretended to rush out.

Maisy halted the roar of approval that erupted throughout the bar by changing yet again, indicating and then miming Snowy sliding down the wall to sit spread-eagled on the floor, an action her audience greeted with a chorus of laughter, catcalls, and whistles. That done and her story told, Snowy's nemesis rose and walked through the uproar to where he cowered and pointed at him.

This totally silenced the audience until Hugo addressed the customers while staring Snowy Widdeson hard in the eye, 'The pig pond, I reckon.'

There was a resounding bellow of agreement. 'Yeah, souse the beggar.'

Snowy, protests and pleas ignored, was wrenched up, raised above their heads by a horde of willing recruits and rushed outside, kicking and struggling. Alston and Hocking and Maisy heard, in the distance, raucous shouts half-drowning the culprit's cries, followed by a sturdy voice yelling, 'One heave, my hearties; two heaves, my maties; three, heave-ho and away he goes!' Followed by an almighty, splodgy splash.

After that, there was a silence that seemed to linger and

linger forever, before it was replaced with someone calling out, 'Yair, there he is. He's found his feet.' And then a chorus of joyous, mock-friendly voices yelling, 'How's the water, Snowy? Oops, sorry matey – how's the mud and muck, Snowy?'

'Enjoying your swim, Snowy?'

'First bath you've had for years!' And the jibes continued as he dragged himself out, an odorous mess.

While the villagers poured back inside to sluice their throats, Alston turned and hugged his mum. 'You warned me he would come down here and make a big story of it. I'm glad you came and I'm glad I was here to witness you.'

'I told you he would,' Maisy said, as she departed, heading up the lane homeward bound. Hocking approached Bob and suggested they ought to be making for Monthrope Hall and alternately shook his head and laughed the whole way back.

Snowy Widdeson sloped off, never to be seen again in Monthrope. Next morning, the story spread like wildfire that someone had found his cottage door wide open, and his few belongings vanished; Snowy Widdeson, clean bowled by shame, was the village verdict.

The outcome reached Laura through Hocking and when she knew it all, she sent a message for Alston. He decided not to wait and obligingly walked up to the Hall and eventually located her alone in the schoolroom, where she thanked him. So, then it was his turn to act out his mother relaying the story to the crowd, while Laura listened enthralled.

Bob hoped the ending would amuse her, but she seemed saddened. 'I hate people being humiliated; I always end up feeling sorry for them.' She gave herself a little shake and added, 'But I'm really glad he's gone away. And I must go and thank Maisy as soon as I can.'

They discussed for a few moments whether Widdeson was likely to remain absent and realised they could only wait and see, and then they both ran out of words. Alston, having leant against the edge of the table for a minute, straightened again ready to leave, but hesitating while she looked up at him.

'I still think you need a hug,' he remarked conversationally. There was no answer, although Laura knew, in her heart, he was right.

'And I think I deserve one.' Laura reddened and racked her brains for a brilliant response, only to find that her wits had gone wandering.

'Of course, if you don't like to hug me, I can wait until you do think I've earned one.'

Dear Lord, he must think me the most ungrateful creature, she fretted, and I owe him so much. 'Of course, you have earned one,' she said, suddenly making up her mind.

She walked across to him, reached around, and gave him a big squash. Bob's arms folded themselves around her in return and he held her close. How nice it felt, how healing it was, to just be clasped and comforted for a moment before drawing apart. They stood smiling rather shyly at each other, glad to find they had at long last moved on to becoming friends.

SNOWY WIDDESON DEPARTS

*M*aisy, walking quietly up the village street on her way home, encountered a bedraggled figure trying to operate the village pump and then clean himself in the water that dropped to the ground, because doing both at once was impossible.

'I'll work the pump,' she announced. He would have liked to hit her with it, but his need was desperate, so Snowy said nothing and stepped up to the spout. As the water sloshed out in the dark, he put his head under and scrubbed his face and hair, before squatting so that the water washed across his body. He then rose and turned round and endeavoured to clear his back. It took many goes and a lot of rubbing but eventually he was reasonably clean and, for possibly the first time in his life, Snowy Widdeson uttered a genuine, 'Ta, Maisy,' and stumbled homewards.

Maisy walked further down the village street to the vicarage, pleased that a light was showing. She went to the back door and the household help, Emmie White, let her in and led her into the warmth of the kitchen.

'Evening, Emmie. I need some clothes, male, middle-sized.'

Mrs White didn't query the request but vanished into a storeroom. She came out with a bundle of oddments and something half-hidden under her arm. In her other hand she held by the collar, a worn, but good quality, driving coat. Maisy accepted them all with gratitude, and Emmie proffered the unseen gift; it was a pair of boots.

'I'll bring 'em back if they don't fit,' promised Maisy and departed.

When Maisy Alston reached Snowy's cottage she found the door shut but unbolted, and she was able to enter. The reason was immediately apparent. Snowy's clothing was lined up along the shelf above the ingle, anchored in place by a branch so it could hang downwards, and she could see it steaming as it dried. He had built up a fine blaze from Mrs Carson's box and the remaining logs he had stored on the shelf and was sitting on his stool in front of it, arrayed only in a ragged vest with a sack across his shoulders.

He looked up at Maisy's entrance but said nothing and returned his gaze to the blaze. Maisy handed him a fustian shirt and he stared at it, mumbled, 'Ta,' and dragged it on. She conquered the urge to straighten it and followed with a pair of fustian workpants which he used unembarrassedly to cover his naked lower self. Lastly, Maisy passed across a jersey which he also donned. The boots were too small, and he nodded at his own which were perilously close to the fire and would probably be rock-hard by morning.

Maisy advised, 'Rub some grease on 'em,' and he nodded towards a pan sitting on the floor. There was certainly plenty of grease in it.

Maisy laid the coat across his three-legged table, carried away the proffered boots and departed for her cottage. She stirred up her own fire and settled comfortably in front of the hearth for 'a cup o' tea and a think' before retiring for the night.

Widdeson remained in front of the ingle, his mind roiling with bitterness against everybody who had affected his day. His focus was on vengeance: repayment of debts in cartloads, and his imagination ranged between beating certain people senseless, to dunking them in the souse-pond and standing on them. Laura and Maisy, being mere women and as he saw it the cause of his problems, headed the list, but he was aware they were untouchable. Maisy was protected by Hardacre, and it was apparent that damn governess was protected by everyone. He knew he would hang if he was caught harming them.

Surreptitious retaliation had never been Snowy's forte. He preferred to knock someone around and it was delicious to sit, comfortably warm now, and daydream of it. Weariness eventually forced him to consider his position. Tonight, he had become the laughing stock of the village and finding any employment, with them all against him, would be harder than ever. It was time to go. He looked around and realised moving would take little effort and then he considered his financial means. He'd drunk all his income from selling those hares. What else could he dispose of? Everything he owned he needed, or was of little value, except perhaps that dratted stool. He picked it up and left his hovel.

Seeing the light still showing at Maisy's, he was tempted to take it there, but he wasn't in a mood to do or ask any favours of someone he preferred to hate, so he knocked at the back door of a merchant who was helpful to people of Snowy's sort and exchanged the stool for five shillings. It was hard to hold out for cash, the buyer preferring liquor as payment, but Snowy persisted and he was pleased with the price. He wondered idly, as he strolled away, if its owner would recognise the stool or even buy it back again.

Maisy had helped Snowy because he was human, and she had the means of alleviating a few of his difficulties. She knew his type and didn't expect gratitude. Having obliged, she considered association with him was over. Sitting by her fire before retiring, her thoughts were largely occupied with the impossible task that lay ahead of her son. He was obviously devoted to the Hardacre governess and, nice as the girl was, she was not the sort to marry a man with no future and the bastard-born son of a housemaid. What influence could she bring to bear on his behalf, and how and when and where to do it?

Meanwhile Snowy Widdeson had returned to base. He looked at the driving coat and decided it would keep him warm until he found a lodging somewhere and then he would sell or exchange it. He greased his boots and caught a few hours kip, packing his possessions into a sack and vanishing just before dawn. Let them not know which direction he took or which town constable to alert to his arrival.

RISING STARS

*A*melia and Richard were quietly married in Monthrope Major, in a wedding where Bertram supported the groom, and Laura the bride, and the congregation was limited to a select few. Those who were not invited were, once again, intrigued with the presence of a governess where least expected, and her attendance deprived them of the opportunity to complain that Amelia remained unspeakably high in her notions.

Amelia and Laura planned to maintain their friendship, only to find the difficulties almost beyond them. Richard and Amelia travelled from the wedding to Bertram's home in London, where they spent a delightful month. Laura received one letter from Amelia during this time, describing a whirlwind of social engagements. It barely mentioned that many of their visits were to Holkham and other progressive farms, or that Julius Wilmott was kindly linking the city businessmen up with the Lukin talent for making money.

 The young couple travelled to Paris for another wonderful month where they explored the many sights of the city whenever they felt like it. They vanished briefly to Holland and Germany to examine beet varieties and a strange – to English eyes – new fodder reminiscent of sauerkraut, called ensilage, which livestock thrived on over winter. They gradually headed for the Mediterranean, examining the Alps in passing, and crossed into Italy. Exploring their way slowly southwards, they eventually reached Rome, decided to defer the Grecian islands, and returned to Marseilles, to be sure of being once again settled at Nirvana before their baby was born.

'Have we really been away so long?' Amelia and Richard demanded of each other. It was heavenly to be home and find all well. In gratitude to their loyal staff, they held a monumental homecoming party for everyone involved and their minions flocked to show their joy. Once settled, they could look around and notice all the changes in Monthrope.

And the two friends could pick up their friendship, unaltered despite the time lapsed.

WEDDING BELLS FOR PEGGY AND PETER

*I*n Amelia's absence, Laura kept her eye open for Peggy and Peter in her comings and goings from Monthrope Hall and paused to chat with them when they met. She found Peggy very straightforward, practical and sensible, with an endearing underlying compassion. Laura called on her once at Sutton House and they strolled around the garden then rested on chairs in the shade to share experiences. Like everyone else, she learned nothing about the two ladies who had lived there, producing the same effect the Sutton House inhabitants had on everyone else: what needed to be hidden and why?

Peter had moved in with Peggy after the two ladies left, and they made visitors welcome. The young couple were poised to move to their new house at the racing stables and lacked furnishings. Laura spoke to Lady Hardacre about their limited financial means, and this resulted in the three of them delightedly ransacking the Hall attics for cast-offs. Beds were found for the couple and the stableboys. A kitchen table was unearthed, and enough kitchen chairs to provide everyone with a seat. Mrs Tillotson and Mrs Carson scoured the cupboards for spare linen and utensils, and Peter and Peggy found themselves relieved of much of their main worry.

Laura asked what they wanted for a wedding gift and was requested to supply two tankards, Peggy and Peter expecting to receive locally made pewter or pottery. Laura drove to the nearest market town in pursuit of tankards and was delighted to find a silver pair, but she was very taken by a silver sugar bowl in the shop and asked that all three be engraved with a linked 'PJ & MP'. The result produced such an exquisitely etched set of initials drifting off into ivy leaves that she could hardly bear to part with them, always a good sign with a gift. She bought some dishcloths as a practical wrapping for her offerings, and a little packet of white sugar to accompany the sugar bowl. As a grocery item only seen in fine homes, she enjoyed the idea of giving the recipients a treat that would probably be nearly as treasured as its container.

Laura attended Peggy and Peter's wedding on a Saturday afternoon, carrying a holdall with her gifts, and was surprised to find a considerable crowd present. She was aware of being among many strangers, but by the time the party had moved to the new house at the racing stables, she had been introduced to Peggy's four siblings and their kin, along with Peter's siblings and theirs. She discovered the guests included the Olsen and Haldon families as well as all the staff from Monthrope Hall and was happy to find so many known friendly faces. The guests were a lively, noisy bunch out for a jolly time, and everyone had brought food and drink and dressed in their best, preparatory to making a roaring success of the evening.

There was a moment's stunned silence when Laura opened her holdall and presented her gifts to the bride and groom. The tankards were unwrapped first, with everyone surprised by the dishcloths and then praising her for the usefulness of the packaging. The newlyweds were expecting to receive tankards, but not in engraved silver, and their astonishment almost overwhelmed them. The climax occurred when she presented the sugar bowl and was greeted by demands from among the crowd to know what it was. She opened the packet of white sugar and filled it to show them. It was Laura's turn to be surprised when both the bowl and the sugar packet were passed from hand to hand in wonder. Some of the wedding guests had never seen either. Laura realised the likely fate awaiting her gifts and made the overawed new owners promise they would use everything and not just confine them to a cupboard in state.

After that, everybody ate and drank their fill and danced. Laura danced jigs and country dances – both line and round dances, with a succession of known and unknown faces, ate and drank to repletion, and hoped she could locate her horse and chaise when it became time to leave. Bob Alston approached her for the last dance before everyone left the newlyweds to their own devices, and Laura remembered how much she had enjoyed dancing with Bob at Monthrope Hall. Here, they were in a group, everyone very noisy and excited, dancing and ducking under the arched arms of each top couple in turn and then along the length of the barn. Laura saw that Bob was as relaxed as she was, and afterwards, he accompanied her as she headed for her chaise. It was pleasant, even on a fine night, to have someone assisting with the harness. She thanked him for his help and drove off down the roadway, hoping Brownie could find her way home. Bob saddled up Thunderer and soon caught up to her.

'Would you like me to drive?'

'No, we're getting along alright and I'm not in a hurry. The lane shows up well enough against the hedgerows, and I don't think I'll miss the gate. It's good of you to offer and I'll be glad to know you're nearby if I do strike a problem.'

'You'll find Brownie knows the way,' he reassured her, but he remained beside the carriage. Arriving at the stables, they found someone had left a lantern hanging from a hook on a post outside a loose box, its waning light showing them where to draw up. Laura leapt down and watched Bob unsaddle Thunderer. He lugged the saddle off to the tack room and came back with a second lantern to find Brownie had taken herself off to the cart-shed and backed the chaise into place.

'Isn't she clever!' exclaimed Laura.

'She must be in a hurry to go to bed.' Bob walked across to unharness the horse.

Laura considered helping him but decided to stable Thunderer. She led the big gelding into his loose box, checked that there was feed in the manger, and unbridled him. She returned the bridle to the tack room, choosing a hook at random on which to hang it. She located a bin of oats and dipped some out as a treat for both horses, pouring a measure into Thunderer's manger and stepping back, intending to find Brownie's stall. From behind, a couple of arms encircled her body and a voice breathed in her ear. 'You're testing me too far, Laura Markham.'

How firm and warm Bob's arms felt. His face rested against hers for a moment and then he kissed her neck, the heat of his breath sending lustful gooseflesh shudders surging down her body. Laura dazedly abandoned the tin, and Thunderer promptly helped himself to the surplus. Bob's hand slid gently but firmly down her body, pressing against her skirts until his fingertips settled just between her legs. They pressed gently, rhythmically and she abandoned herself to enchantment.

It was not to be. Bob abruptly straightened and she realised he had turned away, listening, and then she heard the clatter of wheels and hoofbeats.

'Saved by a miracle,' he whispered. 'You'd better hurry inside – unless you want to be done by every man in the stables.' Laura didn't wait. Mortified, she fled across the stable yard, leaving Bob to regret the arrival of his workmates. With Brownie safe in a stall, he decided not to wait and followed Laura.

The backdoor was not locked. Inside, a lantern was burning rather low, and a line of candlesticks waited on a cupboard for all the partygoers yet to come home. Laura, annoyed at her shakiness, was fumbling to open the lantern and light her candle at the flame when Bob entered, took it out of her grasp and did it for her.

He saw she was nervous, unsettled and avoiding his gaze, and was careful not to touch her. He handed over her candlestick and lit his own and they stood there only a moment before Laura headed for the back stairs. All they could manage was a quick glance, followed by a quiet 'goodnight'. They went their separate ways, both feeling that they'd made a pretty tame ending to a promising evening.

Once again, Laura found herself sitting up in bed worrying. I allowed Alston to go far too far tonight. I never realised I was so susceptible. Well, I'll squash him like a beetle if he tries anything again. He's in no position to offer me a future, so he must be toying with me.

Her concern about what disaster she might have created in her relationship with Alston appeared minor and easily sorted out compared to her sudden thoughts as regards her gifts. She had given an exquisite tablecloth to Amelia when she married, and nobody had thought anything of that, and probably at least some of the wedding guests had assumed it was her own handiwork. Her gift to Peggy and Peter had been given because she liked them, and out of appreciation at being included, without consideration of the conjectures it might raise.

Any guest with half a brain would assume that she had learned about white sugar from working for the gentry. Every housemaid would be familiar with it, even if she had never tasted it. No, that was not a problem. She decided her only real danger lay in the money she had spent on the tankards and sugar bowl. Someone might ask her how she could afford them – would she lie or not? Laura decided that, if anyone asked her whether she had suddenly become a nabob, she would suggest that she had carefully saved up a little of her salary.

This seemed a workable solution because it was true, and she eventually relaxed. It was a waste of energy to berate herself now for harbouring a secret desire to present something out of the ordinary, and perhaps even show off.

Once again, Laura realised she could only wait and see what eventuated. Still, she would try to be more careful in future.

175

TIDY UP AND MOVE FORWARD

*I*t is easier to clean an empty house than a furnished one. Peggy and Peter rose betimes the morning after the wedding, gathered everything they thought they would need, and headed into the village to scrub Sutton House. They started in the attic which was well-endowed with old furniture, carpet rolls, and dust. Nothing there belonged to any of the recent residents, so it was just a case of sweeping down the webs, cleaning the floor and polishing the two windows. Peggy was hard at it when she exclaimed vexedly, 'Oh dash, someone's arriving.'

Peter downed tools and had a look. 'It's Bob and Tilly and Laura.' He rushed hopefully downstairs and sure enough, they were decked in their oldest wear and armed with buckets and brushes. Behind them, a gig was drawing up with Mary, the kitchen maid, and Grimes, looking similarly workaday. What a welcome they all got and what a beavering and a scrubbing ensued.

Such neighbourliness awoke the interest and curiosity of the village. The Jamesons, the Haldons and Olsens dropped by during the day and added their mite. To top it all, Grimes who had been tidying outside, vanished, only to return with Amy Carson who had, of course, brought food and plenty of it.

By evening, the house and surrounds were pin-neat and sparkling. The owner, Claude Sutton and his wife called and approved their efforts. They had long accepted a reduced fee since it was either have no income or accept one that a young couple could afford. Now that the new house at the stud was habitable, Mr Sutton happily sold Peter and Peggy some of the furnishings to supplement the fittings provided by the Hardacres. The only ones doubtful about the new arrangements were believed to be the stableboys, whose shenanigans had brought it all about.

With the removal to Monthrope Stud, the young Jamesons were able to set up house and begin their new life. Monthrope accorded Peter and Peggy the attributes of being hard-working and honest. How would they go, isolated up at the stud with three youngsters and a stable full of spoilt darlings to manage?

Nathan, Isaac, and Jeremy were almost immediately onside with Peter when he began arriving each morning with the master, instead of Grimes. The three stableboys bore with Augustus's severity because his enthusiasm for his horses was infectious and they were of an age to warm to it. Grimes's biting remarks, and something about him, had unsettled them. They appreciated someone nearer their own age who understood their worries and didn't enact a Cheltenham tragedy over a simple mistake. They found Peter could ride anything and that horses followed him around like a string of ducklings. Topping it off, by showing them what to do rather than telling them what to do, Peter was in danger of being hero-worshipped.

Laura visited to see how Peggy was faring and discovered a different story. Peter was having a grand time with the lads and, yes, everything up at the stables had improved, but she had become the ogre. Firstly, she had made the boys bathe, retorting that she would scrub them herself when they objected, and they had sulked off to obey. She had followed this by cutting each boy's head of hair, as a means of keeping down the number of creatures living among it. Boots were now stored in the entryway and hands were washed before going inside to eat.

Her one redeeming quality, in their eyes, was her cooking, but Peggy told Laura she had started by putting a mixture of meat and vegetables on their plates and found they objected strenuously to the vegetables – as dangerous to their health. Peggy hadn't argued and wasn't sure she had done the right thing when she said, 'When you finish your plateful, I'll serve up the apple pie.' This had proved successful, but she knew they felt bullied.

Wringing her apron in her hands, she continued her tale of woe. She had turned the far end of the kitchen into an area where everyone could lounge of an evening, and lounge they did, although Peter set a pattern of doing something useful while he loafed, like his dad at home. Peggy got through the dishes, organised everything needed for breakfast, and then knocked up the bread so it could do its final rising. She finished off the day by attacking the ironing or mending. She felt exhausted, unappreciated, and not even liked.

Laura asked what the best things about her new life were. Peggy thought for a moment and said, 'Peter, of course. And living here is more like my home where I grew up, a house full of people and noise. The lads are eating well this week and beginning to chat among themselves at night. Isaac polished a bit and bridle last night. But I haven't told you it all. I spend a whole day just doing the washing, and I have to say I don't do any more ironing than I need to.

'Gus is quite likely to drop in for breakfast after he's made his rounds, as if I haven't enough cooking to do, already. The other day we had two smiths. Peter's da is going to be the regular here from now on – unless something special comes up, and they came here to check the horses and then both rolled in for a feed. I haven't yet got around to making any stores for winter.' Peggy obviously felt she was a failure.

'Have you told Peter what it is like for you?'

'No, because he's got so much on his own plate. He spends every bit of his spare time working out whether the feed is going to last, what to order, and repairing things. He keeps records and he started a diary, of all things… but I must say, it's proving real useful.'

'Tell him.'

'Laura, it's a woman's lot. I can just hear my mother telling me not to grizzle and I'm thankful that you're putting up with me whining like a baby. I don't want to load my problems on Peter.'

'You're not a spoilt baby, Peggy. You are an overworked wife. Would you mind if I asked Evadne to allow you a laundry-maid? And would you be offended if some of us were to come here and help with the winter stores?'

'I'd be plumb grateful, but wouldn't they feel like I was pretty useless, not to be doing it all myself?'

'They're more likely to think you also need a housemaid.'

'She'd be nice company too but Laura, with three younkers, she'd be expecting within a month. I wonder how I could prevent that? Not have her live-in for a start, but it would be a fair way for a maid to come to work. I'll ask around if you think Lady Hardacre might agree. Maybe there's a girl from one of the local farms available.'

Peggy never told Peter, but Lady Hardacre visited to see for herself, and this allowed Peggy to relay her lifestyle to someone who had never done a week's heavy washing in her life. Her ladyship said very little, but she quickly produced both a housemaid and a laundry-maid.

Realising Peggy had no mother to support her, Peter's mother began to visit weekly, to help however she could, and set in motion the development of a vegetable garden and pigsty fit to rival her own. McPherson the gardener and his crew rolled in regularly with fruit and vegetables for use or winter storage. He joined Beth Jameson in designing and planting out the garden, both of them supplying necessary seeds, plants, and cuttings.

Laura, being busy, found it was some time before she was again able to visit. She was hugged and welcomed by a woman at ease in her kitchen, enjoying the experience when extra souls dropped in because they were no longer a burden.

EUGENE'S INTRODUCTION TO HORTON

*L*ady Hardacre had apparently investigated Dr Humphries's academy at Horton Studley, doubtlessly with her usual thoroughness, because Eugene had been informed that he was to become a pupil there. The first inkling Laura had of this occurred during a music lesson when she was sitting on a settee listening to Michael practising on the pianoforte. Normally she placed herself beside the pianist, but to Michael music was some fascinating form of mathematics, and he revelled in it. Laura thought that he read music much as she read a book and he persisted until he attained the results he wanted. There was seldom the slightest need to correct him, only to soothe any frustration with his own performance.

Laura took the opportunity to seat herself and act as audience. The result was so informative that it was a few moments before she noticed Eugene was standing beside her. When she looked up at him wonderingly, he pressed against her side and, even as she realised something was bothering him and reached up to put an arm around his waist, she noticed again how tall he was growing.

'Mama says I have to go to Horton.'

Laura nodded. He was both angry and on the verge of tears. 'I don't see why I must go. There's no reason to send me away.'

Laura withdrew her arm and looked down at her hands, aware that she had strong views on sending country youngsters away for education, although knowing little about public schooling.

'I think it's seen as part of growing up, Eugene; of learning how to be a man. Certainly, it is part of learning how to run your own life and stand on your own feet. The first step occurred when you were breeched. Maybe learning schoolwork and manners and sport was the second step, training you for later. Now it's come to the next step – learning to be away from home while you continue your schooling and mixing with other people.'

'That's paltry. I can do all that from home. She doesn't care what I want.'

'You'll come home every Friday afternoon and return on Sunday afternoon, because Horton is so close to Monthrope. I think it's quite possible that other parents will hear how good Dr Humphries is and will consider sending their boys to Horton.'

This was received with something like a snort.

'Shall I take you to Horton to see for yourself?'

'You know I don't take readily to strangers.'

'I think you'll find new friends there, people who will be friends for the rest of your life. When you progress to college or to university, some of those friends will be with you.'

Sulkily, he asked, 'When would you take me to see for myself?'

Today was once again Saturday. Laura recalled her pleasant first meeting with the Humphries and replied, 'Tomorrow. I think we'll take Michael, too.'

'Well, at least it gets us out of boring old church.'

Laura pretended not to hear this and hastened off to request a hamper from Mrs Carson. When she returned, Eugene was at the piano thundering his way through his set pieces.

'Isn't he cross!' Michael marvelled over the top of the novel he was ostensibly reading. She aimed a cautionary look at the speaker and sat down, hoping that the exercise might provide some relief to Eugene's feelings. Certainly, he jumped up afterwards in a calmer mood and she wished earnestly for a successful visit on the morrow.

The Fates were kind. Sunday was sunny, and they reached Horton to find the churchyard gradually emptying and the Humphries' contingent heading for the river. The pupils came rushing up, allegedly to assist her with the hamper, but bursting with news. 'We're punting down to Fabian's Pool.'

Laura and her charges were swept along, and she was amused to see how quickly her pupils fell in with the prevailing mood of excitement. A row of punts was lined up along the bank and these were rather haphazardly poled the hundred or so yards to the still waters of the pool and their painters fastened to bushes. Mrs Humphries and Laura were deposited on the bank where they spread rugs and cushions and made themselves comfortable, while the others moved quite some distance away downriver.

The next thing she observed was a group of young naked bodies disporting in the water in a great welter of splashing and diving, some even swimming. She observed Dr Humphries teaching the non-swimmers how to get about and smiled at the excitement of her charges as they mastered an entirely new leisure pursuit that they, of course, had never been able to do with Laura.

Long after she thought they would all have died of starvation, the group returned, rather sloppily dressed, and as hungry as hunting dogs. Both hampers were ransacked and the contents demolished, and then it was time to tidy up the locality, tidy up their appearance, and return upriver.

Laura, Eugene and Michael accompanied the Humphries' troupe to the academy and the boys were shown all over the college by their fellow pupils while the adults regaled themselves with tea and coffee and listened to the chatter floating downstairs.

Dr Humphries then reminded the boys it was Sunday and time for a period of quiet reflection. His pupils promptly retired to their bedchambers, but this aroused the curiosity of the Monthrope contingent and the three of them peeped into the rooms. Each pupil explained that he had read some pages or passage of the Bible and was now busy drawing, writing or making something: the variety seemed endless.

'Time for us to go home,' Laura informed Eugene and Michael, and they made their farewells to the students. She was pleased that both of her boys then went to thank their hosts, but it was two weary youngsters who leant against each side of her as she drove back to Monthrope. She thought, this is the only drive I've ever undertaken with the boys without someone demanding to handle the ribbons and having to be rebuffed.

Only one remark was made and that rose sleepily from the snuggled form of Eugene. 'Adam Wilkins says I can share his room when I go there.'

Laura smiled down at his head and, although Michael had fallen asleep, she whispered, 'That's my brave boy,' but Eugene's eyelids were already drooping.

On her return, Laura handed the chaise over to Titus and saw the boys into Nurse's care. She left them excitedly relaying all the deeds of their day and retired to her room, anticipating some stern remarks from Nurse on the morrow; fancy placing her treasures in danger with all this unnatural business of punts and swimming. She tidied herself up and then went in search of Lady Hardacre.

Her ladyship had just returned from an outing somewhere and Laura thought she looked magnificent as she swept into the Hall, but she realised it was too soon to approach her. Laura took herself off to join Mrs Carson and Tilly over a pot of tea, in the mellow comfort of the huge old kitchen. Rosie and Luke came in and when Hocking followed to ask for a tray for Lady Hardacre, Laura rose and walked up to her ladyship's sitting room.

She wanted to report to Lady Hardacre on the success of the visit to Horton, but she had realised there were sections of it that might not meet with approval. The wait had given her time to think, and she presented a carefully devised summary of the experience. 'I drove to Horton today with Eugene and Michael and they had a very pleasant visit with Dr and Mrs Humphries. We all lunched together and were shown over the academy. Eugene appears pleased that Adam Wilkins has invited him to share his bedchamber when he goes there.'

'You are actually telling me that Eugene is willing to attend Horton Academy?'

'He is looking forward to it, I believe.'

'However did you manage that?'

'It wasn't my doing. It was the outing.' Realising from the inquisitorial glance that there was no getting out of it, Laura continued. 'When we arrived in Horton, Dr and Mrs Humphries were taking their pupils on a picnic and invited us along. We punted down the river to a pool and all the boys had a swim.'

'Our boys had a swim?'

'Yes. Dr Humphries taught them a little. I didn't see much because Mrs Humphries and I waited at the picnic spot and the boys went further down. They enjoyed themselves for such a long time and then they came back and ate a mountain of food. After that, we punted back to Horton to have a good look around the accommodation. Everyone got along very satisfactorily, and afterwards, I drove us home.'

Lady Hardacre seated herself, looking down at her hands and Laura thought her face was a puzzle; surely there was jealousy and heartbreak amongst the smiles and head-shakings. But what a general she would have made. When the advantage lies in the direction you want, strike immediately. Within days, Laura accompanied Eugene and Michael to Horton, seated in state in the barouche-landau, where Adam showed the newcomer upstairs to his room.

Laura and Michael sat on Adam's bed and they both wanted to help Eugene unpack, but he was suddenly too old to be waited on and did it all by himself. Sunday's recruits flocked in to welcome him warmly, before carrying him off to meet two pupils who were absent during the picnic outing. Apparently, two sets of tiresome parents had obliged them to go home at week's end and miss out on the fun.

Dr Humphries walked in, looked at the over-excited group and sent them out to the back lawn with a bat and ball to play rounders. Laura and Michael drove home, solemnly bearing an envelope containing rather a staggering account for Eugene's lodging and education. Warm inside the coach, Michael snuggled under her arm and whispered enviously, 'A whole three years before I am eleven.'

'Two and a half, Michael,' she responded, rather tartly. She was missing Eugene already.

STEP FORWARD BOB ALSTON

*I*n characteristically businesslike fashion, Mr Wilmott wheeled up to the kitchen door of Monthrope Hall, descended from his curricle and handed a box of pineapples to Hocking and the reins to Bob Alston. The latter had heard the familiar sound of carriage wheels and walked down from the stables, and Julius halted in surprise when he received the rather nervous enquiry, 'Mr Wilmott, can I ask your advice?'

'Certainly, Bob. What is it?'

'What do you think I should do? I'm sick of hanging around here, part-groom, part handyman. I need something to be getting on with.'

'Inside or outdoor work suit you?'

'Mostly outside work. As you know, Lord Hardacre sent me to grammar school – I can read and write and cipher, but I'd never make a desk clerk.'

Bob Alston eyed the financier, who was staring at the cobblestones, and realised the old gent was really giving it due thought. His spirits rose and he forgave himself for being so impertinent as to approach someone far above him. He felt he had taken quite a risk and had dreaded being lectured about accepting the role you were born into.

Suddenly, the leonine head flung back. 'Come with me.'

Since Wilmott had arrived without a groom, Bob whistled up Titus to rescue the carriage and ponies and followed Mr Wilmott down a passageway and into the back entrance of the library. Crossing the room to a table by the window, Mr Wilmott searched out a particular roll of paper, spread it across the tabletop and anchored it with several books and the inkstand. They both bent over the sheet and Bob discovered it was a map of east Monthrope.

'All this pink area is Monthrope Hall's land,' said Mr Wilmott, pointing it out. 'But look at this yellow area.' His finger traced a long, irregular lemon-coloured rectangle following the windings of Monthrope Brook. 'That is Monthrope Manor and it's up for sale. I went and had a look at it recently. It hasn't sold because the house and outbuildings need a lot of work. I was thinking of buying it.'

Bob wondered if he was going to be offered a labouring job and remained silent. The older man stared at the map for a lengthy few minutes, sorting his own thoughts and desires into order and considering possibilities before he spoke.

'You are Hardacre's son. You have every right to ask him to set you up on a property. I suggest that you ask him to buy this Monthrope manor house for you. If he agrees, we can look at doing up the buildings. As I said, it will be a big job.'

'Mr Wilmott, I'd jump at the chance, but it will take more money than just buying a property, to set up as a farmer. There's all the repairs. And I know little of actual farm work.'

'Would you like to do it? Can you learn?'

'Yes, to both.'

'Then I'll help you in whatever way I can. And I'll make sure to be there and back you when you face Augustus.'

'Thank you, sir.' They leant over the map together, locating and pointing out to each other its various features: the buildings, the rivulet coming off the river, the woods, and the manorial fields. On cue, the main library door swung open, and Mr Wakefield walked in, closely followed by Lord Hardacre. They stared at the pair by the window and strolled over to see what they were doing.

Bob took a breath and addressed his father. 'I need you to

buy Monthrope Manor for me, set me up in life, Augustus. I'm sick of being a lackey.'

'Good for you, Bob,' interpolated Wakefield before Augustus could open his mouth.

'And I'll back you, Bob,' added Wilmott, deciding to let Augustus know where he stood on this matter.

It was anybody's guess what his lordship felt or wanted, but he saw immediately that a refusal would leave him in the minority, cornered three to one. He advanced to the table, traced the outline of Monthrope Manor on the map and stood considering the issue. With Grimes now heading the stables, Alston was superfluous to requirements. He had been considering what to do to forward the lad's career, and he knew Maisy was worrying about it. He was proud of Bob, liking his straightforward manner and his efficiency around the estate. He even liked the way he trod a middle road between being a servant and master; he was never servile.

Augustus studied the map carefully. The estate abutted Monthrope Hall, separated only by the wildwood. It looked to be an asset with it so handily adjoining the river and, if it went to Bob, it would remain in the family, so to speak. In fact, he could make sure of that by adopting Bob into the family – but enough of that, now. He would tell them of his plans later.

He nodded. 'You'll address this at once, Wakefield.'

'Right away sir. I'll ride over and check it out and put in an offer.'

'You'll need to see Lawrence & Isaacs,' said Wilmott. 'They've been holding it for me and are expecting to hear back. You can tell them that I am backing Alston. But not a word about this to anyone else until we land it.'

He walked over to take Alston by the arm and lead him out of the room, but the young man turned first to Hardacre, shook his hand, and said, 'Thank you,' before going away. Restored to the yard, he turned to Wilmott and again held out his hand.

'This is a dream come true. Thank you, sir.'

'Who'd have thought Augustus would take it so easy,' murmured Wilmott, returning the clasp. On reflection, Alston was not at all surprised. Hardacre had always helped him.

Wakefield rounded up the others a week later and reported that the sale had been made – for a very satisfactory sum, due to the condition of the buildings. 'Let's all ride over and inspect Bob's land,' he suggested. The idea excited and interested them all and they rode across to inspect the new acquisition. Entrance gates, choked with weeds, fronted a winding lane leading to a pleasant old-style manor house. Wakefield handed the house keys to Wilmott and called, 'Come on Bob, we'll ride the boundary so that you know your land and exactly what you own.'

Wilmott guessed that he wanted some privacy with Alston and said, 'Good idea, Charles. Augustus and I will start a list of what needs fixing. What do you reckon Gus, start with the outbuildings?'

'Yes, they're the important ones. Those barns look sound enough from here, but nothing else does.' Wilmott produced a notebook and hurried after him to begin the list of necessary repairs. Hardacre groaned at the disrepair evident everywhere, but his cynical gaze spotted every flaw, and he pointed them out for Wilmott to record. Better to tackle them early rather than let the place deteriorate further.

The pair of young men cantered along the boundary hedges and fences, leaving the older couple to their own exploration. As soon as they were well away, Wakefield said to Bob, 'I've decided I'm going to become your factor: that is, I'll be your agent while you learn the job. Then you can run it yourself.'

'I hardly know anything about day-to-day farming.'

'You'll learn, and I'll teach you all I know, but I want to tell you some personal news first. I know now how I want to lead my own life. It's here in Monthrope and Julius has helped me to buy old Mrs Sutton's house. I'll be much handier to my work. My family are about to move from Surbury, and we'll be together in a real home.'

'That's great news, Charles. Is your wife pleased?'

'Very much so, and the children are absolutely thrilled about it. Now, to get back to the organisation of your place. I'm thinking we'll hire Martin Chugg to be your farmer and cattleman, put the crops in and take them off. Hopkins will probably agree to be your shepherd. He told me he was sick of working for Smithers, and he's the better sheep man. Make sure they teach you what they know. Don't hesitate to tell them it's new to you. Now, this is your south boundary – see the marker.'

Wakefield and Alston returned, elated and excited. 'This has got to be some of the best land in the county. Those flats abutting the river might go under water during winter, but the soil throughout the property is excellent.' The house and barns were explored all over for a second time, and the group rode back to Monthrope Hall full of enthusiasm and plans. Even Hardacre seemed energised and enthused, but Bob swore them all to secrecy. 'For now, let everyone think Hardacre has bought it and I'm his tenant,' he said.

NOT SO BRIGHT AFTER ALL

*I*n October, Leonard and Elizabeth Bright arrived at Monthrope Hall, but without the children. Elizabeth was suffering, and she had asked to come to be with her sister. Leonard helped her up the stairs to a room on the first floor and she was put to bed there.

Although news of this event ran around the Hall like wildfire, Laura first learned of it when she saw Leonard at dinner that night and greeted him composedly, aware that everyone was watching. She asked after the children and was told they had been left in the care of their new governess, Miss Dawson.

Laura was now tutor to only one pupil. She and Michael both missed Eugene, but there was no doubt that Michael flourished with her undivided attention and came on apace in his schoolwork and sporting activities. Julius was immensely proud of him. Eugene resided in Horton with Dr and Mrs Humphries, returning each Friday afternoon, full of the week's events, yet happy to be home again. He joined in readily with their customary activities, particularly enjoying such rides and drives as the weather permitted. He was sometimes accompanied by one of his fellow pupils. This was a mixed pleasure for Michael, but Eugene still found time for his younger brother.

Once settled at Monthrope Hall, Leonard soon appeared in the nursery schoolroom. Michael welcomed him and explained his current activity, but their visitor joined in only briefly before heading off. His sudden appearance had momentarily excited Laura, but she concentrated on a new maths activity she was teaching.

That night, Leonard waylaid her in the upstairs hallway and hugged her. 'How are you, Laura? I've missed you so much.'

She replied coolly, using his name for the first time. 'I'm very well, Leonard. It must be very difficult and painful for you watching Mrs Bright suffer.'

'Yes, dreadful. Be kind to me Laura, I'm so lonely.'

Something or somebody caught his attention and they parted, each hurrying on their way, Laura wondering why his words did not sit right with her. His tone, words and behaviour all seemed overly intimate and inappropriate – and wholly self-focused. She had expected a description of what his wife was enduring and his efforts to afford her the best treatment possible.

Laura no longer daydreamed of becoming Mrs Bright because the thought felt utterly macabre, especially with the patient lying critically ill in a bedroom nearby. As for Leonard, after leaving the schoolroom, she knew he had been out much of the day, joining in with the men's activities. Had he any thought or feeling for, and had he spent any time with that poor woman downstairs? Who had been looking after Mrs Bright? Perhaps it all fell to Nurse. She would try and understand the situation better.

She saw Leonard now only at mealtimes, but Laura did notice that Lady Hardacre and Nurse were often absent from their usual activities. Busy with Michael's education and her responsibilities to the paupers, she learned little more until the situation was clarified towards the end of that week.

Monthrope Hall was deathly quiet that evening. Lady Hardacre had not attended dinner. Laura dined and departed, leaving the men chatting over their port, but her ladyship did not appear in the drawing room. Laura avoided the piano; it seemed unfeeling to make a noise that might disturb the sick woman or to play gaily when someone was dying, or even to play sadly. She decided to retire to her own room and read and selected a book from among those laid out on the table in the drawing room, before slipping quietly away.

The lower hall was empty and lit by a single lantern. She climbed to the second floor and looked along the wide corridors with their beautiful lamps on stands. All was silent except for the sound of her own footsteps and the swish of her skirts, and they may have attracted attention because the door of the nearest room opened, and Lady Hardacre walked out. She looked somewhat less neat than usual and incredibly weary. Laura could see into the room, thanks to a shaded lamp partially lighting a bed and its occupant. So, this had become the sickroom and that must be Mrs Bright.

'Can I help?' she asked.

'Please sit with Elizabeth for a while, Laura. Nurse and Mrs Tillotson are exhausted, and I have been here all afternoon.'

Laura was glad to oblige. Lady Hardacre said that she was going to bed and Laura urged her to eat, to swallow some soup or have a tray sent up. Lady Hardacre, sounding as if she had forgotten all about food, agreed that she would, and left.

Laura examined her patient, straightened the bedclothes and then the nearby table with its plethora of medicine bottles and other impedimenta. She soon saw why these were needed. Mrs Bright's body had changed to a shade of mahogany as her organs shut down, the jaundiced skin shining through her prematurely greying hair. She was not a peaceful patient, squirming when she was awake, mewing and groaning and twisting even in sleep. The most prominent medication on the table was laudanum and Laura fed her drops of the bitter narcotic in warm water when her cries became acute. She stoked the fire but sat near the bed so that Mrs Bright could more easily be assisted, holding her hand gently when she was awake and trying to rest when she wasn't.

Eventually, Laura realised she was about to fall asleep herself and stood up. She cleared the mantelpiece then found a cloth and wiped it down. She was wiping and replacing the ornaments when the door opened, and Leonard Bright walked in. Laura's first thought was that she was glad Leonard should end his day by visiting his wife but there was no trace of such an intention when he spoke.

'So there you are,' he said. 'I wondered where you had got to. I've been looking all over for you.'

Laura decided not to answer. She put the last piece of china in place and moved across to the bed. Her patient was breathing fast and shallowly, high in the chest. Laura knew that sign of depleted strength abandoning the effort to lift the ribs, to draw in further life, and understood its significance. She smoothed the pillows and straightened up, only to discover Leonard was now standing too close to her. Laura was about to offer him a chair when he put an arm round her waist and drew her against him. This shocked Laura. She broke free immediately and said, 'Go away,' and when there was no response, 'Get out.'

'Or you'll throw firewood at me?'

So he'd heard that story, had he? 'Yes,' she said.

'Vixen.' He gave her a quick peck on her averted cheek and left.

Mrs Bright's exhausted body and failing mind appeared to be slipping into unconsciousness, but Laura could only be glad that she was no longer writhing, and she sat down, expecting to see out the night. There was too little light to read the novel she had put down on entering, and now there were too many thoughts for either reading or allowing sleep to overtake her.

There was, however, ample time during the hour that

followed, to think about the scene with Leonard Bright. She was aghast and ashamed that he should choose such a time and place to approach her. What sort of man would seek to make love to a woman in front of his dying wife? Had he no loyalty? What sort of woman must he think she was, if he assumed she would accept or even welcome his advances at such a time? And if that poor creature could still hear, how must she have felt then, or still be feeling?

Even if he had approached me somewhere else in the house, I would have repulsed him, she thought. You cannot, you ought not to be making up to someone else while your wife of many years, the mother of your children, is dying nearby. No decent person would do so.

Nurse came in at midnight and Laura retired thankfully to her room where sleep did, at last, claim her. How nice it would be if Minnie was singing at my window was her last thought as she pulled up the bedclothes; but she soon dropped off and, once again, was not woken until Rosie breezed in with the tea tray and the morning's gossip.

On Friday, Eugene came home for two days and Laura kept the boys busy with activities in the nursery and games in the upper gallery because the weather was uncooperative. But possibly their noise was considered too loud or she was more greatly needed elsewhere. She learned that Michael was to leave Monthrope Hall in company with Eugene, for his first experience of boarding with the Humphries.

Laura accompanied the brothers in the Hardacre barouche and stayed to see Michael settled and happily occupied. She was amused to witness his pride in being grown-up enough to join Eugene, and sad because now her last pupil had passed out of her hands. Fortunately, Grimes was no longer a silent driver and provided a welcome distraction from self-pity. The showers obliged by holding off, so Laura rejected sitting in state and drove home rugged up beside him, while he chatted happily throughout the trip as if he had known her for ever.

Laura was invited to eat luncheon with Lady Hardacre in her cosy writing room and to sit by the fire while they occupied the afternoon with embroidery. They were pleasantly warm with the curtains drawn and the room well-lit by candelabra. Lady Hardacre asked Laura if she would help again with nursing Mrs Bright and Laura replied, 'I am happy to help in any way I can.' She was immediately asked if she was willing to sit with the patient that evening and this became the daily pattern for the final days of Mrs Bright's life.

During the mornings, Laura tidied and ordered the schoolroom section of the nursery and helped Nurse turn out drawers and cupboards in the bedchambers. She saw the family only at mealtimes and conquered loneliness by venturing several times to the kitchen to listen to Mrs Carson and her acolyte, and to the housekeeper's room to spend time with Mrs Tillotson.

Monthrope Hall went into mourning while Nurse and Evadne washed and dressed Elizabeth for her final journey. Mr Bright, suitably clad, accompanied his wife's body back to his own parish, and a funeral was arranged for the following week.

Laura was surprised when Lady Hardacre said to her, the next morning, that this appeared a good time for Laura to take a long overdue holiday. On consideration, Laura agreed; it was now necessary that she should decide on her future. It was important to do so because she now felt less willing to undertake another governessing job, even if one was offered with the three pretty Bright daughters who were so affectionate to her and had now lost their mother.

BOB SPEAKS TO LAURA

With the family in deep mourning, there was no attendance at church that Sunday and silence reigned throughout Monthrope Hall. Having left Lady Hardacre after breakfast, Laura was rather disconsolately approaching her room when she observed Bob Alston walking towards her along the third-floor hallway. She nodded and would have passed on, but he grasped her arm momentarily and said, 'I was looking for you, Laura. I want to talk to you.'

Surprised, she led the way into her bedchamber and indicated the chair by her fire. Afterwards, she was bemused by the instinct that led her to assume it could only be for some extraordinary reason Alston needed to consult her that day. She let the door remain open and drew up the chair from her writing desk.

She was interested to note that Bob took a minute to collect his thoughts before speaking. She had always thought him reactive, but now she realised that he was, like so many in this strange household, a person who thought out his actions before following a course. Also, it was curious that he was no longer dressed as a groom, although perhaps he was wearing his Sabbath outfit.

'Has old man Wilmott, or Evadne or anybody else told you that I now own Monthrope Manor?' Laura shook her head in response. 'I've become the owner of property. Did you notice that I'd left here?' Bob asked.

Laura looked her amazement. 'Really? Nobody has mentioned it and I've been so occupied with nursing Elizabeth or catching up on some sleep, that I hardly notice anything. I suppose there is no reason why anyone should have mentioned it. They haven't seen much of me in recent weeks, and it is, after all, none of my business.'

'I told everyone below stairs that I wanted to tell you myself. It appears they've been kind enough to do so. I knew I could rely on Mr Wilmott and Mr Wakefield, but I did worry that Augustus or Evadne might say something. Laura, I had a talk with Mr Wilmott about my future and he brought it all about. Augustus bought the Manor, as due to his son. Charlie Wakefield is guiding me, and I'm learning how to repair and run a manor, and how to pass for a gentleman.'

Before Laura could think of an appropriate comment, he continued. 'I want you to make this your business, Laura. I want you to consider the matter thoroughly. I've watched you here. I've seen your excellence in everything you do. I know how well you handle Augustus, how delightfully you get on with Mr Wilmott. I've seen how you feel about Leonard Bright and how he feels about you. But I warn you, Bright will let you down in the long run. Don't waste your youth waiting or repining, Laura, because you can do better. Marry me.'

For the first time in her life, Laura knew what it was to be struck dumb. She had viewed Alston as Evadne's man, some sort of virile pawn taking advantage of her ladyship's ambitions. He had told her otherwise, describing an initially bemused adolescent ruthlessly used by his master's wife, presumably because he was related to her husband. Now it occurred to Laura how badly she had underrated him. She had presumed, on no grounds whatsoever, that he flitted from bed to bed: an assumption made because his father was a lecher and Alston had always looked at her with great appreciation. She had never heard even the slightest reference to any laxity but had put it down to staff respecting his relationship with the Hardacres. His previous explanations had given her no grounds at all for that old belief and she had felt obliged to apologise for it. What could she answer him now that he was looking for a wife and possibly a soulmate?

Laura took her time, and she spoke slowly. 'Bob, if I may

call you so now that you are a landowner, I am delighted to hear of your good fortune and I wish you every success. I thank you for the honour you are doing me. You are right. I have been deeply attached, I think now misguidedly attached, to someone else. Perhaps that makes me unfit for anyone else.'

'I think you should get to know me better Laura; you might then transfer your regard. I'm asking you now because I want you to know that I am serious. Laura, I am asking you to be my wife, not offering you the role of mistress.'

He rose as he spoke and pulled her to her feet. She felt all the animal magnetism of this healthy young man, and her lonely body, perhaps remembering previous delights, overcame her intelligence and she unconsciously swayed towards him. She was instantly swept up in his arms and his mouth descended on hers.

He said, 'Laura, darling' and held her close Excited, almost enchanted, and intrigued by the feel of his physical response and the way his voice deepened with passion, she yielded. Her fingers met behind his neck and her bones melted as she responded passionately to his kiss. They then separated slightly but their eyes remained locked on each other. His were smiling down at her, but Laura was shocked, unsteady on her feet, and half-ashamed of having responded so lustily. She realised that showing such enjoyment presaged further acceptance of his lovemaking.

Bob Alston was not a man to let opportunity slip and he bent his head and kissed her again, enjoying reawakening her responses. If he took her now, she might consent because to deny him would be a betrayal of her essential honesty, but he also knew that she needed to decide her own future. A wife trapped into marriage was not his goal. He reluctantly drew apart and smiled again, because she was as slow to part as he was.

'Evadne has told me to take a month's holiday. I'm going to stay with my friends in Surbury and will then travel north to visit my brother and his family. When I return, I'll come and see you in all your new state as soon as I can,' she promised.

Alston headed off to finish clearing out his old quarters and organise his coming week's activities. Laura was left feeling relieved that it was Sunday, giving her time and space to calm her turbulence and decide what she wanted to do. She walked across the room and stared out the window. Oh, Minnie, she thought, what you've missed out on. She walked to the door, decided she was unfit to be seen, automatically tidied the desk chair back into its proper place, laughed at herself, and sat down again.

If Laura thought that she had tied her brain in knots trying to establish and maintain an appropriate relationship with Leonard Bright, it was as nothing to the confusion of ecstatic emotions she struggled with now, as she considered her feelings for this man who had gradually drawn her admiration, and to admit how strongly she felt about him.

How much of it was love and how much lust? It was all delightful turmoil. She acknowledged her desire to belong to someone, to establish her own family, and to be settled in life in a way consonant with her upbringing. She faced again the fact that she apparently had a healthy appetite for lovemaking, and that some underlying need overwhelmed her when a man she found appealing caressed her.

She tried to sort out her attraction to Bob Alston in as sensible and practical fashion as if she were deciphering a mathematics problem, but her brain cheekily refused to comply. Instead, it romped off into a joyful reprise of the scene in her room that morning with all its intertwining emotions.

In the end, she was obliged to consider her usual Sunday

activities and apply herself to reading and writing and leave the thinking and decision-making until she felt calmer.

DUTY CALLS IN NEWCASTLE

When it came to organising her month's holiday, Mr Wilmott, having learned from Laura that she planned to spend a few days with Martha and Ben Wilcox before travelling north to visit her family, proceeded to organise it all. In vain did Laura declare that she could do it herself and that she could pay for it herself. It was all done for her, and she set off in some style, travelling post, to relax in comfort with her friends prior to heading north.

That was the easy part of her holiday. She benefited from the break and the ease of being with such longstanding supporters. She had many qualms about the coming visit, but she felt it was the right thing to do, and it would allow her to understand her remaining family's situation and whether she should provide any further help to them. Once this duty was done, she could return to an exciting new life in Monthrope. She boarded the coach with more optimism than either the long road ahead or the visit warranted.

The journey to Newcastle proved an extraordinary endurance test, partly due to the time of the year: a trip that was not only cold, muddy, bumpy, and sometimes boggy, but lengthy, seemingly never-ending. Thanks to Mr Wilmott, and to the desire of the post boys to complete their stint and return to base, their travelling was speedier than was usually possible, but that was little comfort to Laura, incessantly jolted during long days cooped up in a swaying, bucking vehicle, or dragged along at a snail's pace in the worst stretches. She felt too uncomfortable to daydream of future delights and forced herself to merely endure.

Some overnight stops were pleasant, with welcoming innkeepers bowing her into their hostelry and providing every comfort necessary to a worn-out traveller. Occasionally, the discovery that she had no accompanying relative or maid gained her a frosty reception. In these instances, Laura's cool, well-bred voice, and good quality clothing ensured that she did at least obtain lodgings, although the innkeeper's wife might wonder if she was one of 'them Puritans or Quakers', her apparel was so plain.

Laura praised those who welcomed her to hearty fires and hot food and bore with the suspicions of the remainder. She gradually became aware that her welcome often improved markedly during the evening and guessed that this was thanks to the post boys. Unbeknown to her, they unhesitatingly informed anyone who asked that Laura's trip had been paid for by her grandfather, who was as rich as Midas. Still, after a week of such travel, it was a tired and dispirited young woman who stumbled out of the coach and hammered on the front door of Tyneville Manse.

It was opened by a boy of about eight.

'Are you Thomas?' Laura asked.

When he nodded, she introduced herself and moved to enter. 'I'm your Aunt Laura.'

'Yer can't come in.' When Laura looked astonished he added, 'We've got the sickness here. Everyone in the village's sick.'

'Then I think I'd better come in and help,' she replied and was glad to see that he appeared relieved.

A glance on arrival, at Emily's comatose condition and emaciated frame, revealed her sister-in-law's fate was sealed. Laura gently cleaned her face and hands, moistened her lips with balm, and fed her teaspoonfuls of warm water, honey and citrus juice whenever she stirred, while she waited for the inevitable.

She was washing and wrapping the skeletal body when Moira, the little skivvy who came in daily, suddenly said, 'Do be putting her bubby with yon.' To Laura's horror, she went to the next room and came back with a carefully shrouded chilly bundle which she placed beside the young mother. Laura finished her task, washed her hands and was glad to don her cloak and run out to find the verger and his offsiders busy among the gravestones.

She asked where they could inter the vicar's wife and child.

'Why to be sure, with the other childer,' said old Neill, leading the way across the graveyard. There, she found a row of little headstones attesting that Diana and Morris and Emily-Susan Markham 'rested safely within God's arms'. Now their mother and sibling would join them. Laura was shocked. It was the first she had heard of her family's losses. As a Markham, not only should she have been told, she should have been there to attend them and support her family. There were failings on both sides. That was Laura's welcome to Newcastle and almost all she saw of Tyneville during her first week.

For Laura, Tyneville felt like life on a far planet. Stone buildings and flagged or cobbled streets remained icy all winter. The chill, the drizzle and the muck were tiresome and, at first, so were the inhabitants. They spoke another language, nominally English but known locally as Geordy. She coped best with this blurry dialect if she didn't concentrate but waited patiently for enlightenment. The words gradually sank in, and she hoped desperately that she had understood what was said, or at least what was wanted.

Fearsome diseases raged throughout the north, often arriving by sea, and decimating the population in the docks and mines, the rope factories, and glassworks: the infected rapidly sharing their illness with family and neighbourhood. The elite, some of whom did much good, apparently comprised impregnable groups of Presbyterians, Anglicans, and others. So did the lower orders, except that Tyneville housed a sturdy core of Protestant Dissenters and freethinkers, a combination of chapelgoers and those nominally not followers of a church, but none of them too proud to come in need to the manse door. Poverty was endemic and the needy appeared in dribs and drabs, by day and night.

Laura now understood how Edmund's inheritance had been whittled away and she drew on her bank account for the benefit of her family. She paid for food and sea coal above what Edmund provided and for a fulltime skivvy. Both children attended school. Having bought each of them a coat, cap, and scarf, she was astonished to see them leaving home in their worn-out and outgrown predecessors. When she remonstrated, they solemnly swore that the new clothes would likely be torn away from them by the desperate, and they couldn't bear it.

Laura saw them off in their old coats and tattered tammies but bedecked with their new scarfs. Both children swore to defend these accoutrements to the death and did so. Both mentioned during the evening that they had found it easier to concentrate on their schoolwork due to the extra warmth. Laura, listening in amazement, realised they were obliged to carry out their lessons while all rugged up. The next day she convinced them to wear both their new tammies and scarves and to give their old ones to classmates. This was successful and, the following day, they were able to dispose of their aged coats the same way, literally buying protection for their new apparel.

After debating whether farthings or halfpennies would go further, Laura turned one pound of her earnings into pennies which she doled out, one at a time, when she had no efficacious solution to the never-ending problems presented on the doorstep. She was unaware that this most simple emollient eased her way into Tyneville society. From being a foreigner and an alien, she was promoted to 'our vicar's ain guid sister.'

For Laura, there was an interesting sidelight to her stay

in Newcastle and that was the opportunity to understand her brother better. She soon discovered that he maintained a routine, rising early to pray and read his bible, then practising the Sunday sermon, planning church meetings, and studying ecclesiastical literature. After breakfast, he attended meetings or went on his rounds of the ill and indigent, doing what he could to ameliorate their difficulties.

If he came in at midday, he dined on whatever was quickest to hand then moved to the church or church hall where he was available at need, often for funerals but sometimes christenings or even weddings. He returned home when he could, always too tired to eat straight away, and Laura kept an eagle eye on the front door to make sure he was not bothered for at least an hour. She learned that he recovered best with a hot drink and being left to sit by the fireside. He was then in a frame of mind to take an interest in Charlotte and Thomas and hear about their day and their concerns. Afterwards, Laura would bring him a tray, or he would move to the dining table to eat. He never asked about her activities, and, for a long time, she assumed this was due to weariness; just as she assumed that occasional comments suggesting she needed to earn her keep, meant no more than his being too occupied to notice how hard she was working.

More and more Laura found herself concerned for the wellbeing of her niece and nephew. It was apparent that Thomas endured school because he must, and it was difficult to discover what interested him. Someone had quashed whatever ambitions and ideas he had for his own future, and his solution was to vanish to the seashore and the docks as often as he could. Laura could understand how space might bring peace, and the activities along the dockside fascinate him, but she feared for his safety and his health, glad when he returned safely each time.

Occasionally, he carried a stray kitten or broken-winged gull, hidden inside his coat, which always vanished overnight, and always left him furiously searching next morning. The only time Laura saw Edmund beat Thomas was when his son furiously demanded to know what his parent had done with his pet this time. Laura was appalled; she could not remember her parents ever chastising either of their children. She ended up doing nothing, since Edmund had every right to punish his own child and remained unaware that seeing his sister's eyes fill with tears caused Edmund more remorse than the cries of his little boy.

Edmund's treatment of Charlotte was even harder to fathom and only over time did she guess the source lay far back in time. Certain that it was not good for a little girl to be considered negligible, laden with household duties, and always placed behind her brother, Laura encouraged Charlotte to chat about her day, worked beside her, and admired her excellent progress at school. She was pleased that Charlotte trusted her enough to speak openly, but detected an underlying bitterness that made her seem older than her years.

During the long winter evenings, when there was any let-up in the pestilence or the petitioners, Laura would listen while Edmund talked. He seemed to have no interest in hearing of her own experiences but was voluble on the things that mattered to him. Among an incredible litany of mostly local issues, she was astonished to find he was bitter about his marriage.

'I was nineteen. Both my parents knew I was too young to marry, we were both too young. They should never have allowed it.'

Ah, thought Laura, is this why his regard for Charlotte is so grudging? I thought it was because he wanted a boy. 'Papa didn't want to hold you back from your chosen path and the woman you loved.'

'Nonsense! I knew you would back Father. You were

always his pet.'

'We were certainly close. And, Edmund, he gave you as good a start as he possibly could.'

'He set me on the road to ruin. Fancy giving me at nineteen years of age twenty thousand pounds and leaving it to me to decide what to do with it, so that I sank it in a company that turned into a bubble. No, he only let me marry because we had to.'

Laura had become momentarily distracted by the realization that her inheritance monumentally outweighed his. She roused and said, 'I suppose that you've had at least as much from Mother.'

'Probably; but then I am the eldest, and the only son.' But Laura had now focused on their original topic.

'What did you mean "had to marry"?'

'Oh come on, Laura, you're not a child. We married in April and Charlotte was born in September.'

Laura had always known her views on practically everything differed from her brother's, but the weight of all this evidence silenced her for some time. They sat on either side of the fireplace, where the Newcastle coal she had paid for scorched their faces and toes, both of them deep in thought.

Laura gradually decided Edmund had absolutely misread the situation. Father had dealt with the practicalities of Emily's situation in the only way possible. The poor girl was with child so she had to marry; there was no other choice. It was face up to marriage or run away and hide yourself somewhere, with or without your lover's or your family's support. If Emily had remained unwed, she might have been thrown off by her parents, she might have died. She would certainly have been ruined socially. Edmund must surely know that, so how unkind and unfair it was of him to blame his parent; but it seemed that Edmund thought only of himself.

Now it suddenly occurred to her that Papa might have used Edmund's wedding as a way of throwing off such a burdensome and disappointing son. Was giving Edmund his inheritance a way of shedding, forever, an ongoing problem? And then again, did their hasty wedding explain why the parish he settled in was so far away from all who knew him?

Laura didn't like these thoughts at all because they were incompatible with her memories of the man who had reared her. Well, Edmund was only human, but she had allowed his ugly words to momentarily affect her. She knew her father to be an honest man, most unlikely to abandon any offspring, and she blamed Edmund for presenting such an unpleasant view of the situation. For the first time, Laura wished she knew Emily's version of events, but it was too late. She hoped there had been some joy in the marriage and said so.

This did not elicit any great response and as she got up to light her bedroom candle she thought well, he's devoted to his work, and I think he has some genuine feeling for Thomas and Charlotte. Two months have passed already. I wonder when I can go home. The thought startled her. Home? She had hardly thought of it for weeks. She'd hardly had time to think of anything but the necessities of life, of getting through another day successfully before falling into bed and instant sleep.

Thomas was not correct when he said everybody had the sickness because the epidemic's prevalence appeared arbitrary. Edmund never caught any disease and nor did Laura or the two children, although with winter at its height and disease rife, the vicar was constantly busy among the ailing. Laura sternly informed him that his first duty was to his offspring, and she made sure he washed his face and hands and sat down each evening to hold them and chat with them. She ensured he ate and drank enough to keep healthy, even if it was only thick soup or a bowl of stew eaten with a spoon by the fireside because he was too tired to sit up at the table.

Much of the costs of burying the young mother and child, feeding the family, and supervising the housekeeping fell to Laura. At first, she accepted the responsibility willingly and it took many weeks of day in, day out drudgery before she realised that she was trapped, and Edmund was content that it should be so. He had no intention of facilitating her return south. Laura, at long last, recognised that only if Edmund married again could she be free to pick up her own life. It's time I organised how to get back to Monthrope, she told herself and, adhering to the practicalities, began looking for a successor to Emily.

There were several likely candidates, of varying ages and appearances and qualities, and eventually Laura decided on Nellie Patten, the church organist. She was not only young, attractive and capable but also liked the children. Laura asked her straight out if she would be willing to wed the vicar, and when told she was, if she was a good household manager. Nell professed to be so, and Laura decided to get the children involved and then pressure Edmund to marry as soon as possible.

When Laura thought the relationship between Edmund and Nellie was developing nicely, although pitifully slowly, she spoke to her niece, Charlotte. 'If you don't want to remain here as a skivvy or housekeeper to your family all your life, encourage your father to marry Nellie Patten.'

'Then they'll go having babies, and Thomas and I will be left out.'

Laura considered the moral strictures a devoted aunt should

make in reply to such a statement, on such a subject. She almost immediately decided that, while she was amazed Charlotte could think so far ahead, she admired her niece for being forthright.

She responded, 'Not if you understand Nellie and know how to handle her. In any case, your father is devoted to you both. He's just very busy every day.'

'He is, isn't he? I'm delighted to hear he's devoted.'

Laura ignored the note of cynicism and hoped for the best. She noticed Charlotte making the effort to get to know Nellie, and Thomas soon appeared to have the little organist wound around his finger. She tracked Edmund down to the vestry where he was disrobing after the latest funeral service, and thought he daily appeared older and sadder and wearier.

'This is all too much for me,' he told her, sitting down on a pew and looking as if he would rather lie down.

'You do know Nellie Patten is in love with you.'

He seemed astonished but cheered up immediately. Over the next few days, he began to make time to talk more to Nellie and to observe her with the children, but he still insisted Laura should stay. It really was beneath his dignity to have a sister who was nothing more than a governess; he couldn't approve. In any case, she should remain in Newcastle until he was out of mourning and could conscientiously remarry. Nowhere did he ask Laura about her ambitions or consider that Laura might marry; it appeared her destiny was to remain and be of use. He had never asked about Monthrope or enquired into her own experiences, wishes or associates.

Laura soon realised that even with the opportunity to begin a relationship with Nellie, her brother's insistence that she remain was nothing more than a display of elder brotherly

drove over to offer her a position and to collect her. He found he had two to collect, with Mrs Tillotson having expressed her contempt for employers who cast off long-standing employees like they were house rags.

If his new entourage was shaken by their change of fortune, and income, they had no time to grieve. Both discovered the efficacy of a storm of housecleaning for rebalancing human equilibrium. They unbent sufficiently to accept necessary furniture from the attic storerooms at the Hall and, after a day spent creating bedchambers for themselves, they began to feel at home. After that, they jointly fell on the cooking and cleaning with gusto. Tilly was able to locate a laundry-maid and turn one of the pauper pensioners into something of a yardman, and Monthrope Manor was up and running. If Bob wondered how he was ever to pay for all their activities, he was so grateful for their support that he acceded to almost everything they wanted.

His third month without Laura was a nightmare and it took the kindness of Tilly and the common sense of both Tilly and Mrs Carson to prevent his giving up hope altogether. None of them knew that Julius Wilmott had already left for Newcastle because the Hall was missing Laura almost as much as the Manor, particularly two young lads, full of news from Horton.

Bob's anxiety, however, was intermittently distracted, due to the word of his rise in status having spread like a house fire. The intelligent among the community had realised that, if Hardacre supported Bob Alston to the extent of buying his son an estate, he would likely continue to support him. The young man, therefore, had prospects. Families with daughters to turn off fastened their beady eyes on Monthrope Manor and noted the growing list of improvements.

Bob began to receive dinner invitations, some from neighbours casually dropping in, while others approached more formally by writing. Where he liked the family, he accepted with the proviso that he be excused if he did not stay late. For the remainder, he rapidly developed a formal note of apology: Mr Alston was grateful for their kind invitation but was so inordinately busy at the current time, he would have to defer acceptance.

Needless to say, this had no effect on the ambitious; if he wouldn't go to them, they would go to him. The female variety paid a formal morning call with a currently available daughter in tow. Generally, the young ladies were passable, but they were all appalled at the state of the estate and the lack of servants. It was obvious that females of the calibre of Bess Olsen and Peggy Jameson, who willingly toiled beside their husbands when needed, didn't feature among the gentry.

Bob learnt to absent himself from home during the likeliest visiting hours, although there was a notable occasion when Mellie Whiskoff, wife of a neighbouring farmer he had met just once, tracked him to his hide-out. Bob was recreating loose boxes in the stables with the help of John Smithers, the carpenter. Mistress Whiskoff was apparently overwhelmed by the sight of two muscular young men, heaving posts and planks into place, and sank on to a convenient trestle to recover. It was a wasted effort. Her bold glances startled and almost frightened Bob, and he could see, by his shaking shoulders and stifled mirth, that the whole charade was gradually reducing his assistant to laughter. When Mellie realised this, she flounced out of the stables and drove away, but an exasperated Bob was quite short with young John when he sat down on the trestle and caricatured its previous occupant.

There were other visitors: salespeople, horse dealers, and pedlars of almost everything. Local farmers and estate owners dropped by on horseback or in their carriages. Bob received enough farming advice to have turned him into an instant expert if much of it had been less contradictory.

Apart from the endless advice on pasture and cropping, at least four sheep breeds were recommended to him, and as many kinds of cows and pigs; and, of course, always the breeds each enthusiast was raising.

As Bob Alston saw it, his life was devoted to proving himself a capable and responsible landowner, with a suitable residence for his chosen bride. Nothing shook this until Lady Eger, from a neighbouring county, brought him a seedling plum tree she thought he would appreciate, and at the same time introduced him to her daughter, Zoe. Bob was interested in the plum tree and asked her where to plant it and how to grow it to get the most auspicious results, only to find she could barely tell a plum tree from an oak tree. This suggested that she might be yet another ambitious mother, and she would have received short shrift if curly-haired, brown-eyed Zoe had not been so strikingly pretty.

Alston's future was saved by the fact that Zoe was markedly opinionated for someone nearly eighteen years old. Yes, it was the most darling house and, by the time he had doubled the size of it and added a classical garden, it would be quite suitable. Lady Eger interrupted to enquire if Mr Alston intended to go to town for the start of the Little Season. When he replied that he didn't, Zoe produced a disapproving moue of her lovely lips and asked him whether he intended to buy or only to lease a town house. He disclaimed any interest in such a procurement and she abruptly reminded her mother that Lady Horton was expecting them and really, they must excuse themselves. Bob's withers remained unwrung; she was so pretty he knew she would surely go off in her first season, and he settled back to his own interests.

None of that saved him from worrying whether Laura had found someone else or found something else that interested her more than life in Monthrope. Mrs Tillotson reduced his discomfort by pointing out that Laura's belongings were still present in her room at the Hall. Mrs Carson calmed him by suggesting that Laura was possibly needed by her brother's family and pointed out that she would have written if she was not intending to return. Bob saw the sense in these words, but he began to accept more dinner invitations and grew accustomed to mixing in polite society.

RETURN TO MONTHROPE

*L*aura ventured to the heart of Newcastle and indulged in, what was for her, a spending spree. It took days because she was so careful, but she had several instances of good luck. Her main need was for dresses but her first win was finding a charming pearl necklace in a pawn shop. The Fates remained kind and a mantua-maker she visited looked on her as a godsend when Laura fitted, and had no qualms as regards the price of three elegant gowns, rejected by a client who had unaccountably put on weight. Shifts, aprons, stockings, and even boots, Laura was able to purchase ready-made.

She did not mention any of this to anyone at the manse, because she now felt certain she would need to make some kind of escape. Her delightful new purchases were delivered without incident, followed by an orgy of sorting and packing in her little room at the back of the house. At last, she felt ready enough to think of ordering the post horses and hoping her brother wouldn't turn them away.

Fate intervened the following morning when a hearty knocking at the door heralded the, oh so welcome, sight of Julius Wilmott. Laura flung herself into his arms with cries of joy.

'I've come to take you home. Three months and never a word from you. Have you any idea how much we've all missed you?'

It was absolutely unburdening to sit down and compare their trips north. Laura then related her experiences of the local poverty, the epidemic, and the death of Emily and her baby. She described how willingly she had entered into doing all that she could, to be of help to her brother and his family, until the fateful day when she realised that she would be obliged to remain in Tyneville for the rest of her life. She explained her solution and her ultimatum.

After initially appearing astonished at her interference, Julius laughed and praised her idea of finding a wife for Edmund. 'Definitely time to get you out of here,' he declared. 'I'm putting up at the posting inn in the village centre. I'll need a day at least to recover from the trip north.'

'You'll need at least a week.'

'A day or two to recover and then we'll be off.'

It was one thing to agree but quite another to convince her brother.

'Go off with a man who is not even a relative, and neither man nor maid to protect you? Unthinkable.'

'He's almost old enough to be my grandfather.'

'He's a man.'

'What a cynical mind you appear to have developed, Edmund.'

Laura thanked a benign providence that Julius Wilmott was so well known and so skilled. A few business meetings and accompanying dinners, and Newcastle was flocking to meet him, and the inn buzzed with all the comings and goings and excitement. Thus, when Edmund rather pompously confronted Mr Wilmott, the industrialist produced one short bark of amusement but took care with his response. 'I've had some worries about that myself. At the inns, I shall call her my granddaughter. Do you want me to hire a maid for her?'

This seeming deference to Edmund's opinion soothed the vicar and Edmund raised no further objections. In fact, he seemed resigned to her departure, which made Laura wonder. Knowing his nature, she suspected that, once she left, he would soon persuade Nellie Patten to set the wedding date. If she had been selfish in engineering him into a second marriage, it was all in a good cause –more than could be said about his treatment of herself.

Of course, it was possible that he was anxious not to be at odds with such a renowned person as the great entrepreneur. Laura could imagine him sliding Julius's name into every future conversation where he wanted to enhance his own image, and once again, she had to take herself to task. She acknowledged that experience was making her cynical, and she had already found that it was just as effective as criticism in draining the joy out of living; she refused to think like that.

She was surprised, and a little disappointed, that the children seemed to take her departure without any great concern. At first, Laura feared this was a sign that they were becoming streetwise beyond their years, but she hoped it meant that they had already mentally replaced her with Nellie. She convinced both Thomas and Charlotte to write to her, particularly if they encountered any difficulties, and gave them a sovereign apiece in small change, saying it would pay for lots of letters, and endeavoured to believe their assurances that it wouldn't be wasted.

Once again, it was time to enter a post-chaise, but this one was tooled by Mr Wilmott's own boys. Nobody shed any tears over Laura's departure. She and Julius struggled to hide their elation, the children had routinely departed for school, and Edmund appeared disinterested.

How different was the trip south in Mr Wilmott's care. It was delightful to be greeted by bowing flunkeys and given the best rooms and meals the lodging could offer. For all that, it was a tedious journey, although the weather gradually improved and the road was less hazardous. Seated in the coach, they had the comfort of each other's company: looking out for scenery of interest, watching the weather, and exchanging amused glances at their post boys' lurid comments on the horses, the road, and the populace.

With more than ample time to talk, they rehashed Laura's experiences in Newcastle, and she told him about her shopping spree and, when he looked surprised, about her inheritance. 'There was, and is, no need for you to pay my way,' she finished earnestly. 'Please let me bear my fair share of the costs. I much prefer that.'

'I am delighted that you have the security of money behind you, Laura. It must have been a great relief to learn of it. What did your brother think about it?'

'I'm sorry to say, Julius, that I have been careful not to mention it. I imagine he assumed that all the money I spent in Tyneville on the funeral of my family, on coals and clothes, food, and a skivvy, came from the sale of my home and my governess's salary. Julius, I have tried not to let anybody know about my fortune, and particularly Edmund. It is hateful to say it, but I think it would make Edmund jealous and I don't believe he would ever have allowed me to leave if he knew of it.' There, she had as near as nothing, uttered her most heartfelt fear, that of being at the mercy of Edmund.

Julius sat thinking this over, covertly studying her face while Laura stared out the window, wondering why she felt like crying because she had deceived her closest remaining family member. Julius interpreted this correctly. He moved across and took her hand, causing Laura to look up in surprise.

'My dear, don't flagellate yourself. You have done all that you could and more than should ever have been expected of you, in supporting your brother and his family in their extremity. No tears, no regrets. Edmund is what he is. Move forward.'

Laura leant against him, relieved even as the troublesome tears inched out, and Julius reacted by becoming chattier. He thanked her for the offer to pay her way and hoped she was not offended at his refusing it. As Laura immediately compared him with Edmund, she had to struggle against being overcome a second time. He was delighted to hear of her good fortune and the fact that she had taken time to consider when and how to use it.

'What you've told me has made me wonder if your father was Andrew Markham, a very astute entrepreneur I met in London and Liverpool years ago. We worked together on several major projects early in both our careers, and he was the one of the most likeable, honest men I've done business with.'

Laura smiled and sighed. 'Andrew was my father's name. I miss him terribly.'

'He seemed to become discouraged and gradually withdrew from our circle. He told me he had made enough money. Well, I would have said he'd made more than enough, but he said that he had saved enough to see his family through life and there was no point in continuing. That done, he literally disappeared. I heard somewhere that he owned a home in the country, and I believe he retired there.'

Laura thought her response over, carefully choosing what information to relay. 'I didn't know any of that. Papa came home one day and announced that he was going to grow vegetables and we could consider him retired. That was before Edmund married. I remember Papa was quite upset at Edmund marrying so young and so soon after ordination, and still a curate, but he believed everyone learns for themselves and he was determined not to stand in Edmund's way. He gave Edmund his inheritance when he married. From what you have just said, I imagine Papa was disappointed that Edmund had no interest in, or perhaps I should say talent, for business. Papa may have felt that he had built up a successful enterprise and was disappointed that he had no capable person to pass it on to. Even if the law allowed it, I know I wouldn't have wanted to become an entrepreneur.'

Wilmott moved back to his old seat. 'From what the Tyneville locals say, Edmund seems appreciated and respected where he is. He is making his own mark in the world in his own way.' Laura was comforted to hear this and Julius continued. 'Part of your father's problem may have been, Laura, that he was exhausted. I have seen this in many a nabob; they are driven to check and double-check everything constantly. When you work so hard, I think you would eventually ask yourself, "Why am I doing this?" If Andrew had no son to whom he could trust his empire and no legal permission for a daughter to enter the field, he was sensible enough to think of something else to do.'

'That seems likely. From your report, I wish I had realised how discouraged he was. But you appear to have constant energy, Julius. How do you manage?'

Wilmott smiled and leaned towards her in his enthusiasm to explain. 'I have raised capable men from the worker ranks to trusted positions. They carry the burden nowadays and I encourage them to build a team of satellite assistants to spread the load they are carrying. It is also a way of making sure there is always someone available; someone capable of carrying on each area of the business in another worker's absence. All of them are reliable and some of them are very up to date and forward-looking. Just think, Laura, one of my managers has introduced two women into secretarial positions. I could talk all day about the problems and benefits attached to doing that. The idea is catching on in some quarters and is absolutely denigrated in others.'

'Where would a woman get the training for a secretarial position, Julius?'

'Those two women arrived with sufficient skills to start employment and learnt any new ones readily. Their duties are mostly taking dictation, letter writing, filing, and bookkeeping. I believe one is about to be introduced into planning. I can tell you that employing females has created quite a stir, but the fuss about their appointment is all nonsense. Most married women run big households very competently, and widows have been running local shops and their husbands' businesses all my life. Of course, the facilities for our two have been a problem; for various reasons they need their own withdrawing-room. Fortunately, Finlayson has chosen women of an age and with enough dignity to withstand undue male attention, whether it be negative or positive.'

'May I ask if you plan to retire, Julius?'

'I hope to see my grandsons step into some area of interest to them before I retire. If they want to go a different road, I will place Evadne on the company board as chairwoman and pass the business on to the present managers. Finlayson has given me the courage to try that, and I think Evadne will thrive on it. I have begun encouraging my managers to work out who they want to run their section after they leave, trying to ensure that they are training younger men up to succeed them when they opt out. I find wide experience and firsthand practice essential.'

How lovely to be spoken to as if she had the wits to understand his good intentions. Laura recognised once again how fortunate she was that this liberal and down to earth businessman had entered her life.

Julius also relayed the latest news of Eugene and Michael and from Laura's interested questions, he was drawn to explain that he had visited Horton to discover for himself how they were faring. He had seized the opportunity to remedy such inadequacies as Dr Humphries's clerical income failed to provide. At Laura's surprised expression, he explained that he had supplied sporting equipment and library books. For the following year, he had arranged to supply art equipment, paper, and writing materials. He provided some news of the Hardacres and Monthrope village but less than Laura expected. It seemed to her that Mr Wilmott discussed everything and everybody but the two people she most wanted to hear about. Eventually, she asked him about the Bright family.

'Ah, it's been such a sad time for them, and for us all. Lizzie had a big funeral, Laura, with every observance, and the neighbourhood turned out and did my girl proud. To think, it all happened over three months ago. How hard it is to reconcile myself to her being gone – I still need to remind myself regularly that she is now free from suffering.

Here, Laura wondered to herself if Mr Wilmott was referring to Elizabeth's illness or to the behaviour of her husband.

'The children became quite mifty with wearing mourning and were allowed more colour. They've been sent away to school. I miss them, but I've visited once and I took them out for a meal and bought a few goodies to be shared among their fellow pupils and help smooth their way. I'm satisfied they are well looked after.'

No governess job then, thought Laura, thankful that she wasn't depending on it. She was astonished by Mr Wilmott's boundless energy. She found him amazing – a nabob whose attention was now focused on his descendants. How fortunate that he didn't discount females, but did he never tire?

They stayed that night at one of the great coaching inns, enjoying the hospitality, and more engaged than put out by the constant flow of traffic through the town. The next morning, as they travelled onward, Laura asked about the Monthrope staff.

'Oh, we're very grand now. I think Evadne must have enjoyed that dinner party too much. Of course, she's in mourning, so life remains quiet until she discards it. But she's gone ahead and hired a new French chef and a horde of underservants. You'll get on with that chef like a house on fire, Laura. I can barely understand a word he says and Charlie dives for cover every time he emerges from the kitchen. Evadne's yielded to her mother's persuasion and at long last hired a dresser, and Augustus has a valet. Everyone else is much the same as ever, except Tillotson and Carson have both gone. Apparently, there was a bit of argy-bargy over Carson being superseded when she was expected to remain as cook for the workhands. Mary, the kitchen maid, had to replace her. And old Tilly has been replaced by Mrs Moodle because she stood by her friend.

'Anyhow, Alston's given them a place at Monthrope Manor, and they seem to have settled in happily enough. Alston's become all the rage across three counties. Every mother with a daughter to turn off feels she must make the new young squire welcome to the neighbourhood. Of course, it's all nothing but pretence and toad-eating while they parade their offspring for his edification.'

Laura thought it was possibly the most cynical comment she had ever heard Julius make. Was he just fed up with watching people scrambling to take advantage of someone else's good fortune, or was the trip exhausting him after all?

Laura commented that there had certainly been some big changes since she left but, internally, her self-confidence was quite shaken. She felt less certain about her own future and lost some of her gladness that their long journey was coming to an end. She was about to move on with her life and now it seemed everything was in doubt. She sat staring out of the coach window and wondering how she could cope, and what she should do for the best if she had left her return to Monthrope too late.

The result of all this unexpected anxiety led to further discussion, and Mr Wilmott and Laura prolonged their travel by deciding to make a diversion so she could visit both Mr Davidson and the graves of her parents. The old lawyer welcomed them, and he agreed she could cash in some of the bonds held in safekeeping while the major account continued to accrue interest. The bond money and its earnings were to be deposited in her Monthrope bank, ready to hand for the benefit of whatever future lay ahead.

BIG NEWS

*O*nce these visits were paid, Laura and Mr Wilmott journeyed onwards to Surbury to spend what was for Laura a lazy and restful day with Martha. Julius was up early as usual the next morning to accompany Ben to his workplace, to learn all about it and meet everybody. Laura slept in and had barely risen when he returned. He was followed by a shop boy delivering the armload of treats he had purchased for the Wilcoxes' delectation. Laura wondered if she would ever learn to be as thoughtful as Julius, watching Martha almost bowled over by the soap and scent, the tools and menswear, the food and wine that arrived throughout the afternoon.

The evening was spent in happy companionship but after early breakfast next morning, the travellers made their farewells. They were about to complete the final leg of their journey to Monthrope and, once again, Laura decided she was not wearing black and changed into her familiar grey dress and cloak.

They reached their goal in good time and Mr Wilmott accompanied Laura straight through to Lady Hardacre's sitting room, with a directness that should have alerted her to the fact that he was following orders. Lord Hardacre and Mr Wakefield came in and shook hands with them both, chatted briefly, and asked about their journey in the friendliest way. They then collected Julius and headed for the library.

Lady Hardacre said, 'Sit down please, Laura. I've so much to tell you. I warned the others I wanted you all to myself when you returned.'

Hocking came in with a loaded tea tray and smiled at Laura as he served her. Laura, startled but delighted and curious by all this warmth and familiarity, seated herself and looked enquiringly at her ladyship, solemn in black. She thought

Evadne appeared rather careworn but perhaps it was due to the sombre silk. When she opened her mouth, she spoke with a pause at the end of each sentence, which seemed to emphasise her sadness, while making it plain that she wanted to be clearly understood.

'I'll tell you the biggest news first of all – because I know it will be important to you. In fact, I asked Pa to leave it to me and not mention it. Brace yourself, Laura, for information that I expect you will dislike' She paused and took a breath then continued, 'Leonard Bright married Lady Hester Monteroy two weeks ago.'

She turned directly towards her governess as she spoke and Laura did not try to hide her surprise, although she endeavoured to look as unruffled and non-committal as possible for someone lightning-struck by such unexpected news.

'It's far too soon after the funeral, but he used his poor, motherless children as his excuse and, of course, his own widowed state. He said the children needed a mother and Lady Hester supported him in the pretence.'

Pretence? Laura wondered, while Lady Hardacre paused and sighed and thought, So, it's not just me. Perhaps everyone here is aware of the type of man he is.

Lady Hardacre resumed her discourse. 'The Monteroys must be pleased to have Lady Hester off their hands, even though he's got little more than his estate. My sister's dowry goes to the three girls. Lady Hester is thirty, at least. Of course, she takes Leonard into a different order of society, but I hear they scraped the barrel to make her dowry up to ten thousand pounds, and ...' Evadne came to a halt, shrugged, then added, 'Well, she's no beauty.'

He would have been better off marrying me, thought Laura, amused.

'Was it a huge surprise to everybody, Lady Hardacre? Did Mr Bright discuss it with his relatives before he took such early action and launched into such an unexpected and important event?'

'Not one word. The whole business was done very much on the quiet; one might say it was done almost slyly. We weren't even aware that he knew the Monteroys or that he was courting their remaining daughter. Apparently, the couple were engaged after two months, would you believe, and married a month later, but nothing was published in the papers because of Leonard being in mourning. The three girls were excited to be attendants at the wedding, yet the first thing Lady Hester did afterwards was to bustle all of them off to school so that she and Leonard could "have a honeymoon," although they were away only for a week.'

Evadne was palpably indignant. Laura thought, I would have brought them here or taken them with me. She realised that Lady Hardacre had resumed talking and paid attention.

'I doubt Leonard has told Lady Hester that he is obliged to pay their first governess, Maude Ferguson, one hundred pounds a year until the child she bore is twelve. Or that Grace Fuller demanded and got one thousand pounds outright.' Laura gasped, suddenly remembering the red-headed governess's illness, and surprisingly altered body. Alston's words came back to her.

They sat staring at the fire for a while, both deep in thought.

'Lady Hardacre, thank you for telling me about these events. It's the strangest news, as you said. Quite unexpected. How are Eugene and Michael faring with Dr Humphries at Horton Academy?'

Her apparent indifference pleased and soothed her ladyship.

'Dr Humphries's academy has proved an excellent choice, Laura. They have both settled in happily. They feel very grown up and that makes me laugh, but they are both happy and progressing well in their studies. Sometimes, they bring one or two of their schoolfellows home at the week's end, and sometimes they spend their two days at the home of one of their friends.'

And sometimes they have fun times in Horton, thought Laura, but she remained silent since it would hurt Lady Hardacre's feelings to know that another place might now be sometimes preferred to home. Instead, she said, 'I'm delighted it's working out satisfactorily. I must make up my mind what I'm going to do now.'

'There's no hurry, Laura. No hurry at all. I absolutely forbid you to pack and go when there is not the slightest need for you to rush into a decision. Please don't hasten away.'

Laura thanked her and left the sitting room. She walked upstairs to her room and looked about her. No Mrs Tillotson or even Mrs Carson to discuss all these events with, and she so full of news about being treated so informally. No one would be able to say that the governess had been driven off the property. And there were all the events at Studley or in Newcastle to discuss.

In default, she visited the children's wing to see how Nurse was surviving and found her pining for her darlings. The sight of Laura caused her to weep and lament the passing of time, for she assumed Laura was burdened with all the grief she was suffering herself. 'I know they've got to grow up and go away but they're too young. Too young; it's too soon.'

Laura soothed and listened patiently. 'Of course, you miss them. How could it be otherwise when they've been in your care since birth? But Horton's not so far away. I imagine that you see them every weekend.'

'Yes, but it's barely for two days. And sometimes they visit their friends and don't come home at all.'

Watching Nurse mop her eyes, Laura wondered how she now filled her days, but there seemed to be no expectation that this devoted retainer should be pensioned off or seek other employment. Was that Augustus' influence or the boys'? Having done all she could, she walked back to her own bedchamber wondering what lay ahead of her and what she should do.

She had told Bob Alston she would come and see his manor when she returned, and she had been eager to do so, but now that the opportunity had arrived, Laura felt quite uneasy. Bob was being sought by ambitious locals and she was only a governess. He was unaware that she was wealthy, which she knew meant that he hadn't offered for her because of her inheritance, but suddenly she wondered if it was now her major attraction. After all, marriage was an agreement based around the woman's dowry making it worthwhile for the man to commit himself, while the woman achieved somewhere to live for the rest of her life.

Bob's rise in status might mean he could seek to marry for both money and status. Julius had said the excitement over his advancement had spread through three counties. What would ambitious parents offer Bob Alston, and how strong was his attachment to her? He might be regretting he had ever proposed. How was she to compete and how was she to bear it if he had changed?

Of course, he might be assuming her long absence meant that she had lost interest, or even that she had found someone else – in which case she should present herself at Monthrope Manor as soon as possible. These were happier thoughts, but they raised another issue. If she rushed across to Monthrope Manor, wouldn't it look like she was throwing herself at Bob in a desperate bid against the odds? She could imagine all the interest such an act would arouse in every level of county society, particularly if he had already been attracted to or had even settled on someone else.

Caught between her desire to see Bob and keep her promise to him, and her fear of finding him changed and of becoming a source of gossip, Laura dithered, undecided and unhappy. She couldn't see a way towards visiting Monthrope Manor without embarrassment unless Evadne could be induced to come to her rescue with some excuse to send her there.

Laura fidgeted around her bedchamber until she distracted herself by considering the wealth of news pertaining to Leonard Bright. What a suitable name for a person clever enough to look about him for the worthiest available prey the minute he was free, or perhaps even earlier. She was glad he had no inkling of her own wealth; she felt sure he would have ensured that she had to marry him. Yes, she had to admit to being dazzled for a time by Leonard Bright. Now, remembering her previous devotion, Laura almost writhed with embarrassment. Every piece of information supplied by Lady Hardacre had supported her growing picture of a man without morals, venal, corrupt, and probably just as selfish as dear Edmund.

She considered Leonard's marriage to the unattractive Lady Hester. She could just imagine how he would have gone about it, and the way in which he might have ensured it was necessary. She suddenly realised that whatever approach had succeeded, her ladyship was nothing more than his latest victim, the most recent example of his proclivity for exploiting females. She hoped she would have the opportunity of seeing them together and judging their degree of affection, and how well they were going along together. No, she hoped she would never have to see him again. Would she find them visiting Monthrope Hall? One would certainly expect them to do so, but Lady Hardacre hadn't mentioned it.

She recognised Leonard Bright now as a smooth-tongued seducer and her one source of content was that she had stood her ground and held him at bay, despite her attachment. She felt ashamed that others were aware that she had loved him. Thanks to two brothers-in-law she had met at Monthrope Hall, she doubted whether a woman should trust any man. She resolved to be more careful in future, changed her mind and decided she was glad she knew at least some men with high principles. Her father and Mr Wilmott might not be perfect but they were honest and affectionate and kindly. Why, even the new young owner of Monthrope Manor and Charles Wakefield were incomparably better men than Leonard Bright. Now, when Laura compared Leonard Bright to Robert Alston, character and situation were reversed – one totally self-serving and shallow, the other honest and straightforward. One was working to advance his position in an honourable way. The other had twice taken care to secure his future by marrying solely for money and position and had heedlessly ruined the lives of at least two governesses.

There was no sign of the menfolk when she descended for luncheon, but the two women dined together comfortably before retreating to the sitting room fire. Laura asked if the newlyweds had been visited by Lord and Lady Hardacre or if the Brights had visited Monthrope Hall, and her ladyship revealed an unexpected sensitivity. The couple were recently returned from a trip to Brighton. They had not yet called; it was almost like Leonard had forgotten the relationship. However, the onus was on a neighbourhood to visit a bride and make her welcome, so she might undertake a visit in a day or two. It was apparent that Lady Hardacre felt understandably offended that her poor sister was so easily cast aside, and her family apparently discarded. Of course, Lady Hester, as the daughter of an earl, might prove to be extremely selective in her choice of associates; in which case Lady Hardacre's tardiness in visiting might be due to dreading a snub.

Laura trailed upstairs again, uncertain how to fill the remainder of the afternoon. She was feeling the effects of all the travel as well as the shock of the Monthrope news and lacked energy, but she dutifully sat and wrote to Edmund and the children. She described a little of their journey south and their safe arrival in as lively a way as she could and asked for their Newcastle news, before heading downstairs for some long-overdue pianoforte practice.

Meeting Lord Hardacre in the anteroom that evening, Laura enquired if he had been surprised at the sudden marriage and subsequent behaviour of Leonard Bright.

'Not at all,' he responded, 'Leo's like a cat, he always falls on his feet. He gets in trouble, then walks away and leaves someone else to clean up the mess.'

He took a sip of the whisky he'd chosen that evening in preference to wine and continued. 'I've known him all my life. In fact, we saw so much of each other people often thought we were brothers. Thought so myself; wouldn't be surprised if there was some hanky-panky from one of our fathers or even a grandparent. We went to school together and were sent down from university together. Silly young cawkers both of us, but we thought we were great stuff. Leo was visiting here when I was rapt for a sennight in Rosie's mother, and he quietly appropriated Maisy, who's always been mine.'

He paused again and accepted a refill from Hocking, who then left to discover the readiness of dinner, enabling Augustus to pick up his theme again. 'He goes home, and we settle back into normal life until Maisy comes crying to me, saying Leo was denying his part in her condition. Well, it could have belonged to either of us. I was happy to own it, but Leo didn't visit here again until I teamed up with Evadne. Then he decided the other sister would make an equally good proposition and we had a double wedding, at Julius's expense, of course, being the father of the brides.

'Do you know, Laura, Julius tells me that he travelled all the way to London and Southampton and checked out for himself that Grace and the earlier governess are managing alright? Fortunately, both their parents stood by them, so they have a roof over their heads. But they never hear from Leonard; he takes no responsibility at all. And I'll wager another thing, Laura. In a year or two either Julius or Evadne will have the care of Elizabeth and Leonard's three daughters. They've already been as good as thrown off. What a creature he's turned out.'

What am I hearing? Laura thought, her mind focused on the early part of his speech, and entirely forgetting all the implications of Augustus's own behaviour and all the moral aspects. I've never heard such a tangled web of near-incestuous relationships. He's saying Bob Alston might be Leonard's child. On further reflection, she decided that there was no way to learn the absolute truth and probably far better not to. She hoped Bob would get on with his life, live in the present and be thankful for good health and a sound mind. She thought it best that the whole conundrum never be mentioned or solved for his sake; Bob had endured so much already.

That night, sitting up in bed, she came to understand Augustus Hardacre's acceptance of Bob. It was essential to have an heir to the property and, at the time, he might even have reasoned that his best friend had done him a favour. In any case, so many years later, he had certainly accepted Bob as his own child. He had found in Maisy the person he cared for and his quiet support of her suited them both because she was obviously happy. He was genial towards Bob, but a surprisingly distant father to the two youngest boys.

This awoke a horrid new thought. Had Augustus also

reasoned that his best friend Leo had fathered Michael and Eugene, or did he know the truth? Well, for that matter, why hadn't Evadne turned to Leonard in her hour of need all those years ago, only to find the answer staring her in the face? Of course, Evadne would never betray her sister. She had surely settled on the lesser of two evils. Laura fell asleep with her head full of unsolvable riddles, and a great fear of accidentally implying or even saying too much, and of unwittingly hearing or finding out further revolting details.

THE RIGHT MAN AND MOMENT

The following morning, Laura remained uncertain about the wisdom of visiting Monthrope Manor, but eventually decided she would ride over after lunch. If Bob seemed aloof, she could say she had come to see the estate, as promised, and to visit Mrs Carson and Mrs Tillotson. She spent the morning sorting her own belongings, as a step towards beginning to pack.

Returning upstairs following luncheon on this second day, she found Bob waiting by her bedroom door with his arms folded. He followed her into her room and immediately launched into his grievance. 'You told me you would visit me and see Monthrope Manor when you returned.'

'I know I did, Bob, but I felt shy.'

'You felt shy? Shy! Why would you feel like that?'

'I realised– Bob, you can do much better than a governess now you are a landholder. You could marry into the gentry or even the aristocracy. You must already have seen that.'

'I could marry up, way up. If it wasn't that I'm in love with a governess.'

Her heart gave a great leap of pleasure, lighting up her face. He took her by the arms, pulled her close and said, 'Laura, tell me. Will you marry me?'

'Yes, with pleasure.'

'Then let's sit down and discuss when, because I want it to be soon. I've waited far longer than I ever thought I could.' They sat down drawing their chairs together. 'Oh sweetheart, how I've missed you.' She was drawn close, and some time passed before they settled into any discussion at all.

'I didn't want to propose to you again until you had seen the Manor for yourself, and yet I was worried that it might put you off. It's not in good shape, Laura. Repairs are well under way on the rafters and the roof, and the ceilings come next, but so much else needs doing. I haven't got the money for further repairs to the house. And I want to pay for the rest of it myself, not be running all the time to Augustus or Julius.'

'Is it all right if your wife pays for it, Bob? After all, domestic concerns are the wife's business.'

'Oh Laura, it will take more than the savings from a governess's income to improve the house.'

'I hope it won't put you off when I tell you that I can pay for it. You are marrying an heiress, Bob.'

He laughed and said, 'You're very welcome. I hope you won't be daunted by the amount that's required.'

His tone, rather than the words he used, revealed he had no belief in, and no idea of, her wealth. Laura decided that perhaps it was better Bob should discover its extent after the knot was tied, in case some strange masculine quibble caused him to shy away. She changed the subject to that of the wedding. She wanted just the simplest affair at the local church with Martha to give her away. Bob made no criticism of this and suggested they visit the vicar and ask him to call the banns so they could marry in a month's time. Laura agreed. Let the village think what it liked about such haste; they would eventually find out differently.

'Let's go and tell the family.'

'We can't at the moment, Bob. Everyone is out or resting.'

'All right, I'll invite myself to dinner and we'll tell them then. Now, you tell me all about Newcastle.'

'And you must tell me what you have been doing. I need to learn more about the domestic concerns while you tell me all about running an estate and farming.'

So, the afternoon passed away in talk. Laura listened while Bob described his moment of sudden realisation and panic when he moved into Monthrope Manor. He explained that he was almost overwhelmed with the amount he had to do, and the amount he had to learn and wherever was he to start? Thank goodness he had the usefulness and comfort of Amy Carson and dear Tilly to help him survive her own absence, and to see he got fed properly. Mick and Bess Olsen were proving staunch friends. She heard about how invaluable Charles Wakefield had become and how Martin Chugg had walked over practically every inch of the pastures, shaking his head and just when Bob had decided it was all hopeless, floored him with his announcement.

'Laura, after keeping me on tenterhooks the whole time, he says to me, "Well, you'll be off to the best start of any young gager I know. You may not have any animals but look at the feed you've got. We'll harvest every blade of this, and you can store some and sell some. Then you can stock up gradually or rent the fields out for the first year while you get organised, or you can do a bit of both. That'll give you time to have your stables and cowsheds and barns repaired and tiptop. The barns are the important ones since the fields are nearing harvest." Laura, I was that relieved. Hard work I can handle but now I could see that there would be some returns from all the effort. It wasn't going to be nothing but hard labour and expense.'

Laura exclaimed and praised, and Bob asked again about Newcastle. 'So, nobody up north lured you away from Monthrope?'

Laura smiled. 'It was a near-run thing, Bob, but not in the way you're imagining.' And she launched into a description of her time there and the fear of having to do her duty and support her brother's family, either in person or financially, for the rest of her life. She described her own plans and efforts and the welcome arrival of Julius Wilmott. Bob was not impressed with Edmund's attitude, and it led Laura to tell him more about her family and their upbringing and Edmund's first marriage. Bob limited his comments on Edmund because he was all the remaining family Laura had. He heard her out and restricted himself to saying, earnestly, that he wished he had known her father.

Bob then rode home, saying he would return at six that evening, and he would 'dress right.' Laura wrote to inform her brother of her engagement and her anticipated wedding date, offering to pay all the expenses so that her family could travel to and from Monthrope to attend. She described a little of Bob's history and her hopes of a happy life ahead of them on his new estate. She then celebrated by arraying herself for the evening in the indulgence of a new dress and cashmere shawl, surmounted by her pearl necklace, and once again left her letter on the hall table, when she went down to dinner.

TELLING THE FAMILY

*B*ob arrived punctually and she was pleased at the unassuming correctness of his attire. Laura led him to where the diners had gathered as usual, in the anteroom to the dining parlour. Bob claimed everyone's attention and announced their engagement, to the acclaim of all present. Hocking whisked out a champagne bottle and flutes – trust him to have read the signs right – and they encouraged him to join everyone in drinking to their happiness. Laura found it the pleasantest pre-dinner gathering she had attended at Monthrope, even with the addition of two new footmen.

They were all unusually jolly during the meal and Mr Wakefield began teasing Bob.

'Did you blindfold Laura before you showed her the house? How did she like that archaic inglenook in the kitchen and the old icehouse where the pig moved in?'

'She hasn't seen them yet,' Bob replied. 'Shall we give her the pig for a pet or have it for dinner? She's planning to spend all her wages on one of those new German stoves. It sounds as if it's cast iron and half as big as the house. Probably take five men and a mason to alter the kitchen and install it.'

'Oh well done, Laura,' exclaimed Lady Hardacre, 'I've always wanted one of those stoves. Will it bankrupt you?'

'Not at all,' said Laura. She decided this might be the right time to announce her wealth, momentarily forgetting that servants, including Hocking and Luke, were present, and later deciding that it was possible the gentry were just as gossip prone as their employees. She looked around her assembled friends and smiled. 'I informed Bob when I accepted his proposal that I'm an heiress.'

With one exception, a circle of surprised and incredulous

faces greeted her as she risked a second glance, but Lord Hardacre was the only one to speak. 'Why, how much are you worth, Madam Heiress?'

'Last time I checked, and counting both bonds and savings, it was eighty thousand pounds. My father left it to me. I've forgotten to add what I earned here and my half of the sale of my parents' house.' There seemed to be one, single intake of breath: paralysis, silence, and amazement, everywhere she looked. Luke didn't drop the tureen he was holding, but he jerked its contents and even Hocking was caught momentarily frozen in time, with a bottle raised over a wineglass. Julius alone smiled and nodded at her when she turned to him. However, her auditors took only a little convincing because nobody believed she would dare invent such an astronomical amount.

'Bob, how do you feel about Laura's wealth?' asked Wilmott.

He answered slowly. 'I'm shocked, amazed, but I've no qualms. When I mull it over, I think my main feeling is relief. I can get on with my plans to improve our property and know I can now happily leave all the domestic arrangements to my little gem.' He turned and looked at Laura. 'Why didn't you tell me?'

'I did try to tell you. It didn't seem important.'

'You thought I might cry off.'

'Yes.'

'You were right. Everyone will be claiming that I married you for your money.'

'So what if they do? They'll think you clever, really sharp. But they won't think it was planned, Bob. Everyone here can see you're as astonished and disbelieving as they are.'

'Laura, we do believe you,' cried Lady Hardacre.

From then on, events went almost completely out of hand. Lady Hardacre said that Laura would be married from the Hall and their post-wedding feast would occur right here in the dining room; her French chef would be enthralled to provide a suitable meal. Laura pointed out that some of her guests would feel uneasy at a formal meal. Lady Hardacre and Julius Wilmott then devised a morning wedding, followed by a celebratory noontime feast for the local gentry at the Hall, followed by an evening feast and barn dance for everybody the young couple wanted to include.

Laura explained that she wanted her childhood nurse and dear friend, Martha, to give her away.

'I wanted to give you away,' complained Julius but Lady Hardacre interjected.

'Laura, if your brother and his family are unable to attend, your nurse and her husband should be able to survive one meal at our table. I'll change what I said earlier about inviting the gentry. I promise I'll keep the guest list to just our family and the people you want, so it will be less stressful and more enjoyable for everybody.' Laura gave in as gracefully as she could and hoped her dear friends would not be overawed.

Of course, when they drove to Surbury the next day, so Laura could introduce Bob to the Wilcoxes, Martha announced she would be delighted to give Laura away, but that was it. She and Ben would join Mrs Carson and Mrs Tillotson at Monthrope Manor until the evening feast and barn dance which they would happily attend. It took Bob's best efforts to overturn this dictum.

There was a similar issue with Maisy Alston. After visiting the vicar next morning, the young couple called on her. Maisy professed herself delighted at the engagement and at attending the wedding but flatly refused taking part afterwards. Bob said, 'Well, Mam, you're attending the evening feast and barn dance and that's the last word on the subject.' She agreed so readily to this that Laura suspected she would have a wonderful time and end up being the life of the party.

When they returned to Monthrope Hall, Charles Wakefield sought them out. He and Mr Davidson needed to draw up a proposal for the marital settlement. Laura recalled that the instant she married, her money became Bob's. The thought of being without it made her extremely nervous. She felt all the security she had previously experienced since the long-ago arrival of Mr Davidson's letter, draining away. She remembered that Julius had felt the same way about entrusting a huge dowry to Augustus and had wisely set conditions that allowed his daughter to direct how it was to be used. Augustus had signed that and had possibly since realised the value of doing so; not that she thought he liked it. What man would?

Laura, had, however, reckoned without Bob's own opinion on the matter. He proved a most unwilling recipient of her wealth. He might say in front of the family that he was relieved to be free of money worries. That was camouflage; even knowing that men did not marry unless they were well paid to do so, it galled him to have had to turn to Julius and Augustus for help and even more so to rely upon his wife's inheritance.

He insisted that the savings account be split in half. He would draw on his half to update the property, pay staff, purchase a carriage, and order in the necessary seed and livestock and tools. Profits would be ploughed back into the property at first, but he hoped and intended to gradually restore the balance in his account and then build on it. His will would leave everything to Laura until they became parents.

Laura's half, he suggested, should remain under her name in its current account. This would relieve him of having to set money aside to provide a dowry for any daughters they bore or to assist any sons into a career if he was unable to do so. It would also ensure that she had financial support immediately available for her use if he died or lost his money.

He suggested that Laura's remaining bonds, which had been placed in the Monthrope Bank where they could be more easily cashed in, should be used to pay for the expenses attached to the domestic side of running Monthrope Manor. After all, there was a huge amount for her to do, and perhaps she hadn't realised the extent of it. Not only was there the setting up of the house, and restoring the Manor's flower and vegetable gardens, there was a great need for greenhouses, an orchard, poultry yards, beehives, and a dovecote to be mended or rebuilt, as well as money for her personal use. Laura was relieved and pleased to accept this plan and Charles, steadily copying down the details, noted he would arrange to meet with Mr Davidson who would see the document finalised.

When they were alone, Laura complained about all the fuss. 'I wanted my wedding to be just you and me, Martha and Ben, and your mother. I thought afterwards we might dine at the inn before going home.' Bob urged her to bear with the changes and not disappoint the enthusiastic input of her friends.

After that, it proved a magical week. Laura drove to Monthrope Manor with Julius, armed with the lengthy list of improvements begun or needed. There was a joyous reunion with Amy Carson and Mrs Tillotson and there were new workers to meet. Bob eagerly and anxiously showed her around, and she was glad to note that the basic stone framework of the manor house remained sound. They moved on to the farm buildings and she approved all the recreation and refurbishing of yards and stables and cow byres, agreeing it was the only sensible way to go on.

Lastly, Bob carried her off to inspect his acres where a horde of villagers of all ages, male and female, were busy with sickles and scythes, cutting grass, stooking grain, carting, or gleaning. Laura hurried off to make ginger water to send out to the workers, while Mrs Carson prepared a trayful of bread and cheese. During the heat of the afternoon, it was pleasant to wander through the tangle of the orchard together and plan how to improve it. Laura reluctantly returned to the Hall and she certainly slept well that night.

Such a propitious start was great to build on. The following morning, Julius drove Laura in state to a variety of warehouses and furniture emporia where she selected patterns and samples and ordered carpets and curtains, furniture and household goods. Exhausted by this, Laura then sent Mrs Carson and Mrs Tillotson to town on a never-to-be-forgotten kitchenware, linen, and houseware spree, and she undertook the housekeeping while they were absent. This was observed by the workers at Monthrope Manor, and Laura unknowingly progressed from 'that teacher up at the Hall with funny ideas about schoolwork', to the rank of 'one of ours'.

Suddenly, the week was gone in a flash and the carriage was due to fetch Eugene and Michael home from Horton. Laura travelled with the coachman and visited the Humphries briefly, enjoying a great welcome from the old couple and spontaneously inviting the entire academy to the wedding. She jumped in the carriage with the boys, and they talked all the way home because there was so much to catch up on – life at Horton, their new friends, life with the Humphries, the sports they were playing, and even their studies. The boys broached attending the Bright wedding without a qualm, calling it the dullest show imaginable. That Monteroy family – so high in the instep and as for Lady Hester, the most bracket-faced old gargoyle imaginable. They didn't know how Uncle Leonard could bear to look at her. And nothing for the children to do all evening, but sit and sit and watch for hours on end, Laura, would you credit it? Laura listening to it all, decided to make her wedding more comfortable and interesting for the children. They were entering Monthrope before Eugene remembered his manners and asked after Newcastle.

'Newcastle suffered an epidemic while I was there, the most dreadful affliction,' Laura informed the brothers. 'My sister-in-law, Emily, and her baby both died. But it was good to be able to assist my brother, Edmund and his older children. Charlotte and Thomas are about your ages. I can tell you more about it another day, but now I want to tell you my big news.'

'What, what?' they demanded.

'Bob Alston and I are going to be married next month.'

'Lovely.' Bouncing up and down, hugging her and clapping, both boys were genuinely delighted.

ACTION STATIONS

*I*t was a great joy to Laura that Eugene and Michael insisted on joining her for the trip to Monthrope Manor that Saturday morning. While she attended to her own concerns, they explored high and low, climbing ladders to observe the repair work in progress, and mountaineering over the scaffolding while builders replaced worm-eaten rafters and missing slates. On their return to Monthrope Hall, they hurried upstairs to pour out their stories of the day's activities, and Laura had, once again, to endure some terse words from Nurse that evening on the risks she had permitted them to take.

Sunday, the boys eschewed church for the pleasure of accompanying her again and associating with the chimney sweep; a visit that drove everyone else to distraction and despair as bird nests and soot crashed into the hastily covered fireplaces. They spent the rest of the day helping Bob restore cowshed walls by slapping on buckets of mud, and returned home in fine fettle, as scruffy as tramps. Nurse rushed them off to bathe and it was rumoured the laundry-maid was once again in 'a fair taking' with the pile of washing she was facing that day. After that, the two happily exhausted boys were returned to Horton.

Laura became so busy with renovations at the Manor, she was able to tolerate the buzz of wedding preparations dominating the Hall. There were a few treasured moments alone with Bob. Both were working hard to have the estate looking as trim as possible by the wedding day, so being tired out was a great help to staying virtuous. Bob was astonished and delighted when, two days before the wedding, instead of driving over by herself Laura asked Grimes to act as coachman and return the vehicle to Monthrope Hall. She had told Evadne the previous evening that she planned to remain at the Manor until the wedding day and left her to make what she liked of the announcement.

To Bob, she explained that she thought they ought to have their wedding night prior to the wedding. He was surprised and delighted. Laura continued, saying, 'Look at our wedding day. We'll be on our feet, socialising for all but a few hours in the afternoon when we will probably be content to rest and recruit ourselves for a very busy evening. We'll be dancing and partying half the night and by the time we get to bed we'll be exhausted. I imagine we'll be glad to stagger upstairs to my old room at the Hall and collapse. But what I want is a relaxed, happy, and exciting first night with my husband, so please don't work too hard for the rest of today. I'm looking forward to tonight and I hope you will be too.'

And then, as he rather huskily agreed, she added slowly, in a voice somewhat shaky with anxiety, 'Bob, you do realise I've got everything to learn, don't you?' Bob, eyes twinkling, nodded, but said nothing and Laura continued. 'Thank God, at least one of us knows what to do. You're going to find me shockingly ignorant – but I am very willing to learn.'

She was instantly caught up in a couple of muscular arms to be enthusiastically hugged and kissed. 'We'll manage,' he reassured her.

During the morning, Laura informed Tilly and Amy that she was staying, and both appeared to understand. Work progressed as normal, Laura busily planning garden beds with Tom McPherson – the youngest of old McPherson's tribe, and about to become their head gardener. She was out and about during the afternoon, arranging for new poultry yards with young Mick from Monthrope who was glowing at the achievement of his first employment. They decided on the poultry they would have and where and how they would house it. They were assisted in this by John Smithers, a cousin of the Monthrope carpenter, hired to rebuild the poultry sheds and yards as well as the dovecote.

That evening, Mrs Carson served up their usual early supper, then the young couple said a cheerful goodnight and headed upstairs. What a surprise when they entered their bedroom to find the fire lit, the room decorated with flowers, candles in a candelabra waiting for a taper, and a side-table with a salver supporting a bottle of wine and two glasses. Laura laughed when she noticed a second tray resting by the hearth with the makings for a hot toddy and some biscuits to accompany it. She was sure this toddy wouldn't put her to sleep.

Bob and Laura drank a toast to a long and happy life, and another to such good friends as the pair currently relaxing below stairs, picturing them chatting and rocking comfortably in front of the kitchen fire. Slowly and gently, the lovers undressed each other, kissing and hugging. Bob brushed out Laura's hair, pleasurably and lovingly, enjoying watching her relax. They admired and stroked each other's shapely bodies, before slipping into bed to consummate their union, Bob taking it gently and holding back his own urges to make it more comfortable for Laura. It was a night of discovery and repeated joy.

Next morning, Laura left him sleeping, dressed and went downstairs to the kitchen. She headed straight over to where Amy and Tilly were preparing breakfast at the vast new stove, to hug them. 'You are the dearest, kindest people,' she said. 'You made our bedroom lovely, and we were so surprised and delighted. You made it fun and special and so much easier for us.'

HATE MAIL

*I*t was a surprise, therefore, for these two good helpmeets, when they tracked Laura down later in the morning to where she had hidden herself in the sitting room. They found her in tears. Mrs Carson enquired who had upset her, in a tone implying the perpetrator was about to die, and Tilly rushed to offer a kerchief and back rubs.

Laura explained her distress. 'It's a letter from my brother in Newcastle.'

Yes, Edmund had written straight back. His current missive was lengthy and later Laura would marvel that she ever expected anything different to the unsavoury document he forwarded. She read it out to them.

Edmund had taken exception to her marriage. It was utterly unsuitable for the family to be allied to a man with no known father, and this story of his adoption by the Hardacres had a nasty patched-up sound to it. Surely their county could not be devoid of suitable single men. Certainly, he himself had been prevailed upon by his prelate to marry Nellie Patten four months after Emily's demise, but the bishop himself solemnised the marriage. However, an engagement of only one month prior to the wedding argued a degree of haste on the part of his sister and her fiancé that must arouse prurient suspicions in the most innocent mind.

He continued that he was deeply concerned about their financial welfare; he understood the man was a groom and far below Laura's notice. There was no way they could manage on such an income and this talk of an estate would probably turn out to be nothing more than a tenancy. When children started arriving, he would be unable to support them. Thanks to their own father's poor management he had no idea how Laura was situated but it must have been badly, for her to have been obliged to take up the position of a governess. He had written to Mr Davidson previously to enquire whether he was fulfilling the role of trustee adequately and had been displeased to receive a very terse letter claiming his epistle was actionable. If Laura married, any property of hers would naturally pass into the hands of her husband and he had grave doubts as to the suitability or even the ability of such a person to manage it. He advised Laura to keep careful watch and if she found the residue of her funds was diminishing, through either Mr Davidson's or Bob Alston's mismanagement, to let him know at once.

Laura looked up from the page she was reading aloud, with her eyes streaming. 'It's the nastiest letter I've ever read.'

Tilly soothed and encouraged her to tear it to bits and ignore it, but Mrs Carson had heard Bob come into the kitchen and had already slipped quietly away. She whispered to him that help was needed. Laura had received a dreadful letter from her brother and was crying her eyes out. She paused for a moment, shocked by the fury on Bob's face and decided to focus his attention in the right direction. She said, 'We must help Laura get through this,' and was relieved to see Bob stand back and think the matter through.

The result was that Bob walked into the sunny little morning room, picked his wife up from her chair and moved across to sit beside her on the sofa. He held her while she wiped her eyes dry and produced a grateful smile. He took the letter out of her hand and read it. The three women trembled in anticipation of an almighty explosion and stared when his shoulders shook slightly.

'Laura, you never told me your brother fancies himself a a wit. Or is he just plain witless? If he was here, I would tell him that I consider it utterly unsuitable for my family to be allied to a man who writes letters that show no knowledge of the full story, let alone Christian charity. And I'd add that this account of his attack on poor Mr Davidson has a nasty, patched-up sound to it. It's a tissue of lies and nothing more than an effort to get control of your money.'

He paused for another glance at the letter. 'So, he was prevailed upon to marry, was he? How much will you bet me, Tilly, that it was for the same reason he married Emily, his first wife? How ridiculous for such a pot to call this kettle black. Well, if he can count to nine, he'll find out differently in months to come.'

His mixture of wry humour and contempt had a delightfully soothing effect on his audience and after a few jokes about their poverty and how on earth they would ever afford to raise children, he saw Laura regaining her balance. He stood up and set her on her feet and he then had the pleasure of being hugged by three women. Mrs Carson made them all a pot of tea and they sat round the kitchen table and greatly enjoyed it.

Seeing Laura had cheered up, Bob bore her off to watch the last of the grain and hay being piled up in their barn and she returned to pick up her day's work as normal. Bob put the letter away, in case Mr Davidson ever decided to follow through on his threat to act against Edmund, because he might find it useful. Bob bore no friendly thoughts towards an author whose every word smacked of controlling other people's lives when he couldn't control his own.

Laura decided she was glad she had exchanged her brother's family for a much more congenial one and endeavoured to put the evil document out of her mind. It required some effort to write a civil letter, but she sat down and produced a brief response.

'Edmund, you wrote a harsh letter to me when you had very little knowledge of our situation and you got everything wrong. I am now about to be most happily married and we are well settled on our two hundred freehold acres, thanks to the good management of the Hardacres and Mr Davidson. We do not yet expect a child, but I understand

you do and wish Nellie a safe birthing. Excuse the brevity of this letter, but Lord and Lady Cockram have just arrived with Mr Lang, and I must leave off.'

RALLYING TO HELP

*T*he following morning, she was surprised to receive a letter from Charlotte. On a first reading, it appeared quite innocuous but, for some reason, it worried her. She folded the sheet of paper and put it away in her pocket, then she drove across to the Hall to collect some unwanted curtaining offered by Evadne. She paused for a reminiscent moment in her old room, recollected Charlotte's troubling missive, and took it out for a second examination, pausing a moment to appreciate Charlotte's neat script.

Dearest Laura,

I hope you are well. All of us are in good health. I think you would be pleased with my schoolwork and the way I am helping Tom with his. Nellie says I need not attend school all day, just the mornings and so far, I have been able to keep up with my class and study by the fire at night. I attend to the housework each afternoon and I am learning so much due to all the different tasks that need doing. It makes me look back to your visit and remember what a great <u>help</u> you were to us all. When can we look forward to another visit? Thank you for writing to us. Maisy's cottage sounded so pretty and homely. Now I must show this to Nellie.

We all send our love, your devoted niece

Charlotte Markham.

At first glance, the single page appeared the most innocent epistle possible, but the underlined word suggested something was beyond bearing. Laura was in no mood to think kindly of her brother and felt increasingly sure that the underlined 'help' was the important part of the missive, but what could she do if Charlotte was asking to be rescued? She lived so far away, and Edmund would hardly allow her to be brought south when his own correspondence announced that he deprecated everything about Laura's situation.

If Nellie was keeping an excellent student away from her class and insisting that she do more than her share of housekeeping, what could be done about it? Learning domestic pursuits was a female's lot; everyone would insist on that. If they brought her south, she might receive more affection but what future could they offer her? Wouldn't she just be learning rural domestic occupations and end up as constrained as at home? Well, at least she could ensure that her niece was loved and educated, but how to get her here?

Tired of wrestling with the problem of how to rescue Charlotte, Laura left her bedchamber and descended to the library, hoping Julius might be there and could, as per usual, magically devise a solution. She found a group of four men clustered around the library table, planning and costing the sowing requirements that needed to be stored or purchased over winter for the Hall and Manor. For a minute she felt annoyed – after all, the Manor was hers and Bob's – but then she realised that she would have to give the men some leeway. Bob had a lot to learn, and he had plenty of willing assistance, while farming was something she knew nothing about at the minute. Her role was to attend to the domestic side of the enterprise, and she already had more than enough to do setting that up.

Laura's entry caused a stir because she so seldom appeared downstairs, and she ended up reading Charlotte's letter aloud. Surprisingly, it was Augustus who spotted the significance of the underlined word *help* first, but that didn't solve the problem and they were interrupted by Evadne walking in. Discussion of Charlotte dropped. Evadne went over the figures for the planned seeding project and the men explained that Bob and his team would help the farmers at the Hall with their sowing in spring, and then the team from the Hall would move across to the Manor and help him with his. Laura listened to all this, sitting nearby, with the letter in her hand.

'Are you taking an interest in farming, Laura? asked Evadne, moving to the chair next to her.

'No. I came down with a problem of my own to ask for advice.'

'May I enquire what that problem might be?'

In reply, Laura handed the letter over and her ladyship read it twice through, while everyone else waited in silence. Evadne asked how old Charlotte was, sat silent herself for a few minutes, and then pronounced her verdict to the room at large.

'We have here, a girl like Laura who relishes scholastic pursuits. She has a stepmother who is perhaps ill or lazy or burdened with pregnancy, and perhaps currently unable to pay for hired help. If Charlotte is being maltreated or overworked, why hasn't her father come to her aid? We need to find out more, but I think we can assume he is busy with his own duties and impervious to his daughter's needs.' For a moment, she was silent as she reviewed possible strategies.

'From what Laura has occasionally said of him, it seems her brother is sensitive to anything affecting his idea of his own consequence.' (Here, Laura and Bob's eyes met for one delightful moment.) Evadne continued, 'The only way to rescue either of the children would be to offer him something that intimates some considerable benefit and éclat for himself or his family. With the boy, that is easy. Pa can readily call on someone to offer the son training for almost any future employment; I can think of influential people in any number of fields of endeavour who would respond. We would only need to know where the child's talents and interests lie. It is less simple with the girl because she is expected to remain at home until her marriage is arranged, or until there is some desperate reason for her to leave. Firstly, Laura, what are your nephew's interests?'

'He reminds me somewhat of Michael because he is so good at arithmetic, but he has become very much a child of his township and is always to be found down the docks.'

'Then that shows us the bait we'll need to use – that of building Thomas's future. Find out if Thomas is happy to leave where he is now and come here. We'll put him in Nurse's care, complete his education and Pa can select an area to slot him into. We'll insist on Nurse travelling north at our expense to collect him and bring both children south in state, a real entourage – I think the travelling coach with its crest, and a couple of postilions or outriders. We'll add a few concerns about bringing such a young person away from his family and make a special request that his sister be allowed to accompany him, for fear of it affecting him adversely. I have realised that I absolutely must have a companion, not that I will tell your brother how sudden this awareness is, but I will offer to pay all her expenses and find some way to promote her interests. I don't expect that they will refuse the offer of help for Thomas, but we may have to insist that Charlotte accompanies him. If your brother and his wife refuse to let Charlotte come permanently, we will repeat the request that she accompanies Thomas on the journey and see how long we can prevent her return.'

'You ought to be running the country, Evadne,' interposed Augustus.

She nodded and surprised them all. 'I know – but neither while it is being run by an aristocracy, nor if it ever becomes run by *les sans-culottes*, and that means I had better remain where I am.' She rose. 'I'll write at once. Come up in half an hour, Laura, and see what you think of my letter.'

She turned around and suddenly laughed. 'I've thought of the perfect fillip to my proposal. It's a pity the children will miss the wedding, or I'd say that Laura is so stricken by the absence of her dear family at her wedding, that I must plead for the presence of her niece and nephew to support her through the ordeal. Instead, I'll have to slant it so that your brother gains the impression that the children's arrival will help her recover from the absence of her dear family at her wedding.'

'And I was going to arrange two witnesses and a luncheon at the inn,' muttered Laura.

'I've always wanted a daughter,' said Lady Hardacre, 'and, if I can't have you, your niece will do very well. I like the sound of her.'

'She's quite cynical for her age,' remarked Laura.

'Now, why might I understand that?' mused her ladyship, strolling out. The men looked at each other and Laura decided to follow her.

'Cognac,' muttered Augustus and headed for the decanter.

Lady Hardacre was not one to waste paper. She paced her writing room then sat and mentally practised her letter, over and over. She eventually decided Edmund would respond most favourably if she presented as very grand and formal and emphasised the Hardacre's superior position to a village cleric. The finished letter was markedly briefer than the one she had originally intended:

Lord and Lady Hardacre, hearing good reports, present their compliments to the Reverend and Mrs Markham and are pleased to offer their assistance in forwarding the career of their two eldest children, Thomas and Charlotte; now near-relatives. They are prepared to raise Thomas and see him settled in whatever niche of Mr Julius Wilmott's mercantile empire best suits the young man. Lady Hardacre, being in need of the benefit of a companion at Monthrope Hall intends, should Charlotte present as suitable, to employ her in that position, and undertake every care of her.

'Should Lady Hardacre receive a reply in the affirmative to this proposal, Nurse will travel north to fetch both children, who will thereby be spared the ordeal of a lengthy journey alone or accompanied only by a stranger. Doubtless, Reverend and Mrs Markham will be relieved and happy to know that Monthrope Manor, the home of his sister and her husband, lies less than a mile from Monthrope Hall, the estates adjoining. Constant support and communication will therefore be possible between family members. Assuring the children's parents that every care of these new relatives as well as all expenses, will be borne by this estate, I remain...

Yours etc.'

She handed this missive, impressively inscribed on her best notepaper, to Laura, who exclaimed that Edmund ought to be most affected; she could just imagine him gloating over it. The letter was elaborately sealed and sent off by post express. After that, it was a case of waiting.

During the day she wrote again to Nellie, full of housewifely news. She mentioned, in passing, that Lady Hardacre was proving almost as philanthropic as her esteemed parent, Mr Juius Wilmott, and enclosed the customary sovereign.

WEDDING JOY

*L*aura and Bob's wedding was less tense and more surprising than either of the main participants had imagined. Ben and Martha arrived a day early and were happily welcomed as the first guests at the Manor. On the great day, Laura removed to her old room at the Hall and dressed in one of her new gowns, under Lady Hardacre's supervision. She donned a plain bonnet and Lady Hardacre draped over it a veil as fine as gossamer, her own wedding veil. It was about this time that Laura recognised that Evadne seemed to be becoming warmer and more human daily, and she confirmed this by repeating the sentiment that she had always wanted a daughter.

McPherson, the Hall's old gardener, arrived with a bouquet and announced that he had made it specially for the young couple: that the rosemary was for remembrance of and by old friends, the lavender was for health and healing, the thyme represented years of happiness, and the white and red roses symbolised the couple's purity and love. Laura was delighted and gave him a peck on the cheek.

She donned her pearl necklace and waited with Mr Wilmott while the Hardacre family and Mrs Wilmott drove ahead to the church to ensure that they would be in place before the bridal party arrived. There were none of the Monthrope staff about as Mr Wilmott led her out to his town carriage and, as they drove into Monthrope Village, she looked about, pleased that the day was fine, no mud.

Laura had pictured going quietly to the church on any ordinary Saturday. What she found were empty carriages lining every roadway and the entire village turned out to observe the spectacle. All the pauper pensioners she had so patiently visited for Lady Hardacre were lined up at the lych-gate with their hair crowned and their hands full of flowers, so she and Julius paused to admire and thank them for making the day special.

Martha was waiting in the entry and Laura stood between her nurse and her friend while the pensioners ambled in to join the congregation. She looked around and discovered the staff of Monthrope Hall and Manor filling the back rows. The rest of the church seemed to be packed with gentry and tenantry. The organ struck up and the trio paraded solemnly down the aisle to where the vicar, Bob Alston and Charles Wakefield were waiting. Martha and Mr Wilmott carefully drew back the exquisite veil and Bob looked at Laura as if his heart was melting. They went through the service without faltering and emerged man and wife. If some of the service seemed to pass in a dream, Laura retained a clear remembrance of Maisy Alston's radiant face; a mother absolutely swelling with pride in her son. Laura felt it made the whole day worthwhile.

After the service, the Monthrope staff hastened back to the Hall to attend to the last-minute details of the feast while the pensioners scattered their flowers, and Bob and Laura paused to accept or endure the good wishes of every family in Monthrope. It took time but they relished the warmth and goodwill as the gentry passed in revue, followed by a mingling of village and farming fraternity.

Eventually, they were able to approach their waiting carriage, admiring a flower-bedecked Grimes and carriage horses, and thankfully sit down.

Bob whispered, 'Let's order Grimes to flee the country.'

Laura laughed, but after a moment, she replied, 'It's such a brilliant idea. I'm so tempted, but when I think of all the good-hearted people who've worked themselves to the bone to make today special for us, I couldn't do it to them.'

They arrived at Monthrope Hall to find the staff lined up in welcome, with the house servants grouped in front of the entry, male and female each to its own side, headed by Hocking, Mrs Moodle and Monsieur Bodine. Gardeners, grooms, and farmworkers were gathered along either side, led by Grimes and McPherson. Again, it took time, but they paused to acknowledge every person before moving to the anteroom where Hocking, Luke and Theo circled with drinks, and the newlyweds could relax.

Lady Hardacre had kept her word, so Martha and Ben and Maisy were faced with meeting only four groups: the Hardacres, the Wilmotts, the Wakefields and the Humphries team from the academy at Horton. When they entered the dining room, Laura smiled to see Lady Hardacre chatting and getting to know Mrs Wakefield and Lord Hardacre educating Ben Wilcox on his favourite topic. Dr Humphries' pupils joined Eugene and Michael at the centre of the table and enthusiastically tackled the gargantuan feast the French chef had prepared. During the meal, speeches and toasts followed in droves as everyone remembered and thanked everyone else. Sounds of riot from the servants' hall suggested that, if the staff were getting a little above themselves with an endless litany of toasts and songs, they were enjoying the occasion and were neither thirsting nor starving.

After the meal, most attendees were happy to find a quiet nook in which to doze like boa constrictors, but Laura took the children up to the gallery and introduced them to the games she had taught her pupils. Dr Humphries accompanied her, and she was delighted to see he took a real interest in their activities, perhaps intending to use some of them at Horton. Everyone enjoyed themselves, but there was no complaint from any quarter when Mrs Humphries appeared and announced it was time to return home. Full of thanks, and loud in admonitions to come and visit them, the party disappeared down the driveway, leaving Laura to seek a well-deserved rest.

Bawdy jokes were made about Bob and Laura retiring to her old room before attending the evening's entertainment, but both were glad to rest for an hour before walking across the farmyard. They discovered the barn splendid with greenery and flowers, and McPherson's crew earned a grateful 'Thank you'. The throng of revellers, from both estates and the village, meant a rising tide of noise while kegs of ale were rapidly depleted and Buff Haldon hastened off for more. Pigs and sheep revolved on spits turned by youngsters glad to earn a shilling, and tables sagged under the weight of food and drink until the guests drew in and fell to. Afterwards, the centre was cleared for dancing and the watchers stood around or found somewhere to sit. A fiddler-led band played and everyone, children included, jigged and pranced. It went on for so long that, as Laura had predicted, she and Bob were glad to totter back to the Hall for the remainder of the night.

They heard no sound at all from the tower room, but the next morning, Laura made time to lay her bouquet in friendship on Minnie's grave. After that, it was pure joy to drive home to Monthrope Manor, now emerging from the turmoil of repairs, and begin to settle into a new life.

Ben and Martha proved to be the kind of welcome, helpful guests one encourages to visit regularly. Maisy visited occasionally, preferring Laura and Bob to visit her, but Laura was surprised at how often Lady Hardacre dropped in, wondering at first if it was because she was missing Elizabeth, but eventually deciding they really had been adopted by her employer.

NEW ARRIVALS

*L*ady Hardacre's first visit following the wedding was made on Sundancer, and she arrived enthusiastically waving an envelope above her head as she reined in at the gate. The Newcastle response to her letter had been positive. It was obvious from her excitement that the grand touch had operated powerfully on Edmund and she was proud of it, and deservedly so.

When Laura and Bob read the letter, they found Edmund had replied at his most formal. The kindness of Lord and Lady Hardacre to his poor sister was eclipsed only by their unsought but extremely welcome offer to take his two oldest children into their care. Their generosity in sending a vehicle and nurse was praised and they would endeavour to have everything in readiness for Nurse's arrival. He was happy to report that both children had readily acceded to the change, despite the long distance from their home.

Lady Hardacre reported that the news she was to have two children in her care had wrought marvellously on Nurse's spirits and she was enthusiastically packing to head north and collect them. Laura was glad that the travelling coach was called into use but still found herself wondering how she could possibly survive the rigours of the trip. Nurse was driven by Grimes and Titus with a couple of farm boys in uniform as outriders and she departed, waving happily through the window to everyone in Monthrope who rushed out to see her pass by.

Once again, it was a case of waiting, but just over two weeks later the coach hove into view and Nurse tumbled out of it. Unlike everyone else, she had made the trip up and back without an intervening rest period and the children reported that she had slept much of the return journey.

The Alstons were sent for and saw Charlotte established in Laura's previous bedchamber and Thomas next door to her. Laura showed Charlotte the bolts that guaranteed her privacy but made her promise not to alert Thomas to the secret passageway, expecting it would prove irresistible.

The long drive had ensured that Nurse was now an old friend, but Hocking introduced the children to Mrs Moodle, the housekeeper, who had moved into Mrs Tillotson's old room. Tom instantly rechristened this unfortunate lady Mrs Muddle, but Laura decided to say nothing. She had discovered that the poor woman was called 'The Poodle' by everyone else because of her woolly hair. Lady Hardacre immediately began planning new clothing for both offspring but was interrupted by the arrival of a person who had seen her advertisement for a tutor.

He was the vicar's son, newly looking for employment, and his erudition would have armoured Thomas against him if it wasn't for the fact that he loved all sports, but particularly sailing. When Adam Greenaway found he was to teach two children and one of them was a girl, he was concerned, but his father persuaded him that, with some circumspection on his own part, it would not be at all dangerous. Laura and Bob drove home that evening feeling that the children were well-enough settled and Adam would likely prove an excellent tutor for Charlotte and Thomas.

Eugene and Michael came home for the weekend to a great surprise and the adults had to hide the fact that they had nearly forgotten to collect the two absent boys. Their presence introduced the newcomers to the existence of horses, and Grimes rapidly recruited ponies from neighbours whose children had outgrown them, while Evadne hastily cobbled up a riding habit for Charlotte. Neither of the newcomers was interested in the piano until they heard Eugene and Michael enthusiastically playing and then both decided music was exciting. After dinner, everyone sang around the instrument, then Adam Greenaway read them the first chapter of an adventure story, and it was bedtime.

Laura and Bob saw their family again on Sunday at church and joined them at Monthrope Hall for breakfast. Augustus had given Tom a puppy, thereby earning his undying gratitude, but Laura made Augustus and Grimes promise to see that it was well-trained. Adam Greenaway reported that trying to teach a boy interested only in boats, and a girl who wanted to study all day, had stretched his ingenuity to the limit. Laura discussed with him how to convince Tom he would be useless afloat unless he could read, write, and do arithmetic. She knew Charlotte would largely teach herself if she was given the correct material and didn't fall in love with her tutor, but she made her niece promise to get some exercise daily. Perhaps not surprisingly, both Evadne and Charlotte developed an interest in archery and bowls, and Laura later discovered that Evadne happily joined Charlotte during her riding lessons.

TRAPPED

*L*uck tends to run out when you rely on it daily. Snowy Widdeson, after living hand to mouth in Monthrope Major, in constant fear of being consigned to the workhouse, moved to Studley. His unsavoury appearance deterred anyone from employing him and he often relied on his forest skills to feed himself and raise money. He was still wearing the outfit Maisy had provided him with, including the driving coat. He had never acquired shelter long enough to dispose of it and many a night it had been his only covering in some unsuspecting farmer's barn.

This day, he entered the back door of The White Hart with a couple of prime coneys to trade, glad to be out of the unending drizzle and looking forward to imbibing something warm. As luck would have it, just as he turned towards the kitchen door, two gentlemen entered behind him, taking a shortcut to the bar foisted on them by the inclement weather.

'Well, look who we have here,' exclaimed one of them. Widdeson didn't waste time checking to see who spoke. He knew Ascot's voice of old, usually while it was uttering 'twenty-eight days and no argy-bargy, or I'll double it'. He closed the kitchen door behind him, hastily sold the coneys to the cook for two shillings and a handsome cut off the roast on a crust and nipped out the kitchen door. He found a corner in the stable, ignoring the protestations of the ostler, and consumed his meal slowly and enjoyably. The damage was done, however. Lord Ascot, very much a horse and hound man himself, was accompanied by his bosom friend, Philip Ainsley, the Master of Hounds.

'Keep your eye open for that villain,' Ascot warned his friend. Ainsley did better (or worse?) than that. He informed his gamekeeper that a known poacher was in the area and to be sure to keep a lookout. The gamekeeper, preferring to spend his nights in bed, set mantraps near a few preserves, and two nights later he came across a pitiful sight. Widdeson was lying on his side in the bracken, his broken left leg clamped in hard iron, and almost unconscious from pain and loss of blood. There were signs he had tried to lever the jaws open with a stick and failed.

It was a great surprise to Laura when Lord Ascot rode up to the Manor and, leaning down from his saddle, greeted her amiably. 'I wanted to bring you news of someone you may be glad to see less of.'

Laura invited him to come in, but he refused. 'No, thank you kindly. I bought a flock of sheep at Monthrope market this morning and they're making their way along the lane, so I must keep moving. But I wanted to tell you that Snowy Widdeson came up for sentencing at the quarterly assizes last week and was found guilty. He's on his way to the hulks and facing transportation.'

Laura was shocked but she realised Ascot meant well and, perchance, was wanting to relieve her mind, so she said, 'How kind of you to come out of your way to tell me.' He waved and cantered off, and she walked indoors, a prey to mixed feelings.

Later, she heard more details of Snowy's detention, and it fretted her. She almost hoped Ainsley's gamekeeper would get caught in one of his own mantraps. Fancy using such a wicked implement on a fellow human – and all for the loss of a few paltry bunnies. Widdeson was a pauper and doubtless, he was starving. She wondered how crippled the trap had left him and could only hope that he would do better in a new environment.

FINDING THEIR PLACE

*T*he next event occurred on Saturday when Charlotte and Thomas joined the Hardacre sons in a visit to Monthrope Manor, Eugene tooling the chaise and taking care because he knew retaining the privilege depended on his completing this trip successfully. He and Michael greeted their welcoming committee of Laura, Tilly, and Amy Carson with enthusiastic hugs, before rushing off to the barns and byres where they located Bob setting up cow stalls.

Thomas wandered all over the house and house-yard, eyed the possibilities of the orchard, and then drifted after the boys, wondering why everyone was so excited about the place. He was amazed to see the brothers enthusiastically helping Bob and some carpenter fellow with their building efforts. They were chattering away like magpies about their week and how they weren't coming home next week because Dr Humphries had something special happening. Thomas sat on a crate and listened to it all and wondered why they visited Monthrope Manor when all it meant was work.

Charlotte spent the day shadowing Laura and understanding what she was doing and how it was done. She didn't find much of it interesting until they sat down during the afternoon to attend to some sewing and had time to talk. Laura asked Charlotte how she planned to use this book learning she was so earnestly pursuing. After all, the likeliest thing to happen was that she would be married off and become a housewife like herself. When Charlotte realised that she was not being sneered at, she expressed her opinion as forthrightly as she had done before in Newcastle.

'I'm never going to marry. I'm going to start a school that will educate girls properly. I'm a bit undecided. I might train poorer girls up enough so that they can find better employment than being a skivvy, but I would really like to train clever girls to work in whatever field they want. I would like to be a doctor or a scientist and I am sure there are other girls like me. I just haven't met any yet. There were some jolly clever girls at school in Tyneville, but all they talked about was being married so they could get away from home.'

Laura remembered Julius's manager who had taken the unorthodox step of employing two women in secretarial positions. She said to Charlotte, 'By the time you grow up there will be more employment available to women. And I don't mean working on the mill floor in factories, but decent employment. Keep in touch with Julius and with his managers after he retires; Evadne might just support you. Make sure you let her know what you want to do, so that she doesn't get swept away and treat you like a living doll to dress up and parade around. If you are not interested in working for one of Julius's companies, some of the girls you train up may be.'

This was the first time Charlotte had dared mention her ambitions to anyone and Laura's ongoing support would hold her steady through years of upheaval in achieving her goals.

Thomas was very much enjoying life at Monthrope Hall where he was warm, well-fed, and attended to by a bossy and talkative, albeit willing, slave, for reasons unknown called Nurse. He had rapidly learned how to be cajoling when he wanted anything from her, but he lorded it over the other staff members who bore with him while happily anticipating a fall would follow.

Adam Greenaway and Julius fretted because they had yet to find anything that genuinely enthused Thomas other than his puppy, and they disliked his manner of ordering the staff around. 'I'll have to find him a niche in one of the colonies, I imagine,' opined Julius disappointedly. Thomas's immediate future was saved by Augustus's gift of a puppy whom he called Brandy. In this little creature, Thomas at last found something to love and protect; later she would return his affection by being a most resolute guardian of his own wellbeing.

The breakthrough with Thomas was not to come until Julius and Adam included him in a contingent from Dr Humphries's college. They travelled as a group, to have a look at a canal Julius had invested in. Thomas had once haunted Newcastle's dock areas and the canal was a relief to his need to be near water. Julius responded to this by introducing him to a variety of boats and they eventually settled on a sailing dinghy. Three miles from the Hall was the nearest they could get it to his home, but from then on, Thomas willingly rode to Horton, where he stabled the pony, and spent many happy days on the river. He had promised to always take someone with him. Michael or Adam accompanied him whenever they could, but sometimes his only partner was Brandy. Few people, of any age, had the stamina for a whole day in a small boat and it was some time before he made any local acquaintances, and years before he was allowed to upgrade his vessel.

Adam Greenaway had seen the difference in Thomas's schoolwork, and he rarely had to use the threat of no trip to Horton to induce obedience, because now there were things that Thomas needed to know and was eager to search for. That they all applied to sailing, watercraft, fishing, water creatures, and waterways, didn't worry his preceptor. His pupil was learning and, although his knowledge was highly specialised, he was sure it would one day lead to suitable employment.

During this time, Eugene often felt rather left out and he invited himself to stay overnight at Monthrope Manor, following Bob Alston everywhere and appearing glad to be with him. Bob realised the importance of this one Sunday morning, when he was taking off a week's growth of beard in his dressing room, prior to the trip to church.

Eugene wandered in and stood looking over Bob's shoulder, watching the process in the adjustable mirror. It was a careful procedure with the cut-throat razor and, as Bob finished his task and once again wiped the blade on the cloth hanging ready, he caught Eugene's fixed gaze. The lad's nearly as tall as I am, he thought, as he rinsed his face.

'Are you my brother or my father?' Eugene demanded and he threw himself at Bob even as the other reached out for him.

'I'm your friend,' Bob stated. He led the boy into his bedroom and let go of him so that he could finish dressing and added, as he pulled on his Sunday coat, 'Don't you ever forget that.' They walked peacefully down to join Laura in the carriage waiting at the door.

After the Sunday service, Evadne asked Bob and Laura to join the family for breakfast. Julius arrived and announced he had a hamper with him because it was high time that they all drove to Horton to inspect Thomas's dinghy. This created quite some excitement, but Bob and Laura had been looking forward to a day by themselves while Tilly and Amy had a break, and they preferred to drive home. Once in the chaise, Bob told Laura about Eugene's question.

'Whatever did you say?'

'I told Eugene I was his friend and he seemed to prefer that and didn't make any further enquiries. I was relieved because I feared he might trace further back. My father, Eugene's grandfather, is a pretty poor apology for a man.'

Laura said carefully, 'I find Augustus quite bearable these days. He's doing the best he can and there are things he quite shines at.'

Bob sent her a quick sideways glance. 'Any person with a few wits can see that Gus was never my father. I wasn't talking about Gus at all.' He looked across and saw Laura had assumed her anxious face. 'I worked that out for myself years ago. If he had been my father, how come my mam never had half a dozen children?'

'Bob, I suspect even Augustus knows that, but he is happy to have you as his son.'

'I am grateful for a lifetime's kindness. He has always been good to me, and generous, but I like to think it is mostly for my mother's sake, rather than anything else.'

Laura said, 'I think any father would be proud of you and your boys.'

ACCEPTED

Some months later, Laura visited Evadne on her way homewards from seeing Bess Olsen about borrowing a clucky hen to sit on a clutch of eggs. They had a pleasant chat and then her hostess surprised her.

'You and Robert must come to the next Monthrope Assembly. You need to be known here, to be one of the families we mix with.'

'Evadne, it will just lay Bob and I open to being snubbed in public.'

'Not at all. The County is eager to know any rich young woman, and now Augustus has formally adopted Robert, the young man who stands third in line to Monthrope Hall is not to be despised.'

'This is just the sort of distinction I don't want and which I despise.'

'Yes, I know, Laura. Remember I've been through all this myself.'

'Oh, lord, forgive me, Evadne. I didn't think before I spoke.'

'Just say you will come.'

'Certainly, but I'll leave if anyone sneers at Bob.'

'You'll do or say something brilliant if anyone is so inclined. Monthrope will just have to get used to the strange sight of a happily married couple.'

'I said we would come, and I meant it.'

Laura travelled home, thankful that she already owned dancing slippers, and that the most elegant of the gowns she had bought in Newcastle could act as a ballgown. A quick trip to town would supply her with the myriad accompaniments necessary. Thankfully, Bob was already suitably supplied. Possibly all the effort would be for nothing because Bob might refuse to attend and, just when she hadn't time enough to think about it, there was a letter from Nellie. It proved to be somewhat different in style and tone to the missives Laura had grown accustomed to receiving from Emily.

'I was brought to bed yesterday week of a darling baby boy and we are both well. When I am recovered, we are to leave Newcastle and try the west, which I hope will go better and be less demanding on both of us. I hear Manchester is very forward-looking. I'll write when I can give you a definite address. Thank you so much for keeping in touch, I am glad to learn that all is progressing so satisfactorily on your manor. The children have written once each and seem happy at Monthrope Hall.'

Laura put the letter aside and braced herself for the task of pleading Evadne's request that they attend the Assembly. She found she had guessed rightly that Bob would refuse to go, but she was wrong about the reasons.

'I can't dance well enough.'

'We'll practise before we go,' she replied.

He was too tired after a hard day's work to go anywhere except to bed. Really, he was so worn out each evening it was all he could do to provide her nightly satisfaction for his wife, before sleeping ten hours straight.

'You will have a relaxed couple of days prior to the Assembly,' replied Laura, nobly refusing to be distracted. 'We must socialise a little. It will do us good to blow a few cobwebs away.'

Well prior to the great event, Laura rolled up the carpets so that they could dance. She played on her new pianoforte while Mrs Tillotson and Mrs Carson partnered her husband, or they sang and clapped while she and Bob circled the floor, or they all sang and danced together. Tiredness appeared to melt away with this new interest and both were looking forward to the outing as well as the dancing, and both decided independently that they would just enjoy themselves and not worry.

Unlike the village, Monthrope Major boasted a library and assembly-rooms. Bob had the forethought to book them accommodation at the best hostelry the market town afforded, allowing them an overnight stay before driving home, and they delighted in this luxury. They drove to the inn, dined, and changed into their evening clothes.

Not yet a year married, extremely busy at the Manor, and unused to socialising in Monthrope, Laura had been barely aware of the distinctions allocated to a bride when all the local families visited her. The Assembly was to educate her further. Evadne, Augustus and Mr Wilmott met the young couple at the door and formally introduced them to the Master of Ceremonies and gradually circulated them through the principal families in the room. Laura, with the Master, and Bob with Lady Evadne, led the first dance and the gentry did their duty and partnered them through every following dance.

Early in the evening, they realised Lady Hester and Leonard Bright had arrived, but Laura was more excited to find that they were followed by Amelia and Richard with Lord and Lady Ascot. She hastened across to welcome her friends and the two parties merged. It made a world of difference to have Amelia chatting away with her. Gradually, Laura and Bob relaxed, and all feelings of formality vanished.

At suppertime, Lady Horton swept up and collected their enlarged party to share the Horton table in the supper room, and Laura suspected that she and Bob were being well-guarded. When it was time to resume dancing, Amelia led out the set, followed by Laura, and Lady Hester came several places later, her expression boding ill for those close to her.

Following that dance, Leonard approached the Monthrope party, greeted his late wife's family and introduced Laura and Bob to his wife. He asked Laura for the honour of the next dance, and she accepted as gracefully as she could. She suspected that Bob would be refused if he asked Lady Hester in return, and she wondered whether Leonard realised this, but the issue never came up. Mr Wilmott promptly resolved the situation by approaching her ladyship and she walked onto the floor with him.

As they promenaded during their dance, Leonard said to Laura, 'Well, you certainly kept your light under a bushel.' He sounded aggrieved and the glance he sent her bore no resemblance to those of the past.

Leonard's running true to form, she thought, remembering Augustus's depiction of his friend, and rather amused by his chagrin. No congratulations or well-wishes tendered on our marriage, no enquiries as to how we go on, or how we fill our days. I have committed a fault; I neglected to inform him I was rich and he, therefore, missed out on a golden opportunity. That makes me so happy.

She replied only by raising her eyebrows at his tone. He reacted instantly. 'None of us knew you were as rich as Croesus,' he explained, sounding just as hard-done by as at first.

Oh, hooray for gossip, thought Laura. Word has got around to him. I'm so glad he knows I'm wealthy and he hasn't got a farthing of it. She gazed back at him and wondered what she had ever seen in this imitation of a gentleman.

After a moment, she responded quietly, 'One learns to avoid fortune-hunters.' It was enough to silence him on the subject and apparently on every subject. Laura had no interest in talking to him, and they finished the dance in silence. He led her back to her party where she was confident of being welcome.

Julius brought her a drink and she sat enjoying it and watching the participants moving through the formality of a minuet. We've been so well treated tonight, she thought. The Hardacre family and their dependants have shown me for a long time that they appreciated my assistance. Monthrope village showed it accepted me when it soused Snowy Widdeson. I have a real friend in Amelia and many others. Tonight, thanks perhaps to Evadne and Lady Horton, the county people have shown Bob and me that they are prepared to socialise with us. Truly, my cup runneth over. And later tonight I have some very special news for Bob that I expect he'll be pleased to hear. It will be a winter baby but very welcome.

For Laura, the final dance was the peak of the evening's events. It was the adventurous new dance destined soon to take Britain by storm, but imported by and more commonly seen among foreign servants and called the waltz. She turned at once to her husband before anyone could claim either of them. She and Bob moved confidently onto the floor, noticing how few of their fellows were rising to join in this new form of entertainment. They swirled around the ballroom, happily absorbed in each other's company, each secretly anticipating a delightful end to their evening when they retired to the inn. However, the crowning moment really occurred for Laura during that last dance, when Bob smiled down at her and said, 'I'm glad we came.'

ACKNOWLEDGEMENTS

The author remains deeply grateful to the publisher and her acolytes, to her assessor, and all the friends and relatives and fellow academics who have supported and encouraged her writing over recent years.

So many of you.

Thank you, one and all.

Helen.

ABOUT THE AUTHOR

Helen BeDe took up writing historical romances in retirement after a lifetime in which she was a farmer's wife, teacher, psychologist, and sociologist working mostly in rural Australia.

Helen won an A.N.A. poetry prize as a teenager, followed by the Chiron Prize for Verse and the Lee Steere Award for History while a student at Claremont Teachers Training College. She wrote professionally throughout her working life, gave talks and ran workshops.

Her major interest has been helping others.

Helen still enjoys growing and processing food and enjoys contact with a wide range of friends and relatives.

Her first novel, Marvellous Miss Markham, is an historical romance set in England during the reign of George IV.

Extensively researched, this novel explores our very human need to belong. It has been followed by two further novels... so far.